ANDREW HALL is a ginger-haired disabled writer and alternative film poster maker from the United Kingdom, and he finds that whole situation simply hilarious. Often dealing with themes of the bittersweet, defiant laughter, and finding beauty within the chaos, he believes that tears should be allowed to fall. *Green Laughing* is his debut novel.

Find Andrew on X/Twitter @CripOnATrip21

CW01502021

GREEN LAUGHING

ANDREW HALL

Northodox Press Ltd
Maiden Greve, Malton,
North Yorkshire, YO17 7BE

This edition 2025

1

First published in Great Britain by
Northodox Press Ltd 2025

ISBN: 978-1-915179-69-2

Cover and Interior Design by T J Keane

This book is set in Caslon Pro Std

Printed and bound by Imprint Digital
Unit 1, Seychelles Farm, Exeter, Devon, EX5 5HY

Chapter One

Waking up to Darkness

It felt familiar, but something wasn't right. Everything had been amplified to the point of extreme. It was like her body had been submerged in water, but her skin was still dry. She could feel it was all wrong before she knew what she was feeling. The blood rushed through her veins, bringing colour back to her skin, and her lungs began to plead for air as a subtle breeze fell across her face.

Poppy opened her eyes as the transparent covering above curved itself away under the narrow bed. They were dry and sticky and saw only brightness. She closed them, the intense light burning a black spot across her pupils, before opening them again. The more she looked, the more the black spot seemed to change. It morphed around the edges, turning purple, then green, and yet dodging her gaze directly whenever she tried to focus. Behind it, she could just see the white ceiling tiles shining down, and to her left, she became aware of the boxy monitors that were stacked on top of each other like bedside furniture.

She reached over and blindly fumbled for the tray, finding the small bottle on top and the tiny pipette that went with it. She unscrewed the lid, her fingertips numb and clumsy, and filled the pipette, bringing it shakily to her face before squeezing the drops into her eyes. She swore, and blinked, allowing the dark mass in the middle of her vision to slowly dissolve as the room focused in front of her.

'I can't move.'

Poppy jolted to her left and saw Teela staring back at her from the adjacent bed.

'What's happened? Why are we awake?'

Poppy lifted her head the best she could and craned around to see the monitors. A warning flashed across the screen in slow repetitive cycles, followed closely by dates and times she did not recognise.

'We're early,' she said, coughing.

'Why?'

Poppy sipped on a tube that hung down from the ceiling and coughed again, vomiting the liquid back up all over the floor. 'Damn,' she said, bringing her legs round and dangling them off the bed, her ankles loose like a puppet's.

'I can't move like you can,' said Teela, her voice cracking. 'Why can't I move?'

'Have you had your eye drops?'

Teela shook her head, trying to make out the blurry form beside her. 'I can't reach; my arms won't-'

'Okay, hold on. I'm going to try and walk towards you.' Poppy shuffled forward to the edge of the bed and slowly pushed down through her fists, trying to lift herself off the mattress. Her ankle buckled under the pressure. She folded to the cold tiles as if she hadn't any bones, her knees cracking hard as she just managed to catch herself with her hands.

'Poppy?'

'I'm okay,' she said, trying to remain calm. 'It'll wear off. It always takes a few minutes.'

'Not like this. I can't fucking feel my skin. I'm numb.'

Poppy dragged her body the short distance between the two beds and used a monitor to slowly pull herself to her feet. 'Okay,' she said, unscrewing the lid off the small bottle and filling the pipette, 'keep your eyes open, I'm gonna give you the drops.'

Teela swore as they hit her pupils and covered the irises. She blinked fast as the liquid welled across her bottom lids before dripping down the side of her nose.

'I'm going to get the blood flowing,' said Poppy, using the monitor as a crutch. She pinched the skin around Teela's arm and dug her elbow into her thighs, kneading the flesh.

'It's not working,' said Teela. 'I know I'm moving, but I can't feel it.' She took a sip from the tube and hurled it back up, leaning over the side of the bed instinctively.

'See,' said Poppy, 'you can move. It's just taking longer because we're in shock. It's like someone's turned the lights on in the middle of the night and we're still groggy.'

'What are the dates?'

Poppy looked over at the monitor. 'I don't know; they're not correct. What do you think?'

Teela awkwardly lifted her head and took in the information. 'It's like there's nothing programmed, like it's gone back to default settings or something.'

'What does that number two mean?' Poppy pointed to a smaller readout at the bottom of the screen as it quickly changed to a one.

They both watched, staring at the digit before it suddenly switched to a ten, then a nine, then an eight.

'It's resetting,' shouted Teela. 'Get me off the bed!'

Seven.

Six.

Five.

Poppy dragged Teela's hips and rolled her over onto her side, letting the momentum take her off the bed and onto the floor.

Four.

She landed on the tiles, and a good portion of Poppy's legs, as they both watched the countdown from their crumpled position.

Three.

Two.

One.

The transparent coverings on both beds silently curved across, forming a lid, enclosing the two mattresses like glass coffins, and behind them, a green light on the wall flicked over to red.

'The door,' said Teela, rolling off Poppy, slowly trying to get to her feet before collapsing.

Poppy clambered up and stumbled over to the door. 'It's locked,' she said, trying to force it open.

'I don't get what's going on,' said Teela, still in a pile on the floor.

Poppy wiped her brow and assessed the situation. 'Let's go over the facts. We took our pills as normal.'

Teela nodded.

'We went into hiber just as normal. You didn't feel any different?'

'No.'

'Then it woke us up too early.'

'Then reset itself,' continued Teela. 'As if we were back at the start.'

'Causing everything to lockdown and go back into stasis.'

'We're gonna have to bash the door down,' said Teela, only half joking.

'No,' said Poppy, 'we just need to get it out of stasis.' She walked over to the monitors. 'Can you rig it?'

'I've never tried,' said Teela. 'Help me up.'

Poppy crouched down and wrapped Teela's arm around her shoulder, hoisting her up. They both stood for a moment, before Teela's knees buckled underneath her.

'I can't stand.'

Poppy lifted her back up. 'Yes, you can. I just let go too soon – it's my fault. Give it time.' She held her for a while, making sure Teela had gained some sort of control, before separating. 'You good?' she said.

Teela nodded. She was a little wobbly, but getting stronger

by the second. 'All my tools are in the Control Room,' she said.

'What do you need?'

Teela examined the main monitor. 'Something thin and strong to prise open that panel and get to the screen.'

Poppy looked around the room, her eyes settling on her eyedrop tray. 'What about this?' she said, picking up the shallow metal dish, running her finger across the sharp, flat rim.

Teela hobbled towards the monitor and took the tray off Poppy. She turned it sideways and forced it under a thin strip at the base of the screen. She rammed it up and down, warping the metal, as the panel popped off. It clanged on the floor, revealing the control screen. Poppy watched as Teela held her fingers across the black strip, causing it to illuminate into life.

'I've never used one of these before,' said Teela, working her way through various menu screens. 'Seems fairly standard, though.' She reached the section for reprogramming. 'I can't change the time period; it's set. That can't change below three months for obvious reasons, but,' said Teela, nodding as if to convince herself, 'I can change what the computer thinks the current date is, so it's like the three months have already happened, hopefully.' She slid her finger across the strip as the numbers on the monitor changed, whirling in blurred streaks with each spin.

'Time travellers,' said Poppy.

Teela scrolled until she reached a date that worked, before backing out of the menus and resetting the computer. They both watched as the monitors faded down before slowly pulsing back into life as the numbers flashed back on screen.

'It's not working.'

'It's booting up,' said Teela. 'Give it a moment.'

They stood in silence, waiting, before a couple of large clicks made them jump. The transparent coverings rotated back around, revealing the mattresses like flowers in bloom, with the light on the wall switching from red to green as the door unlocked.

Teela stumbled towards Poppy. 'Now what?'

'We're gonna have to call this in. Can you make it to the Control Room?'

Teela nodded.

'Here,' Poppy walked her over to the drinking tube. 'Drink the rest of it. It won't be nice, but it'll do you good.'

Teela placed the nozzle into her mouth and gagged, watching as Poppy did the same. 'I'm gonna throw up.'

They both bent over and heaved by the side of their beds, retching up a little, but keeping the majority down.

'Whoever said the first drink after waking up is the best wasn't drinking whatever that is,' said Teela, wiping her mouth on her arm.

Poppy nodded and headed to the door. 'You ready?'

Teela followed her, a little slower, her legs still a bit shaky. 'It's like when you've been ill,' she said, as they walked down the main corridor of the ship. 'Y'know when you're better, but you just don't have any energy?'

'It'll wear off in an hour or two,' said Poppy. 'I'll call it in, then we'll get some food, have a shower, and by tomorrow it'll be like it normally is.'

They continued to walk, the ship as boring as it ever was, their concentration trained on putting one foot in front of the other.

'You got any theories?' said Teela, after a while.

Poppy shook her head. 'It's probably just an error. How old is Vitula? It was only a matter of time before something happened. You never know; this might mean we get some upgrades.'

'You joking?' said Teela. 'We'll be lucky if we get new bedsheets.'

Poppy looked back at Teela, wearing just a t-shirt and shorts. 'Speaking of which, are you cold?'

Teela nodded.

'We'll make a detour to the bedchambers and get dressed,' said Poppy.

'Fine,' Teela gestured down to her jelly legs. 'But you're

going up. I'm not climbing two ladders like this.'

'One day,' said Poppy, as they turned the corner to the bedchamber landing, 'we're gonna think to leave some clothes in the Hiber Room so we don't have to walk around in our pyjamas.'

'I don't get why they put it so far from the bedchambers,' added Teela. 'Why design it like that?'

They both looked up to the landing one level above, then to the metal ladder right in the middle of what looked like the sheer side of a cliff face.

'Right,' said Poppy, planting her foot on the first rung of the ladder, 'I'll see you in five.'

Teela watched as she slowly climbed up towards the bright lights before disappearing over the ledge. Her eyes dropped down to the foot of the ladder. They transformed into the thin legs of a chair. It was tilted, leaning back, almost past the point of no return before righting itself.

Teela watched it from the back of the classroom. Each time was like a test, seeing how far it could be pushed before reeling it back in; and each time her stomach seemed to sink, her breath held, before a beautiful relief that never lasted long as the whole process started again.

'How many times have I told you not to swing on your chair?' The teacher raised their eyebrows and turned back to the board as the chair's occupant carried on regardless.

Teela knew it was going to be this time. She could feel it. Just after being acknowledged, that's when it normally happened, when all eyes were on it. She watched as the chair tipped again on its back two legs, the knees catching the table as an anchor. Except, this time they missed.

She saw the head hit the corner of the table behind and shatter, the blood leaking out from the wound. The teacher screamed, then the rest of the class screamed.

'Think fast.'

Teela looked up to the landing as Poppy threw down some

clothes.

'I didn't know what you wanted, so just grabbed what I could see.'

'These are fine,' said Teela, clumsily stepping into the trousers and pulling the stiff fabric of the jumper over her head.

They set off down the corridor in silence.

'How you feeling now?' said Poppy, listening to the slight limp in Teela's gait. 'Will you be able to make it up this one?'

'I reckon so,' said Teela. 'It just feels weird, like pins and needles.'

They walked down to the far end and reached a ladder that was enclosed by surrounding walls, pushed back in an alcove.

'I think you better go first,' said Poppy.

'What, so I land on you if I fall?'

'Better than landing on this.' Poppy stamped her leg on the metal grate. 'I wouldn't let you fall anyway,' she added, 'I'd catch you.'

Teela raised her eyebrows and placed her slightly shaky foot on the ladder. Poppy followed, three steps behind, making sure she was okay.

'God, it stinks,' said Teela as she went over the top of the ledge.

'Air filters must've gone again,' said Poppy, climbing up to get her first look at the Control Room.

It wasn't very big, made smaller by the filing cabinets and boxy containers around the edge. In the middle, two large chairs had been abandoned in front of a chunky desk, filled with monitors and strip panels that angled across the width of the room in three jagged motions.

Teela went over to her seat as Poppy rummaged for a document in the largest of the filing cabinets.

'Can you remember the log-code for error comms?'

'It's the fifth one down,' said Teela, holding three fingers to the screen of the largest monitor.

The desk quietly illuminated, the monitors slowly glowing brighter, hitting an intense white, overshadowing the smaller lights that dotted themselves around the keyboard panels and strips, before falling back as various numbers and diagrams appeared on the screens.

'Flightpilot seems to be fine,' said Teela, studying a smaller monitor to her left.

'Okay,' said Poppy, sitting down with a clipboard. She scrolled her finger down the page and highlighted the fifth code down. 'Three, seven, six, seven.'

Teela typed in the numbers, and a message appeared on the screen. 'It says to specify.'

'Hiber,' said Poppy.

'Okay, wait - shit.' Teela reached into a cupboard under the desk and brought out a thin, cylindrical receiver. She paired it to the desk and handed it over to Poppy. 'You'll need this, obviously.'

Poppy coughed.

'Okay,' said Teela, starting again, 'three, two, one.' She gave a thumbs up.

Poppy held her finger across a black strip sensor at the base of the receiver. 'This is Captain Poppy Talib of Star Express Transit Ship – Vitula to base.' Her tone shifted to a more casual one. 'I bet you weren't expecting to hear from us so soon. I'm not quite sure how to explain this, but we've had a slight problem with the hiber monitor, and we've been woken up earlier than expected. In terms of health, we're completely fine. We had a bit of trouble at first, trying to adjust, but we seem to be doing better. No health concerns. As for the ship, not quite sure what happened. First Officer Teela Rose is currently running diagnostics. Flightpilot is still working. I guess there's nothing we can really do except to just carry on, but I just thought I'd call it in and let you know what's happening. We'll update further after we get any results. OVER.' She read her words back on a small screen next to the receiver before lifting it back up to her lips. 'Send.'

A green light ran around the edge of the monitor before disappearing.

'Did that sound alright?' said Poppy, putting the receiver down.

Teela nodded. 'How long do you reckon it'll take them to reply?'

Poppy shook her head. 'Your guess is as good as mine. It's not an emergency, so—'

'How is it not an emergency?'

'I mean,' Poppy stretched her red eyes. 'I mean, we're not in any immediate danger, are we? Think how many ships we have. They're not going to send out the cavalry for a dodgy wakeup call.'

'So that's it?'

'That's it,' said Poppy. 'Listen, we're not even halfway into the route. We'll wait here for a bit, do as we normally do. They'll find us, and bring us back home.'

There was a small pause as Teela thought. 'Oh great, I see.'

'What?'

Teela twitched in her chair. 'If we get brought back home, that means an undelivered cargo.' She nodded as Poppy began to see where she was going. 'We're not even gonna get paid, are we?'

Poppy thought for a while. 'No.' She resolved it in her mind before repeating herself. 'No, it doesn't work like that. This wasn't our fault. We should still get paid. We won't get any bonuses, but we'll still get paid. They can't pin any of this on us.'

'Oh yeah?' said Teela. 'Just watch them. Mark my words. I bet we don't get a pix, not a single pix.' Her mind coiled back on itself as she thought. 'In fact,' she said, after a moment, letting it spring out, making Poppy jump slightly, 'in fact, I reckon we have grounds to sue.'

Poppy laughed.

'No, seriously. We got woken up out of hiber unsafely, before the correct dose, didn't we? That's the company's fault for not maintaining equipment. Pix pinching.' Teela let herself believe the idea, knowing full well that none of this would ever come to fruition. 'Do you think Star Bird Delivery still has this shite?' She pointed towards the desk. 'Nothing works. Nothing makes sense. We've been woken up randomly for no reason. Your door is knackered.'

'Hey,' said Poppy, 'don't talk about Vitula like that.'

'Did you know,' said Teela, ignoring her, 'that all the panels and grates downstairs should be covered in carpet? I saw the original décor in an old advert back at base. Oh yeah, everything was complete luxury. We should be able to walk around in our bare feet.'

'Rubbing up against the walls?'

'If you like. They took them out because the grates and panels were easier to clean, not that they ever do. I'm actually surprised we have beds in those prison chambers up there.' Teela leant back, her tone lowering. 'I don't know.' She looked down at the dull floor beneath her feet, her eyes tracking over the thin joins between the tiles.

'I like Vitula,' said Poppy. 'I like these jobs, with you. They're longish and they're quiet. Half the way asleep, wake up to check the cargo, tick the boxes, then park us up and drop off the delivery. It's simple. I like it.' Her tone became more animated as she spoke. 'Could you imagine doing the Red Run every day, with all that traffic? On and off planet every two minutes, going back and forth for those pompous rich guys? No thanks. I like the scenic jobs. We're the canal boats of the stars.'

Teela looked at her. 'What the hell is a canal boat?'

Poppy laughed. 'My Dad told me about them. These tiny-thin, narrow boats that used to travel up and down canals and rivers delivering cargo in the old days. I mean, old, old days. Before we first left.'

Teela, only half listening, didn't reply, allowing the conversation to quietly end.

Poppy closed her tired eyes and imagined herself slowly drifting along a small stretch of water. She tried to picture what it was like. In her mind, she constructed the shapes of the buildings, the speed, even the boat itself, but knew none of it was real. She tilted her head back and focused on the sky, her creations disappearing as soon as they had come. Far above her, a single cloud seemed to follow, the breeze pushing it along as if it were tied to her wrist like a balloon.

'I'm just sick of getting dealt the bad hand.'

Poppy opened her eyes and gave an understanding smile. 'I know.' She let the word dissolve in the gloom before starting at a different pace. 'Listen, I'll tell you what. I'm gonna go and do a recording in the booth, okay? You do what you want. If you feel well enough to go down and check the cargo, fine. If not, just leave it and I'll do it later.' She gestured loosely to the desk. 'See if you can find anything. And then we'll meet back here in an hour or so and I'll bring you something to eat. We might have some news by then.'

* * *

Poppy walked down the long corridor, her mind still a little foggy, craving more sleep.

In the middle, about halfway down and seemingly randomly placed, a black booth jutted out from the white panels of the wall, cutting into the floor grates by half, sitting like an abandoned wardrobe in the middle of the aisle, waiting quietly for somebody to enter.

Poppy swiped her hand across a black strip panel and went inside, sitting down on a small chair that faced towards a circular camera.

'Speak to initiate recording,' said a voice.

Poppy stared into the glass lens of the camera, seeing herself. It was the first time she had seen herself since she had woken.

'Speak to initiate recording,' said the voice again, stark and without emotion.

Poppy coughed, and a small red light in the corner flicked over to green. 'Captain's log, on board Star Express Transit Ship – Vitula. Poppy Talib.' She gave a smile. 'We're awake,' she said, holding her hands out as if it was a surprise she had been planning. 'I'm not sure why, but here we are. We're fine, just a bit groggy and waiting to be picked up.' She switched to a more serious tone. 'Just for the record, legally speaking, there should be no blame attached to us. Whatever happened was no fault of ours. We have done everything by the book, followed all the usual routines in the signed papers. I don't know what happened, but it's not our fault.' She smiled, as her mind wandered back to home. 'Didn't expect to be going back so soon. Mum will be glad. She hates that I'm away for so long.' She quickly brushed her hair back. 'That wasn't a criticism, by the way. I like the job. I was just telling First Officer Teela that I like the slower pace.' She thought back to the dream of canal boats as she slowly drifted down the soft, flowing river. 'Anyway,' she said, 'I'm waffling. I never really know who this is for, you or me? Life help anyone who has to sit through these after a delivery.' She paused. 'This route probably won't have many logs anyway, but I'll keep you updated as things go along.' Poppy stood up.

The light clicked back to red. 'Recording session terminated. To continue recording, please remain seated.'

* * *

Poppy swore under her breath as she tried to navigate, holding the overfilled bowl in one hand whilst trying to grip onto the ladder with the other.

She reached the top and pushed it across the Control Room floor before clambering in. 'Chocolate mousse,' she said, proudly presenting the bowl as she sat down in her seat.

Teela didn't reply.

'Okay,' said Poppy, confessing, 'I found some Choco Powder sachets and mixed two with some Milk-Repro.'

'Poppy.'

'I know, but it's the best you're gonna get.'

Teela pushed her chair back. 'Poppy.' Her voice was low, but sharp.

'What?'

Teela's gaze stuck straight to her screen. 'There's something wrong.' She squinted her eyes across the charts, triple checking. 'We're not where we should be.'

'What?' Poppy dragged her chair closer, abandoning the bowl. 'What do you mean?'

'I mean what I just said. We're not where we should be.'

'Yeah, but,' Poppy leant in towards the screen. 'Remember we've woken up earlier than we should have. We won't have reached our first marker post-hiber yet.'

'No,' said Teela, trying not to let the frustration bubble in her throat, 'we haven't reached any marker since Mark Twelve. After that, nothing.'

'I thought you said the flightpilot was working?'

'It is,' said Teela. 'It's still functional. Everything is working. I just don't know where it's been taking us. Something happened after Mark Twelve, I don't know when, but...' Teela paused. 'Poppy, I don't know where we are.'

Poppy studied the charts, the thin lines creating a net over their section of space, each tiny square equating to an area too great for the human mind to comprehend. 'I don't recognise any of this,' she said, staring blankly. 'We could be anywhere.'

'What are we going to do?'

'We're going to have to call it in.' She saw the worry on Teela's face. 'It'll be okay. These charts aren't right, can't be,' she said, convincing herself. 'As soon as they get our message, they'll be able to find us.' Poppy picked up the receiver again. 'Get me the log-code for emergencies,' she said, pointing to the clipboard.

Teela reached over and scrolled down the long list, all the numbers merging into one. 'Okay,' she said, standing up in order to hold the paper closer to the light, 'three, six, three, seven.'

Poppy typed in the numbers as Teela stood behind her, scrolling through the various log-codes and inputs.

'Three, two, one,' said Poppy, counting herself in. 'This is Captain Poppy Talib of Star Express Transit Ship – Vitula to base.' She gave a long pause. 'I recently sent a message to Error Communications about having been prematurely woken. I stated that after initial minor health concerns, everything was fine and that flightpilot was working and we were still on course for our delivery destination.' She read the words as they appeared on the screen. 'Following that message, First Officer Teela Rose has discovered that, although flightpilot is still functioning, we are not on course, and are', she paused. 'In fact, lost.'

Teela's gaze drifted up from the screen to the slit window that ran horizontally across the wall behind the desk and looked over the front of the ship. 'Oh my God.'

Poppy turned round, gesturing for her to be quiet before seeing the look in her eyes. She followed her gaze out of the window, and slowly stood up, the receiver dropping to her side.

It was like the front third of the ship had been melted, as if a scalding blade had swiped its way across with one slow and deliberate action, mangling the variously sized cubicle cells that ran down the length of the ship on either side, some as big as buildings, their top halves bent and warped out of shape and their surface scorched.

Teela jumped onto the desk to get a better look.

'Is it all the way down?' asked Poppy.

Teela squinted, trying to see through the slit. 'I can't tell.' She edged forward, knocking a monitor.

'Be careful.'

'It seems to be okay nearer to us, then it gets worse. All the cells…' She paused, taking it all in the best she could. 'Then, I can't see. It's too dark.'

'Can you see the mast?'

Teela bent down. In the very far distance, just visible, she could see the wiry frame of the transmitter mast sticking up from the front tip of the ship. 'It's standing,' she said. 'It looks fine.'

'Thank God,' said Poppy, her heart pounding in her chest.

'I don't think it-' Teela's mind changed pace. 'Wait, what was it?' She jumped down off the desk and brought up a plan of the ship on her screen and examined it carefully. 'There's no internal damage,' she said, zooming into every room before moving on to the next. 'Nothing exploded from inside. We're okay.'

'Are you sure?' said Poppy.

Teela examined the inside of the ship again. 'We're fine. I don't know how, but we're fine. We hit something, though. Or it bloody hit us.'

'Clusters?' asked Poppy.

Teela's mind raced. She brought up the charts and cycled through them trying to find something along their original route. 'There's nothing here.' She looked over at Poppy. 'What are we going to do? Something isn't right.'

'I'm gonna have to… I'm…' Poppy stumbled over her words. She looked down at her hand and found the receiver. She wiped the half-spoken message from the screen and held the receiver to her mouth. 'Poppy Talib of Star Express Transit Ship – Vitula to base.' Her tone was as clear as it could be, but wavered slightly at the end. 'This is an emergency distress transmission. We have been hit by something, presumably a small cluster-' She took her finger off the sensor. 'This is impossible,' she said, pulling the receiver away from her mouth. 'What are the chances?'

Teela shook her head in disbelief, both agreeing and

disagreeing at the same time. 'Look,' she said, gesturing to the window. 'There's nothing else it could be, other than debris from something else.'

'Debris from where?' said Poppy, a little more forcefully than she meant.

'I don't know, do I?' Teela rubbed her stinging eyes. 'Does it even matter? We've been hit.'

Poppy returned her finger to the sensor and held the receiver back up to her mouth. 'We've hit something and taken considerable damage. We also seem to have been knocked off course.' She paused. 'We're completely lost.' Her heart rose in her chest. 'We're not in any immediate danger, but advice would be very much welcome. Once again, this is Captain Poppy Talib of Star Express Transit Ship – Vitula...' she looked over at Teela, 'with First Officer Teela Rose. OVER.' Her eyes flicked across the words on the screen without really taking them in. 'Send,' she said, collapsing down.

The green light travelled around the edge of the monitor again before disappearing.

They both sat in silence, staring out of the slit window to the blackness beyond.

Chapter Two

Somewhere Close to Nowhere

'We still don't know.' Poppy took a deep breath and stared directly into the camera. 'We're still waiting on a reply.' She contemplated the words before rising from her seat.

The light turned from green to red. 'Recording session terminated,' indicated the dry voice. 'To continue recording, please remain seated.'

Poppy left the booth and stood in the corridor, leaning against the wall until her eyes had adjusted to the bright light.

'Just one more try. You can do it; I know you can.'

It was her mother's voice. She could hear it as if she stood right next to her. Poppy looked down to her feet, the harsh light shining on the metal boot buckle. She closed her eyes. She could smell her mother's perfume; it floated up to her face as she bent down next to her, untangling the knot that had just been made in her size-two shoes.

'Look, Catherine can do it,' her mother said, pointing to her younger sister.

A proud little girl on the back doorstep stomped her feet on the concrete, causing lights to flash down the sides of her trainers.

'Come on, another try.'

A small bleep made Poppy conscious of her surroundings. Her eyes were dry, and she wondered how long she had been staring into the empty space that lingered just in front of her face. A small rectangular watch on her left wrist read, "10:00 U.T."

It bleeped again.

* * *

Poppy reached the end of the corridor and climbed up the cold metallic ladder to the rusted doorway of the Control Room, her trousers providing a suitable surface to wipe the condensation from her hands. 'Any updates?'

'Nah.'

She took her seat to the left of Teela and leant forward, looking intently at the monitors in front of her, remaining quite still as she tried to make sense of the maps. She lifted herself out of the chair and strained her neck above the desk to get a better look through the slit window. The ship below, illuminated by various spotlights, drew her eye away from the sea of empty black that surrounded them and towards the damage.

'It won't be long now.'

Teela stirred from her tablet. 'If you say so.' She caught Poppy's eye. 'What?'

'It's normal for them to take their time,' said Poppy. 'You know what they're like.'

Teela shook her head. 'It's normal for them to take their time when the shower needs fixing, or the washing trolley needs new sensors, which it does, by the way...' she paused. 'I don't know. I just thought this would have been priority.'

'It was priority when we didn't have the right import documentation on those storage units last year,' said Poppy, 'and they still left us hanging around off-planet for five days.'

'Six days,' said Teela.

'Exactly.'

'Well, I wish I had another hiber pill until they decide to show up.' She gave a fake laugh. 'Oh, that's right, we shouldn't even be up yet - another thing that's wrong.' Teela paused for a moment before starting up again. 'There's nothing in them, y'know?'

Poppy looked over, but didn't reply.

'There's nothing in those bloody cells out front, the damaged ones.' She leant back against her chair. 'They're superficial.' She held her finger in front of her face and played with the light, creating shadows across her eyes. 'They could be used for stuff, but ours aren't.'

'Like what?'

Teela shrugged. 'I don't know. Stuff this company can't afford to put in their ships. There's a reason we're flying to the arse-end of nowhere with just three containers.' She snorted. 'I bet it'd be impossible to update this ship even if we wanted to. How old is it? The tech that could be in those cells has probably long since died out. Extinct.'

'Listen,' said Poppy, 'we've done everything by the book. We've followed the procedures and protocols. It's fine. Just kick back and enjoy your extra time awake.'

'Extra time awake? Like this life isn't bad enough without more of it.'

Poppy smiled and stretched. 'Well…' she said, standing up, leaving the word hanging, slowly ending the conversation, 'I'm peckish.' She tapped her stomach. 'Do you want something bringing?'

'One small vine of plump, red cherry tomatoes,' said Teela. 'Fresh and crisp to sink my teeth into. Yeah?'

* * *

Poppy's footsteps reacted violently against the grated floor as she walked back down the main corridor. Pipework and tubing were naked where sections of the once brilliantly white covering had been removed or broken, and two strip lights ran parallel to each other, creating a runway that buzzed monotonously above. She turned off the main corridor and went down a short side passage before reaching the kitchen. A sign, written in Teela's handwriting and stuck to the entrance read, "The Morgue". The hairs on her arms stood to attention as she stepped through the threshold, pulling her skin upwards in a thousand tiny bumps.

Inside, all the surfaces were grey-brushed steel, cold and sparse. In the corner was a fridge, which Teela often joked was where she kept the bodies, and a drainage system, embedded into each worktop that ominously waited for any miscellaneous spillages, as if willing them to occur.

Poppy walked over to the dominant fridge and tentatively touched the long bar handle, waiting for the customary static shock. A piercing sting entered her fingertip and travelled up her arm in a sharp nip, but the anticipation was always the worst part. She grabbed the handle again with more conviction and yanked the door open, quickly pulling out a cylindrical can of corned recon-beef before slamming the door shut, as if taking revenge for the hostile greeting.

She walked over to the worktop opposite and studied the can. The once red labeling, now faded, had been replaced by a murky maroon shade, and on top, an outer layer of frost had encompassed the rather rudimentary ring-pull. She took a knife from the top drawer and started to scrape and scratch at the frost. She jabbed the blade under the pull and leant her weight into it, forcing a crumpled opening and bending the knife under the pressure. She swore, examining the warped metal, before taking a plate and encouraging out the contents with a couple of firm taps. A greyish-mauve substance landed on the surface with an audible thud.

Poppy stared at the gelatinous brick that occupied her plate and thought of home, of her father's Speciality Pie, steaming hot with a crusty top, and her mother's glorious roasts with all the trimmings. Her stomach rumbled as she imagined the delicious smells that used to greet her nostrils when she arrived back from school. She allowed herself to sit at the old table. She could see Catherine setting out the plates and serving up, and could hear the sound of cutlery as it willingly helped with the delightful task.

'How was your day?' asked her mother.

'Fine,' she said, digging her fork into the piping hot potato crust on her plate. 'I got picked to do that presentation I was talking about.'

'Yeah? How do you think it went?'

'I… My voice cracked at the start…'

'But?' said her father, spooning a bit of the gravy into his mouth.

'But I think I did okay.'

'Told you,' both her parents said in unison, smiling.

Poppy begrudgingly sliced the brick, placing the resulting slabs between a folded piece of flatbread that cracked into a crumbly mess. She did her best to clean up the bits before leaning her back against the worktop and holding the plate ready in her hand. The sandwich crumbled as she picked it up. She bent over and tried to lift it to her mouth, taking an awkward bite that she immediately regretted. The beef had a dry, fibrous texture, not helped by the thin and tasteless bread. The stale substance stuck to the roof of her mouth like cement, loosened only by her tongue, which scratched around in her mouth, persuading it to be swallowed. She took another bite and tried to imagine she was back at home and that the meal in front of her was glorious, but no matter how hard she tried, nothing could disguise from how her jaw clamped shut with each arrival, as if begging for the end.

She swallowed the last few bites almost whole, trying to hurry along the process, before loading the plate into the washer and reaching for a bottle of chilled water. Her dry throat glugged as she poured half the contents down her neck. She gasped for breath and took another mouthful to rinse, swashing the liquid around the insides of her cheeks before performing an exaggerated swallow.

* * *

Poppy climbed up the steel ladders to the bedchamber landing, the water bottle forced into her back pocket. She swiped her finger across a small black panel on the wall and waited as the door jolted open with great strain, just enough for her to squeeze through, before juddering shut behind with the same pained sound.

She placed the water bottle on her bedside table and sat on the edge of the bed, letting her head hang low.

'That was lovely,' said her mother, piling the plates into a neat pile. 'Compliments to the chef.'

Her father gave a little bow. 'It's all in the science of the seasoning. It's amazing how far just a little garlic salt can take you. Now,' he said, taking the plates and standing up, 'who wants dessert?'

Poppy tapped her watch, and it sprung into life, cycling through a multitude of colours before settling on a deep grey as a set of small red digits slowly appeared on the screen. Her mouth moved as she read the time aloud in her mind before swinging her legs round and collapsing on the bed. She rolled over to face her pristine room and watched the light as it passed through the bottle, refracting and dancing with the water amongst the subtle vibrations of her movements.

'Go on, Poppy!' shouted a voice from the crowd.

She could feel the anticipation as her thirteen-year-old self stood on the diving board looking down at the water, the light bouncing off the waves and blue tiles, creating a silver net that seemed to want to lure her in.

'It's all in the science,' she said, under her breath, her lips hardly moving. 'Toes pointed, arms straight and clasped, aerodynamics, gravity. Science.' Poppy hit the surface and comfortably broke through the silver net, the cold water gushing around her ears, turning the cheers of the crowd into a drone.

The drone was still there as she stared up at the lights, only this time without the joy that she knew was waiting for her as soon as she resurfaced. Poppy tried to distract herself, concentrating on the small, frosted words printed on the side of the bottle. She wondered how many bottles she had drank during her time on board. She closed her eyes and began to whisper under her breath, 'Natural mineral water. Made especially for space travel. Please store in a cool and dry place. Drink within three days of breaking seal. Natural mineral water. Made especially for space travel. Please store in a cool and dry place. Drink within three days of breaking seal. Natural mineral water. Made especially for space travel. Please store in a cool and dry place. Drink within three days of breaking seal.' She repeated herself again and then again, slowly drifting into a doze, but still aware of her surroundings.

* * *

Another bleep.

A relentless tapping on her brain. It seemed to start quietly before growing into a sharp annoyance. Poppy rubbed her slightly sticky eyes and peered down at her silent watch. She stretched her face and stared, confused, at her wrist as another bleep knocked on her skull. She sat up and allowed herself to regain full consciousness before recognising the higher pitch of the rectangular intercom flashing on her bedside table. 'Hel-' Poppy coughed; she could feel the dust in her throat. She took a swig of the water and tried again. 'Hello?' Her voice was gruff.

'Just the four calls, Poppy.'

She coughed again. 'Sorry, I was asleep… nearly. Captain's prerogative.'

'Not when I'm due a break,' said Teela. 'You coming?'

'Yeah, hold on.' Poppy sat upright. 'Has there been any news?'

There was a short delay as Teela seemed to distractedly rattle around with something.

'Teela? Any news?'

'Of course there hasn't been. I would've told you if there had.' She paused. 'Are you coming up or not?'

'Yeah, I'll be there in a bit.' Poppy slid her finger across the intercom and stood up, holding her arms out for balance as the blood rushed to her legs, before entering the washroom via the open doorway at the end of her bed.

The room was barren and clinical, consisting of a small sink and mirror, complete with shelf and a small metallic toilet. At the far end, there was an open space for showering, and a rusty showerhead fixed to the wall drooped down pathetically, seemingly dazed by the uneven floor that sloped towards a circular drain in the middle of the room.

Poppy rubbed her temple. The lack of furniture seemed to make the lights shine brighter. She stood by the sink and took off her shirt, splashing a fair amount of water over her face before the mirror forced her to stop as her eyes caught sight of herself. She had her father's face.

Her mind drifted to the old bathroom. She pictured herself stood on the small stool, trying to see her face in the mirror as her father swung his arms around in gargantuan sweeps, talking about everything and nothing, slopping water over every surface as he dealt with the dark bristles across his chin.

Poppy picked her damp shirt off the wet floor and swapped it for a fresh one before heading back out onto the landing and beginning the descent down the ladder. It reminded her of the bunk beds they used to have at her grandparents' house as she dropped one foot below the other. She thought about the old single bed she used to have in the spare room before Catherine was allowed to stay over and realised, as she reached the bottom of the ladder, that Catherine had never experienced that house when it was at its fullest.

* * *

'You got them?' said Teela, as Poppy walked through the threshold. 'The tomatoes?'

Poppy made an extravagant gesture with her arms. 'All out, I'm afraid. The guy said he'd just sold the last vine, as well.'

Teela shrugged, the disappointment in her eyes almost believable.

Poppy tucked her shirt into her trousers and edged her chair towards the monitors. 'What do we know?'

Teela raised her eyebrows. 'What, you mean from the last time you asked me five minutes ago? Nothing.' She stood up. 'We're on our own.'

'Give them time,' said Poppy.

'Well, I don't like to be kept waiting.' She handed Poppy her tablet. 'Make yourself useful.' She tapped the surface, and a chart of the System glowed on the screen, illuminating their faces. 'These markers show exactly where we're not. Your job, whilst I'm away, is to find exactly where we are.'

* * *

Teela climbed two-thirds of the ladder before sliding down the rest, the insteps of her feet clamping tight against the outer railing whilst her sleeves, pulled over her hands, dealt competently with the friction. The grating on the floor jolted and clanged as her boots beat up the metal with each step as she hurtled down the corridor at full pelt. She reached her chamber, panting slightly, and clumsily slapped the panel on the wall. The door opened smoothly, compared to Poppy's, and revealed a cave of chaos and disorder. Odds and ends, footwear and clothing, resembled a jumble sale across the floor, and propped upright in the corner was a dirty white panel that had previously fallen from the ceiling, nearly knocking her clean out.

She stared at the mess, a smile on her lips.

'Up! Up! Everybody up!'

She was in a small bed surrounded by white partitions that hung from the tall ceiling like empty sheets of paper. She sat up, listening to the shufflings and murmurs outside that began to grow louder.

'Come on, up!'

A silhouette, seemingly of a bear, grew larger on the furthest partition. She watched it for a moment before lying back down and pulling the scratchy duvet over her head.

'Teela Rose, why aren't you up?'

Teela braced as the partitions shot up at a tremendous pace towards the ceiling, revealing a long dormitory filled with at least twenty-five exact replicas of her bed, each one bland and without any noticeable human interference except for the child that stood sleepily beside it.

'I won't ask you again.'

Teela flung back the cover and stood up on the bed, glaring at the intruder face-to-face, her eight-year-old frame only just reaching eye level even with the platform. She studied the beast of a woman that used to scare her, but no longer held power over her. At least ten-foot tall, nearly the same width, with slicked back hair and bright red lipstick.

'For the third and final time, why are you not up?'

'They keep calling me Basket.'

The children either side giggled at the word.

'Teela,' she said to them, shouting. 'My name is Teela.'

'Basket,' whispered one of the children.

'I'm less concerned about what they call you, Tee-la,' said the beast, 'and more concerned about why you're not out of bed yet.' She pointed towards a small bedside table where Teela had left a hair band. 'What's that doing out? Put it away. The cupboard is there for a reason. We are not pigs.'

Teela pulled off her stiff boots and threw them onto the

mound of clothes by her feet, watching as they slowly slid off the peak and landed on the floor with a clomp. She stepped forward and swore as her toe stubbed on something hard, concealed by a molehill of socks, before regaining her balance, swiveling precariously on the spot, and clambering over to the washroom.

Vests, underwear and hair bands were strewn across the floor, but seemed less obvious in the spacious surroundings. She used her sleeve to wipe away a murky smudge from the mirror before picking a random hair grip from the sink and sliding it into her mousy brown hair that came to just above her shoulders. She stared at the youthful face before leaning in towards the mirror and toying with a small scar above her left cheek. She studied it for a moment and smiled.

'Just let me do it,' said Teela, as Poppy stood watch.

'It's not going in.'

'It is.' Teela measured the trolley with her hands and moved them across to the door frame of the Utility Room. 'It'll fit. I'll make it.'

'On your head be it.'

Teela took a run and rammed the trolley as hard as she could. It hit the frame, scraping along the side and jamming itself tight into the doorway as Teela went over the top, hitting her face on the rim before landing upside down in the cart.

* * *

Her feet sank between the slats of her bed as she hobbled about trying to find scraps of clothing, the reflective surface of the locker doors on the opposite wall doing nothing except to magnify the clutter. She pulled the final layer over her head and jumped down, scrambling for her boots, before backhanding the empty water bottles from her bedside table and sliding her finger across the intercom. 'Poppy, just thinking,' she paused, slightly breathless. 'I'm gonna go down to the cargo and check on the parcels.'

* * *

Teela jogged leisurely to the back of the ship, making sure not to break into a sweat. She reached the small rusted lift and opened the door, before stepping onto the cramped rectangular platform. It droned into action with a jolt, the temperature dropping dramatically as she descended, the chill hitting her unprotected face with a vicious bite and her breath, now visible, billowing out of her lungs, disappearing as quickly as it came with each inhalation.

The metal pallet hit the bottom, and she stepped off, leaving the tight compartment as a shiver ran across her skin. She stopped. In front, a space the size of a large aeroplane hangar enveloped the lift, dominating over her with condensation-lined walls and a maze of peeling white pipes and tubing that snaked across the floor. She reached for the tablet fixed to the wall and made her way down a narrow walkway towards the centre of the hold, each step echoing throughout the nether regions of the ship like deep cymbals.

She approached the far end and stepped off the walkway to an open area. Large dirty plastic strips hung down from the ceiling, partially concealing three great black containers, as tall as multiple houses and the same wide. She stood in the middle of the open space and absorbed the threatening magnificence of the giants. Her back straightened as she looked up, right to the top, where the high edges were hard to decipher from the roof of the cargo hold, the two blending together in a darkened mist, as the containers stood proudly to attention, dwarfing her into insignificance.

A twitch of a smile appeared on her lips. She grasped the tablet like a lion tamer would a whip and purposefully marched towards the container furthest to the right. She found a small serial code etched under the handle and positioned the tablet's camera. It took a few moments to process the information before a message appeared on screen, indicating that the code had been successfully read and added to the report.

Teela refreshed the screen and repeated the process for the next two containers before beginning her inspection around the circumference. She walked slowly, as close to the metal giants as possible without touching them, her head tilting up occasionally, looking for any signs of peculiarities on the corrugated sides, before always seeming to fall back to the join where the bottom of the containers hit the floor.

A small superficial crack in the surface layer of the floor caught her eye as it always did. It darted across her path like a bolt of electricity before disappearing under the middle container. She bent down and traced the crack, the tip of her finger sneaking into the opening, entering a couple of millimeters between the ground and the metal lip. She imagined herself lifting up the whole container with the one finger, holding it above her head and tossing it away as if it were nothing.

'I bet Basket couldn't lift it.'

Teela looked into the face of the ringleader, and then to the vase. They were both twice as big as her, with the latter being made from some sort of dark frosted metal. 'I can lift it,' she said, pushing through the small crowd of children.

'No, you can't,' said the ringleader. 'If I can't lift it, how are you gonna lift it?'

Teela crouched down beside the vase and wrapped her arms around it with a bearhug, pushing down through her thighs until it lifted a centimetre or two off the ground.

'Higher,' said the ringleader.

Teela straightened her back and pushed the vase against the wall, lifting bit by bit until its base was almost at her eye level. She smiled, her face red, but shaking with satisfaction.

'Now!' shouted the ringleader.

A child from the crowd ran towards Teela, pulling her trousers down to her ankles before moving out of the way for the rest to pelt her with pebbles of wet paper tissue.

The cold sting of the black metal container bit at her skin, and Teela quickly pulled away, finishing her inspection and leaving the open area almost embarrassed, as if she had been caught out by her own fantasy.

She climbed up to the walkway and returned the tablet to the wall. Taking a last look at the bleak scene, she was deserting before boarding the lift. The shaft wall scrolled slowly past her face in a parade of marks and scratches as she rose to the main level. A large dent, which had been there ever since she could remember, seemed to knock at her subconscious. She thought back to the crack in the hold. She imagined the ground underneath the containers suddenly buckling under the pressure as a crevice developed around the base, creating an opening that dragged everything into it before anyone knew what was happening. She could see the contents of the ship floating around, bobbing aimlessly in the empty blackness, the containers now small, dwarfed by this new unlimited ocean.

The kick, as the lift reached the top, woke her from the idea. She returned to her room and sat on the edge of her bed, her heart beating slightly faster than it had before. She slackened her bootlaces and rested her heels on the back of the boots, pushing down and squashing the heel-tabs. She let the air circulate underneath her soles before slipping her feet back in, leaving the laces untied.

Her thoughts turned back to the crack again before drifting onwards. She was on board the Gulliver's farming ship, inside their newest barn. It was her thirteenth birthday, and Mr. Gulliver had told her to shift the hay bales. She could smell the dust, just like it was, stabbing at her eyes and nose as if she was there. Her hands were raw from the rough netting, and her sweltering feet felt like they were about to burst out of her ill-fitting boots. Harold Jnr was sat at the top of the pile, throwing bits of straw at her head as she worked.

'Is there any more?' she said, her voice dry, as the sun punched through the convex glass of the high domed ceiling and into the barn.

'Aye. Those.' Harold Jnr pointed to the landing where three bales hid in the upper shadows. 'Happy birthday, isn't it?' he said.

Teela ignored him and climbed the ladder to the second floor. 'Why doesn't your Dad buy some equipment for this sort of thing?'

'He did,' said Harold Jnr, 'you.'

He snorted at his own joke as Teela tossed a bale down with great strain. It landed at the bottom, bouncing off a corner before lying completely still.

'Temper,' said Harold Jnr, as he spat towards the new addition.

Teela awkwardly approached the second bale, edging along, the metal roof beams not far from her head. 'You were supposed to be helping.'

Harold Jnr shrugged as Teela grabbed the second bale. She lifted through her legs, pushing down on her swollen feet.

'I just-' Harold Jnr spun round, a loud crack clipping his ears as Teela fell through the flimsy boards to the ground below.

A flashing light on the intercom poked the corner of her eye. She reached over and played the message.

'Teela, come up when you get this.'

* * *

'What is it?' said Teela, as she entered the boxy confines of the Control Room.

Poppy spun round on her chair. Worry seemed to edge further across her face the closer Teela got to desk. 'Have a look at this.' She pointed to a small monitor.

Teela leant towards the screen, squinting at the mass of seemingly incomprehensible letters and symbols. 'What exactly am I looking for?'

'Exactly.' Poppy rubbed her brow. 'There's nothing there. The messages... our messages... they never sent.'

'But it said...' Teela reached over and studied the code. 'They went. It said that they went. You saw me send them.'

Poppy shook her head. 'It just gave confirmation of the command, that they were going to be transmitted. It didn't confirm they had actually gone.'

Teela paused, staring at her flat expression. 'Let me try again.'

'I already did.'

'But let me again.' She shuffled her chair to Poppy's position at the desk, brushing her aside. 'Reload last message,' she said, purposely, and text appeared on the screen. 'Send to last recipient.'

A green light ran around the perimeter of the monitor before disappearing. Teela brought the mass of letters and symbols back up on the screen. They stared towards it in anticipation, but nothing happened.

'It should be there,' she said, pointing to an empty line.

Poppy didn't reply, choosing instead to sit down and shunt her chair over to Teela's usual spot.

'Show the recipient's profile.'

A grid, listing various numbers and codes regarding the base's communications, appeared on screen.

Teela studied the form carefully and seemed satisfied. 'Pair,' she said, in a loud clear voice.

The green light danced around the perimeter once more, but this time turned to red as it reached the top.

Poppy placed her elbow on the desk, resting her head on the tight fist of her left hand as Teela repeated the process. They watched as the green light ran around before turning again to red.

'Try somewhere else.'

'Where?'

Poppy thought for a moment. 'Try the Winter Hill Outpost. It's the closest Comms planet to our original course.'

Teela selected the outpost and waited as the green light went around the screen before turning to red. Poppy's head sank.

Teela tried again, only to be met with the same result. 'I don't know what to do,' she said. 'It won't lock on.' She stared at the monitors. 'I knew something was wrong. I told you. I knew it was taking them too long.'

Poppy stood up and pushed the chair away.

'What we gonna do?'

'Nothing we can do.' Poppy fiddled with the edge of the desk and tried to give a comforting smile. 'Just have to wait it out.' She strained her neck, looking out of the slit window beyond the desk. 'Sooner or later they'll realise we're not where we should be and come looking,' she said. 'Until then, looks like it's just you and me.'

Chapter Three

The First Contact

Poppy waited for the light to change from red to green. 'Captain's log, on board Star Express Transit Ship – Vitula. Poppy Talib.' She shifted in her chair. 'I thought we might have heard something by now. I-' she stopped herself. 'Morale is pretty good. Just carrying on, standard duties, routine cargo checks, etcetera. First Officer Rose is still focused on the transmitter. We're just carrying on.' She looked down momentarily at her hands. 'Could do with a bit of good news, if I'm honest.' She gave a fake laugh that was tired. 'Feel like we've been stood up.'

* * *

'Any news?' said Poppy, as she entered the Control Room.

Teela didn't reply, her face buried inside a tablet.

'Still mardy?' Poppy sat down at the desk, accidentally knocking a panel with her foot.

Teela looked up, as if only just realising someone else was in the room. 'You finished lecturing?'

'Yeah.' Poppy leant back in her chair. 'Not really much to say, is there?'

'Right, well...' Teela clambered to her feet, ignoring her. 'I need a break.'

Poppy nodded and pulled her chair closer to the desk. 'Anything you want me to do?'

'Yeah,' she said, gesturing loosely to the monitors, 'fix it.'

Teela cracked her knuckles as she meandered down the clanking corridor. A double door on her right, with glass cutouts, broke up the tiresome repetition of yellowing wall panels and pipes. She went through and entered a large dimly lit room, longer than it was wide and far greater than both of the bedchambers combined. A small settee lined the sidewall, with a table in front and a medium-sized monitor that allowed various sorts of entertainment to be played, but none of it mattered.

Teela's gaze immediately anchored itself to the Window – a wall of glass, free from any frames, which stretched uninterrupted along the length of the room, allowing the magnificence of the universe to break into the ship. She ignored the settee and the monitor and walked across to the opposite side, choosing instead to sit on the floor, as close to the Window as she could get. She pushed her head forward, so it was almost touching, and looked down. Around the rim, she could just about see the protruding exterior of the ship as it clamped the glass, forming a tight housing. She leant back and stared outwards, trying to ignore the reflections of the room inside.

In the distance, stars became fish, their iridescent scales catching the rare streaks of moonlight able to break through the water's surface. Her mind wandered. She imagined herself swimming through the vast ocean of the galaxy. The ripples of water bursting away from her strokes like supernovas before fading into nothing. Below her, planets danced in synchrony, spinning so fast that it was as if not at all, moving in circles, weaving in and out of each other, repeating themselves over and over.

Teela climbed out of her bed and crawled under one of the hanging partitions. Her head poked into the long dormitory, followed by the rest of her as she scurried to her feet. The room was completely dark except for an emergency exit sign that glowed a horrible lime green, and the dimly lit corridor that leaked into the room through the glass window of the door. She turned around and headed in the opposite direction, right to the far end where two large windows sat quietly behind two enormous blinds. She found the gap and slid her body inside, perching herself on the cold metal of the windowsill. The blind wafted for a moment, gently swaying from the interruption before falling still as she tucked herself away in the corner, resting her cheek against the glass.

Outside, the grounds had been illuminated by various spike lights that had been pushed into the grass along the edge of the wide path leading to the exit and the street beyond. Teela squinted, dissolving the surroundings until all that was left was the small orbs of yellow light in her vision. She played with them, making them grow in size by carefully opening her lids, before shrinking the golden dots by closing her eyes tight. She looked up to the sky and tried to make out the real stars. She held her hands to the side of her face, like binoculars, trying to create a seal and block out the light, but it was no good. All she could see was the glow of the city reflecting off the clouds.

* * *

Her eyes were dry by the time she woke. She had barely blinked since she had sat down, as if her body refused to let her look away from the Window for even a second. She could hear Poppy's footsteps clunking down the corridor and readied herself for her arrival, wiping her eyes and moving back slightly from the glass.

Poppy walked over and stood beside her, staring out at the vast ocean, her hands resting purposefully on her hips. Teela watched her face in anticipation as a thought moved slowly from her mind to her lips.

'I'm doing a wash.'

Teela tipped her head back in disappointment. 'I thought you were going to say something then.'

'I did.'

She shook her head and walked over to the settee. 'Nah, I meant something, y'know, with bite. Important.'

Poppy smiled. 'Putting a wash on is important. What kind of world would we be living in if nobody put a wash on?'

Teela slumped in her seat and rested her eyes on the glass. 'How far away do you reckon we are from the nearest person?'

'Further than we've ever been, I reckon.' Poppy turned her body to match Teela's gaze.

Teela thought about it for a second, repeating the notion in her mind.

Poppy shrugged. 'Can't be certain, of course, but I think it's likely.'

'Still too close for me,' said Teela.

Poppy smirked and turned round to face her.

'The pile on the right is getting a little frisky,' said Teela. 'Don't touch the things near the bed.' She paused. 'I'll go back up in a bit, I'll just have a few more minutes.'

Poppy nodded and left her to the Window. She headed down the hall and towards the bedchambers, stopping off on the way to collect a bulky wire trolley that followed her closely behind like a puppy, the temperamental sensors on its front copying her movements the best it could.

She approached the bedchamber ladder and groaned as the wheels wobbled in the steel grates of the flooring, knocking it off course and into the shallow channels either side of the main walkway. She dragged it out and positioned it under a square funnel in a cavity behind the ladder, like an open air-vent, before climbing up to the landing and entering Teela's chamber.

The room was worse than last time, the clothes somehow multiplying between washes. Poppy stood, struggling to differentiate the pile to the right from all the other mounds of clothes that surrounded it. She flicked her eyes over the various possibilities and navigated her way towards a mountain in the corner whose summit seemed slightly higher than the rest. She pushed up the battered shutter of the hatch, embedded in the wall near the washroom, and began tossing the clothes inside.

'Are you going to say something?' said her mother.

Her father stood with his hands on his hips, staring out of the window. 'It's his garden. What can I do?'

'It just looks a state. It's like a jungle.'

'A jungle, you say?' said her father, bending down with a mischievous look to his face.

'Hey,' said her mother, pushing him back. 'Kaleem, I didn't mean like that,' she said, giggling, causing Poppy to giggle as he tackled her down onto the settee.

'But we all know Mr Tiger Tickles lives in the jungle,' said Kaleem, as all three began to squirm in throes of laughter.

Poppy's face was flushed by the time the last white sock, which she had almost mistaken as a black sock, had been thrown down the chute. She collapsed down in Teela's chair, surveying the scene, using the hard surface of the desk to prop up her head. To her surprise, the workspace was actually relatively tidy. A small light occupied the far right of the desk, accompanied by a file stack and a small set of plastic drawers. To the left was a tablet, and at the back, rolled against the wall, was a small upturned stationery holder that she had knocked over with a casually tossed vest.

Poppy picked up the elegant stylus that had fallen out and returned it to its small black tube. A small ting rang out as she let go. There was something she couldn't quite make out glistening at the bottom. She pushed her little finger inside, touching whatever it was with the stub of her nail, before gently tipping up the tube into her hand. An exquisite ruby hairpin landed quite comfortably in the crevice between her index and middle finger. She brought her hand closer to her face and studied the ornament. It was about ten centimetres long with the main body of the clasp seemingly made from silver or possibly platinum. Her eyes ran up the length of the perfectly straight stem. Towards the top third, the metal twisted and contoured to form an elegant knot that held tight a deep ruby stone, circular in shape. She rolled it between her thumb and finger. The gem, intense and hypnotic, twinkled as different cut sides were suddenly bathed in pools of light.

A contracting, heating pipe cracked outside and drew her attention away. She picked up the holder and placed the pin on the inside edge before slowly tilting it up, gently enough as not to damage the seemingly fragile ornament. She carefully rested the stylus on top before returning it to its original position.

* * *

Poppy headed towards the Utility Room, the heaped trolley of washing dutifully following her as she walked.

Her mind wandered again. She could see her mother standing by the kitchen table, proofreading an article she was about to post.

'Look, look,' she said, tugging at her clothes. 'Look what I've done!' Poppy dragged her up and led her towards her bedroom.

'Whoa,' said her mother, in an overly dramatic voice, as Poppy proudly showed her the bed where all her clothes had been ordered and placed into seven neat small piles. 'You did this all by yourself?'

'Yeah,' she said, nodding. 'Look,' she pointed to the nearest pile. 'This is for Monday.' She moved along a pile. 'This is for Tuesday.' She moved along again. 'This is for'…

Poppy entered the Utility Room and immediately regretted the notion, the trolley bumping repeatedly against the narrow doorframe as it tried to follow her.

She looked back, a smile forming on her lips as she noticed two large scuff marks on either side of the frame. She went over and halted the trolley before grabbing an armful of clothes and dumping them in a large drum that squatted in the corner. There was a soft whump as they hit the bottom, and her mind drifted back to Teela's bedchamber and the hairpin. She went for another armful. The red stone reminded her of a brooch her mother used to have.

Poppy looked down and was holding a piece of glossy paper. She tapped on a bold headline, and a video started to play.

'What do you think?' said her mother, barging into the room. 'I've asked your father, but he's as useful as a-'

'Bikini in the Arctic,' said a voice, interrupting from the other room.

'Yes… Thank you, Kaleem!' she shouted back, sarcastically. 'So,' she held up a red dress in one hand and a white dress in the other. 'I'm wearing my poppy brooch. It goes with the red better, but it stands out better against the white. What do you think?'

Poppy moved forward to the edge of her bed. 'Mum,' she held the paper, which was still playing, towards her mother. 'I got it.'

A large masthead flashed, "Accepted", in bold letters, and underneath, a man in a suit was waffling on about the Star Express Postal Service family.

Poppy swiped her finger across the thin black panel on the side of the drum. A large gushing sound crashed into the room as the trollish machine sprang into life and filled itself with a soapy solution. She picked up a small pile of separate clothes that had been drying and unhalted the trolley. It shot away from her, fiercely, like two magnets repelling each other, before crashing into a nearby wall.

* * *

Poppy entered her room and retrieved the small pile of clothes waiting for her in the hatch, sucked up by the funnel below. She folded them neatly and placed them into her locker. A rectangular photograph of her family, perched on the inside of the locker door, caught her eye as she moved away. She opened the door a little and let the light touch the faces. She waited a moment, just staring at the still image, before sliding her finger along the top of glossy paper, causing the picture to move in looped footage that played again and again. She watched as their mouths widened to cheesy grins and then returned, only to widen again as the loop repeated, their hands waving continuously.

Poppy could feel the spring air on her face as it swam through the grass, and she could taste the contents of the picnic box she knew lay just out of frame.

'Will it hurt?' She took her socks off and gave them to her father. 'It looks spiky.'

'Hurt?' said Kaleem, digging his toes into the freshly cut grass. 'It's one of the greatest sensations known to humankind; your toes won't know what's hit them!' He turned to her mother. 'Honestly, Alice, love, we shouldn't have waited this long.'

Poppy's eyes traced across the faces she knew so well. Her father, Kaleem, with his thick, bushy eyebrows; Alice, her mother, holding up Catherine, trying to get her to wave; her aunties and uncles and her cousins in matching overalls; and then her grandparents, Grandma Iselda and Grandad Richard Lehrer. Her gaze lingered on the face of her grandad who was at the front of the group in a wheelchair that seemed slightly too big for him, his face gaunt and tired through the smiles and waves.

Poppy slid her finger back across the photo, and the loop froze before returning to the original starting pose. She closed the door slowly, watching as each face gradually disappeared into shadow before being obscured by the rim of the locker. A click sounded from the mechanism, and a light above the lock turned red as a sad breath left her lungs.

'It tickles,' said Poppy. 'It's tickling my feet,' she said again, laughing.

'Really?' said Grandad Lehrer.

'Yeah!' She paused, noticing her grandad's feet were still on the metal footplate of his wheelchair. 'Have you ever felt it?'

Grandad Lehrer nodded. 'Oh yes, I have. Not for a long time, mind.'

Poppy stood motionless for a moment as she thought, before quickly bending down and yanking a tuft of grass from the ground. 'There,' she said, sprinkling it from a height on top of her grandad's feet, 'it tickles, doesn't it?'

Poppy picked up a couple of Teela's clothes, left over from the pile, and walked across the landing. The light turned green, and she stared in at her sparse locker, just the one photo stuck to the wall. She slid her finger over the image, and it burst into life. She watched as Teela pushed her out of shot and stuck up two fingers towards the camera, the two of them both laughing uncontrollably. A smile quietly spread across Poppy's face as she remembered the feeling. She watched the loop again and again, not able to tear her eyes away from the joy, as the room seemed to disappear apart from her hand and the photo. Smile, push, Vs, laugh, repeat. It was the first time she felt she had met the real Teela. The first time she could see slight cracks on the brickwork of her impenetrable wall.

A vest slipped from the top of the pile, and Poppy caught it with an outstretched knee. She reset the photo and returned it to the locker before neatly placing the pile into the small compartment and shutting the door. She picked up an empty food carton by her feet and threw it towards the overfilled bin in the corner.

* * *

Poppy sat in the Control Room, studying a chart of the nearest bases to their original route.

Teela waffled aloud to the room, an indignant expression on her face. 'Can you believe it, though?' she said. 'We have to be rescued? We've turned into one of those pitiful ships that need to be rescued. Can you believe it? It's embarrassing. It's bloody embarrassing.'

Poppy smiled vacantly, but wasn't really listening. 'Teela?' She threw the chart on the desk and fenced with the idea of asking her about the hairpin. 'I found something before.'

'Oh yeah?'

'It was in your room… in the stylus case on your table.'

Teela sat up. 'You been searching through my things?'

'No,' said Poppy, 'it wasn't like that. It was by accident. I knocked it over, and the stylus fell out.'

Teela listened, but was no longer in the room. She was stood at a horrible, once clear, but now yellowing reception desk, her bags by her feet.

'You have to sign this,' said a middle-aged man, handing her a piece of paper. 'What you came in with.'

Teela scrolled down the list as the man rummaged in a back room. A yellow blanket. A peach babygrow, size three-six months. A pair of white socks. A pair of white shoes, size one. A wicker flower basket. Envelope and hairpin.

The man returned carrying a box. He set it down on the desk and opened it up so Teela could see the contents.

She stared at the tiny clothes, the shoes, still perfectly white, not big enough to place her toes in. 'I don't want them. Or the basket.'

'Fair enough.' The man shoved the box to one side. 'You still gotta sign the form.'

Teela slid her finger across the paper, scrolling to the dotted line at the bottom. 'Wait, where's the hairpin?' She spun the form around, pointing to the tiny black letters. 'The hairpin?'

The man feigned to look in the box before giving up the pretence. 'There,' he said, bringing out a yellowing envelope from the back room.

Teela tore it open and tipped the contents onto the desk. She stared at the elegant pin, the red gemstone glinting up at her, standing out from the grey top of the desk, offering hope for the first time in her life. She picked it up nonchalantly, as if it were only a pencil, not wanting to give the man any satisfaction of the elation rushing through her skin, before dropping it into her jacket pocket and crunching up the envelope.

'Okay?' said the man.

'There,' she said, copying his tone, signing the paper with her finger and picking up her bags.

Teela looked over to Poppy who was staring at her. 'It's none of your business. Just stay out of my things.'

Poppy opened her mouth to speak, but was interrupted by a loud, high-pitched tone that pierced the cabin.

'It's them,' said Teela, hastily tapping the screen marked, "Allow Audio Transmission".

They waited anxiously, Poppy looking at Teela and Teela looking steadfast at the screen, but for a millisecond where her eyes flicked towards Poppy.

The tone stopped, replaced by a grinding sound that echoed around the room as the two ships tried to connect, followed closely by another high-pitched tone.

Then silence.

'*Star Express Transit Ship – Vitula, this is Captain Jason Sheridan from the Department of Search and Rescue. OVER.*' The voice was clean and confident and seemed to be from a man slightly older than the two of them.

Poppy held her thumb across the sensor on the receiver. 'Captain Jason Sheridan, this is Vitula. GO AHEAD.' She lifted her thumb and waited.

'*Star Express Transit Ship – Vitula, this is Captain Jason Sheridan from the Department of Search and Rescue. Do you read me? OVER.*'

Poppy covered the patch again. 'Captain Jason Sheridan, this is Vitula. We read you loud and clear.' She smiled. 'And may

I add that it's so good to be able to say that. OVER.' She let go of the receiver and waited. The pause was longer this time.

'*Star Express Transit Ship – Vitula, this is Captain Jason Sheridan from the Department of Search and Rescue. Do you read me? OVER.*'

Poppy looked at Teela. 'Captain Sheridan, this is Vitula. We read you. OVER.'

'*Vitula, this is Captain Jason Sheridan from the Department of Search and Rescue. Do you read me? OVER.*'

'Yes, we read you. OVER.'

'*Vitula, this is Captain Jason Sheridan from the Department of Search and Rescue. Do you read me? OVER.*'

Teela took the receiver from Poppy. 'We read you!'

The two of them stared at the monitor, both tacitly agreeing that this should be the place to focus their worry as the room filled with a long silence.

'*Vitula, this is Captain Jason Sheridan from the Department of Search and Rescue. Do you read me? OVER.*'

Chapter Four

Same Way, Different Reasons

Teela held the paper by her side and tried to match the face with a person sat at one of the tightly packed tables in the overly lit room. She scanned across the jumble of people, all trying to do the same, before she saw one staring back at her, smiling.

Teela fought her way across, sidestepping through the narrow aisles between table and chair legs, before reaching the match.

'You must be Teela?' said Poppy, standing up and holding out her hand.

Teela nodded and shook it.

'I'm Poppy, Poppy Talib.' She beamed a smile that was almost too big.

'It's busy,' said Teela, pulling out a chair and sitting down.

'Yeah,' Poppy straightened out the pleats on her trousers and sat down. 'Yeah, we're packed in like sardines here.'

Teela nodded, not quite sure what sardines were.

'I'm…' Teela watched a nearby pairing greet each other for the first time. 'I'm not really sure what's going on, to be honest. I've never-'

'Don't worry,' said Poppy, interrupting, 'this is my first job too. It's not something I ever really imagined doing. My parents are both in education, in one way or another, and I just assumed I would end up there myself. I just remember them constantly talking about all these great things,' she gestured with her hands. 'Out there when I was growing up, and then I saw the advert for the Star Express and I thought, why not? Why not go out and actually see some of it firsthand, so to speak? Why not go and see some of that beauty and magic, and all those things that are going on firsthand, instead of through a screen?' Poppy took a deep breath and continued on. 'Of course, being captain on my first attempt, that was just a bonus. I was really happy with that…' She noticed Teela's polite nods becoming less and less pronounced. 'Sorry, here I am just waffling on. What about you?'

Teela didn't reply straight away. Poppy repositioned herself in her chair, happily waiting for the answer.

'Oh, I dunno,' said Teela, at last. 'I guess, I just wanted to get away from it all.'

'Away from what?'

Teela tapped her finger on the desk, scraping off a bit of the flaking paint. 'All that stuff you just mentioned, all those things that are going on.'

'Oh,' said Poppy, nodding, not sure of how to respond.

They sat in silence, letting the droning chatter from the other tables fill the space as they both tried to think of what to say next.

'I…' Poppy lowered her voice. 'I didn't know whether to mention it, but I guess we've both read each other's files?'

Teela nodded. 'I reckon mine is quite a bit smaller than yours.'

'Yeah, well… that doesn't matter,' said Poppy. 'I guess as my first action of note as captain, I just wanna say, if you ever wanna-'

'No,' said Teela, doing her best to look everywhere around the room except in Poppy's direction.

'Well, that's okay too,' said Poppy. 'It seems like we're going the same way for completely different reasons.' She gave an awkward laugh.

Teela nodded.

* * *

'There is no need to worry; this is not a test. Those have already been completed. It's why you're here in this room and not somewhere else.' The microphone reverberated around the room. 'This is simply another bonding exercise, to get you used to your new crewmate. It's… fun.'

Teela eyed up Poppy who was standing beside her and looking attentively at the speaker like a puppy to its master.

'Remember, your crewmate is your family. They're your partner. Yes, one of you will outrank the other, but both of you have important roles to play. One is no use without the other.'

Teela noted Poppy's perfectly pressed cuffs. Even the upturns on her trousers were just as immaculate as when the new recruits had first been issued the uniforms a month ago. She wasn't quite sure what she imagined when she first read Poppy's name on the pairing papers, but this wasn't far from it.

'Of course,' continued the speaker, 'you're going to have your differences, like any family, but we have done our best, using all the data from the tests and your account profiles, to pair you with someone complimentary, someone who you should ultimately get on with.'

Teela swapped her weight from one foot to the other and let her eyes drift around as the speaker ploughed on with their monologue that everyone could tell had been said a thousand times before.

The room was big, but smaller than she expected for a company of this size, packed with about twenty or thirty partners, all standing in slightly haphazard little rows of couplets. Without turning her head too much, she weighed up the people closest to her, trying to gauge whether they were a captain or a first officer, before allowing herself to look at their lapel pins to see if she was correct. She got the first four almost immediately before being stumped by a chubby man with messy blond hair diagonally to her left. She fidgeted forward a couple of centimetres, trying to get a better look at him through a couple she had already identified.

His stance gave the impression of confidence, a waft of

superiority seeping from him that suggested he was almost too good to be there, but this very same arrogance was the thing that made him shrink next to his partner. A scrawny-looking man with an open face and a ready smile who gave the appearance of someone owning a knowledge of life the blond-haired man could only dream of.

'And that is why,' the speaker droned on, 'the job that you are all going to do is so important. You really are,' they gave a corporate smile. '"*Removing the space between us.*"'

There was a small ripple of annoyance around the room.

'But that's enough of me waffling on,' said the speaker.

A few small pockets of concurring grumbles echoed off the ripple, forcing the speaker to inject some positive energy.

'Let's just get on with it, shall we? If you make your way to the side of the room, you will find a piece of paper and your main puzzle. One of you will instruct; one of you will construct. It's completely up to you who does what. And remember, it's not a race,' the speaker paused for dramatic effect. 'Or is it!' They paused again, waiting for some sort of reaction, but were met with apathy. 'Let's go!' they shouted, trying to raise the enthusiasm of the whole room as everyone began to move from their spots.

Teela kept her eyes on the man with the blond hair as he slowly turned around, ambling towards the side of the room with the others, a gold pin badge stuck upside down in his lapel.

'So,' said Poppy, turning to face Teela.

Teela pursed her lips and gave a nod as they followed the rest of the couples.

'Do you want to be instructor or constructor?' asked Poppy.

Teela shrugged. 'Up to you.'

At the side of the room was a row of small platforms each pushed tight against the walls where the instructors stood, holding their piece of paper, looking down to their partners who each stood next to a small table with a metal case, no bigger than a jewellery box.

'I don't mind doing the physical stuff, if you wanna read off the sheet?' said Teela, as they watched everyone else take their places.

'If you're sure?'

Teela nodded, her jaws numb from the forced niceties.

'Okay!' said the speaker. 'Now, as I say, it's not a race and there's no time limit, but we all like a bit of competition, so the first one to finish gets a ten Pix coupon you can use in the canteen.

'So, it's a race,' mumbled someone a few platforms down, causing a few rebellious laughs.

'That's ten Pix you can use on any item in the canteen,' said the speaker, ignoring them. 'Okay, remember, everything you need is on the paper. Three... two... one... go!'

Poppy slid her finger across the edge of the crinkled instructions, causing the paper to illuminate and reveal the set of neatly bullet-pointed commands. She squinted her eyes and began to read out loud before lowering her tone to a forced whisper. 'Okay, first we need to unlock the case.'

Teela examined the lock.

'What do you see?' asked Poppy.

'It's a load of symbols. Six spaces.'

'Do you recognise any?'

Teela shook her head. 'No, they're just shapes-lines and dots as well.'

Poppy scrolled down the page. 'What's the first symbol?'

'It's a square with a dot in the middle.'

'Is the dot filled in or hollow?'

'Filled in,' said Teela, waiting for the result as Poppy went silent for a moment.

'Okay, type two and then one.'

Teela swiped her finger across the lock and typed the first two numbers.

'Second symbol?'

'A circle with a line going through it, straight down.' Teela waited.

'Is the line dotted or just a line?'

'Just a line.'

'Okay,' said Poppy, 'type zero and then five.'

Teela did as she was told before moving on. 'It's a triangle with the point at the top and two lines on the outside edge of the sloping bit.' She turned round and held her arms like a pyramid, her fingers pointed at the top. 'Like this,' she said, noting that a few of the other teams had managed to get into their cases.

'Dotted?'

'What?'

'Are the lines dotted?'

'No, I would've said.'

'Okay, a one... and a nine.' Poppy's mind clicked into place. 'Oh, I get it.'

Teela had already realised and typed the next two numbers. 'Yeah, I know. It's our dates.'

'Twenty-one, zero five and nineteen, zero four,' said Poppy. 'It must've signed me in when I touched the paper-'

'Yeah,' said Teela, interrupting the revelation, 'what's next?'

'Inside there should be some glasses and a pair of gloves.' Poppy looked up. Teela had already put them on. 'Okay, what do you see?'

'It's like a ball,' said Teela. 'No wait, it's Earth, but it's all cut into blocks and segments, like a jigsaw. I don't know what I have to do. What are the instructions?'

'It doesn't say anything yet. Try touching it,' said Poppy.

Teela reached out her hand and pressed a large section of the blue and green orb.

'Anything?'

Teela waited. 'Yeah, hold on,' she said. 'They're moving, coming apart.'

'I've got it,' said Poppy, as a diagram of the puzzle appeared on the paper. She watched as all the curved segments slowly drifted apart, revealing, for a brief glimpse, how they all slotted together, before rotating in one big shuffle and halting as they all suspended themselves in space. 'I'm glad this wasn't on the tests,' said Poppy, twisting her fingers on the paper, surveying each segment in its entirety.

'Any idea?' said Teela.

'I guess we just have to put it back together.'

'Yeah, but how?'

'I'd start with the smaller sections; they were probably in the middle, and then work your way out.'

Teela nodded in a way that implied she was hoping for a better suggestion, before grabbing the smallest piece she could find and setting it right in front of her. She found another that looked like it vaguely fit and pushed it towards the first. A small red line darted around the peripheral of her glasses in unison with a small buzz of a claxon as the two segments pushed themselves apart like opposing magnets. She swore under her breath and grabbed a few more pieces, twisting them in the space before pushing them together at different points. One pair turned green, giving a satisfying click, as the rest pushed themselves away from each other. 'Can you not see anything that could help? What's on your paper?' she said, pulling down the glasses so she could see where the other couples were.

'I just see the pieces move when you pick them up, that's it,' said Poppy. 'I can suggest pieces if you want but-'

'No,' said Teela, 'it'll just get confusing.' She glanced back at the others, struggling to tell how they were doing as each constructor fumbled around, seemingly swatting at fresh air, with their instructor gesticulating behind.

She pushed the glasses back up to her eyes and carried on, flicking her gaze over each curve and corner, trying to form some sort of logic. She grabbed a few more segments and jumbled them together, some clicking into place, some falling apart, before trying another set, and another, each time having minimal success. 'This is pointless,' she said, after the sixth attempt to jam two pieces with similar bevelled ends together. 'There must be a hundred… two hundred pieces here. I don't understand why they've given us this problem when it's so one sided?' She wiped the sweat from her brow. 'They wouldn't set a task that only involved one person.'

Poppy didn't reply.

'What is it?' said Teela, taking off the glasses again, noting the sheepish look on Poppy's face.

'I didn't see this…' Poppy showed the paper to Teela, her finger hovering over the small diagram of scattered segments. 'When I tap and hold one of the pieces,' she explained. 'Numbers appear at the top of the page.' She gave a sorry look. 'I didn't notice the numbers.'

'And all the segments are numbered, and it tells you which go with which?'

A cheer interrupted them as a couple at the far end finished the puzzle, closely followed by a second, and then a third.

'I'm sorry,' said Poppy, as the speaker began to congratulate the frontrunners.

'It's okay, just come on,' said Teela, forcefully, ignoring everything that was going on, 'we're finishing this.' She shoved the glasses back onto her face. 'Just read out the numbers when I pick one up.'

'We don't have to,' said Poppy. 'Everyone else has stopped.'

'I don't care,' said Teela. 'I want to finish it.'

Poppy could feel the room emptying around her as she held the paper in her hand.

'Just come on,' said Teela, pulling the glasses down to see what the delay was. 'Ignore them, just read out the bloody numbers.'

* * *

Teela stared at the ceiling, her jaw clenched and her mouth dry. It was like she had an itch inside her stomach that she couldn't quite scratch and was trying her best to squeeze away. Her eyes flickered as a set of footsteps she had learnt the rhythm of quietly grew louder from the far end of the corridor, and her body tensed even more, hoping they would walk by.

The knock was soft, but rattled around the room as if the walls were made of paper. She waited a second, just to give it a chance to change its mind and leave, before dragging herself from her bed and to the door.

'A peace offering,' said Poppy, holding a slice of nutcake.

Teela moved out of the doorway to let her in.

'I didn't want to leave for the week on bad terms,' said Poppy, moving a pair of casually flung trousers off a chair so she could sit down.

'We're not on bad terms,' said Teela.

Poppy put the plate on the bedside table. 'You were pretty cut up about-'

'It was just a game,' interrupted Teela. 'I just hate losing.'

The slow drip of conversation struggled along.

'We're good, though? This is going to work, isn't it?' asked Poppy. 'I feel like I've done something wrong. I can't tell if you're angry with me or just quiet.' She spotted a scuff mark on her boot and rubbed it off before turning back to Teela. 'We've done alright in a lot of the exercises, but I just feel like you want me gone, like I'm in the way or something?'

Teela slumped on the bed. 'You haven't done anything wrong. You're nice... too nice.' Teela paused. 'It's just... it's always just been me. It's weird having a person there all the time.'

'Is it not nice to have someone beside you for a change?'

'Yeah,' Teela shrugged, 'it's just a learning curve. When I first signed up, I thought I'd be going up alone. I didn't know there would be someone else.'

Poppy laughed. 'Well, here I am.'

They both waited for another drip.

'Well,' said Poppy, standing up, 'I just wanted to make sure we were okay before we start next week.'

'I take it you're going back home for a few days, then?' said Teela, slowly following her to the door.

'Yeah, and you?' Poppy's heart nipped at the edge as she realised what she had said.

'I'll probably just mope about here for a bit, and then get packed.'

Poppy hesitated. 'You could come with-'

'No,' said Teela, cutting her off, 'I'm happy with my own company. I'll be ready when you come back.'

Poppy stepped back into the corridor. 'We'll look after each other when we get up there, won't we?'

Teela nodded.

'And who knows,' said Poppy, laughing, 'we may even enjoy each other's company.'

Chapter Five

The Diagnosis

'Captain's log, on board Star Express Transit Ship – Vitula. Poppy Talib. It's been three months,' Poppy leant against the back of the booth. 'Three months since we established an audio link with a Captain Jason Sheridan from the Department of Search and Rescue.' She looked up to the ceiling join of the booth. 'He still can't hear us.' She bumped her crown against the wall in frustration before sitting up. 'He can't hear us...' She shifted in the hard, uncomfortable chair. 'He leaves us a message every hour or so. I think it's meant to reassure us that he's not left.' She shifted again, agitated. 'In other news, a cupboard door is jammed shut in the Morgue...' she corrected herself, 'in the kitchen. And a couple more side panels have fallen off along the walkway to the Control Room. We've tried replacing them...' she paused. 'Sorry, I don't know why I'm telling you this. It's not important.' She stood up inside the booth, her hands on her head, so that the camera could only see her from the waist down.

The light turned to red. 'Recording session terminated. To continue recording, please remain seated.'

She twisted round and stared at the back of the booth in a vacant dream, the dreary tone of the automatic voice slowly numbing her ears as it repeated and repeated. She squinted her eyes, trying to make out the surface of the darkened wall, the camera's red light providing the only source of light. She was aware of what she was doing, but at the same time, didn't know why she was doing it.

'What?' said Teela, as she threw a dried mango flake into the air and tried to catch it in her mouth.

Poppy realised she wasn't the only person sitting on the settee. 'Nothing,' she said, looking at Teela in the reflection of the Window. 'I was just thinking.'

'What about?'

'Nothing.'

Teela threw another flake in the air. It bounced off the side of her bottom lip and onto the floor.

'Can you stop doing that?' said Poppy.

Teela nodded, slightly shocked at the outburst, and poured the rest directly into her mouth. 'There's something eating you,' she said, swallowing.

'Nothing. I just...' Poppy coughed. 'If you're gonna eat them, eat them. 'You've dropped two on the floor already.'

A small click from the camera turning off cut through the fog and provided a focus. Poppy checked her watch and left the booth.

* * *

'Anything?' Poppy entered the Control Room and slumped on her chair.

'You know the answer.'

Teela was on her back, lying underneath the main desk, caught in a rubble of protective coverings and panels that were scattered across the floor. The inner workings of the controls exposed to the room in a copper maze of frustration.

Poppy picked up a small square section of circuit board that had been discarded. The neatly painted lines seemed to form a city, with each copper strip a road, leading on to another, which lead in turn to either another, or a dead end. She could see her hand through the transparent material. The strips now looked like veins, wrapping themselves across her dark skin, bleeding momentarily in the light, before quickly dulling.

'I tried to fix the door in the Morgue,' she said.

'Right?' replied an uninterested voice from under the desk.

'I took it off, but couldn't get it back on.' Poppy scratched her head. 'Well, I have got it back on now, actually..., but it still doesn't work. So I shouldn't have bothered.'

'Right,' said the voice again.

'A couple more panels have fallen off, as well.'

'How many?'

Poppy took her time counting in her head. 'Six... maybe seven. I've put them in the Storage Room.' She watched Teela's feet as she busied herself with something in the shadows. 'I was just thinking before, have you checked the-'

'Yes.' Teela's tone was harsh. 'I've checked everything.' There was a pause before her head emerged from underneath the desk. 'Sorry. It's just, I've been through it all countless times.'

Poppy tossed the circuit board onto the floor. 'It's okay.' She looked at the mess, trying to find herself a job. 'Is there anything you want me to do?'

Teela shook her head. 'No offence, but it'd be easier if you just left me to it.' She watched as Poppy's face attempted to hide its feeling of inadequacy. 'Saying that,' she tried to think of something on the fly. 'If you wanted to do us a favour, you could get us a couple of light-patches from the Storage Room?'

Poppy jumped, quickly heading towards the door. 'Just the two, or do you want more? Three, four?'

'Yeah, whatever.'

'I'll get four, just in case.'

Teela watched as her face disappeared from view, the sounds of her feet hitting the lower grates chiming throughout the shaft. She waited until the last clanked footstep had succumbed to the silence before collapsing on the floor under the desk. She stared up at the map of copper circuitry and began to follow each golden-red strip from start to finish. Her eyes were raw, yet she didn't dare blink in case she mistook one strip for another and lost her place. 'Fuck.' Her right eye twitched as a stabbing pain in her left hand distracted her from the futile efforts. She looked down and slowly loosened her clenched fist, revealing a small set of pliers she had been unwittingly strangling. They stuck to her skin through a mixture of sweat and ingrained pressure. She shook her wrist, freeing the pliers from her palm, and they hit the floor with a clatter. Holding her hand to her face, she noticed a small red mark left behind, embedded in the flesh. It was quite deep, and itched. She used her teeth briefly to scrape at the sore before realising she was making it worse. She stretched her fingers and tried again to trace the copper strips, but her mind kept wandering, the copper trails sedating her with their intricacy.

She swore again and peeled off a light-patch from inside of the compartment before emerging from the hole. She sat down in Poppy's chair and watched as the patch faded from a bright white orb to a dull piece of circular plastic, shrinking slightly as it cooled. With her foot, she dragged out a box from underneath the desk and tossed the impotent patch in with the others.

'Come on, Teela. I know you know this.'

The eyes were on her. She stared down at her tablet and then to the board at the front. The numbers seemed to blur, splitting in two and scattering off in different directions, as if suddenly hit with a bright light, creating ten separate hazy flares in her brain.

'I don't know,' she said.

The teacher walked over and tapped her finger on the tablet. 'We'll do it together.'

Teela nodded and watched as the perfectly manicured finger hit the numbers in a sequence that suddenly, for that moment, seemed to make sense.

'Now you go,' said the teacher, pointing to another child.

Teela followed it on the board as the boy tapped on his tablet, forcing herself to concentrate on the squiggly lines as they lit up one by one.

She looked around the room and scanned every surface, hoping that a mental spotlight in her mind would illuminate an answer and isolate itself from its surroundings, becoming the only thing she could see. Her lips moved as she slowly went through the checklist again and again in her mind. She stared at the desk. Her eyes hovered over the monitors and keys. There was nothing. She let her gaze fall to the hold under the desk and the circuit sheets that lay at the entrance. Nothing. She looked up to the circuitry that ran across the ceiling and out of the room. Nothing. She followed a strip that travelled along the coving behind the desk before disappearing entirely. Nothing.

Her eyes settled briefly on the slit window before being distracted by the time on a small monitor in front. It was close to the hour mark. She watched as the numbers slowly faded into each other and waited for the habitual high-pitched tone as it burst into the room. She didn't flinch, except for a small glance towards the flat-disked speakers on the wall.

'Vitula, this is Captain Jason Sheridan from the Department of Search and Rescue. Do you read me? OVER.'

Teela got up and slumped over the receiver. 'Yes,' she laboured, changing from one leg to the other, 'we read you.' Her eyes fell once again to the thin window as she waited for a reply.

'Vitula, this is Captain Sheridan. I've failed to read you. OVER.'

She let go of the receiver and waited as Sheridan repeated his lines again. His methodical voice fizzed around her head, and she tried to picture a face to match. She imagined him as an overgrown and over-tanned man with floppy hair, who never had to try at anything. She smiled as she allowed herself to write a whole character profile on him. She thought about his status as captain and reckoned he had probably gained it through friends in high places. His father was probably high up in the company, or maybe even a politician. It would be easy for him to follow in the family business, ignoring the fact that working as search and rescue for a postal company wasn't actually the family business. She continued, focusing on his demeanour and tone of his words, which reeked of entitlement, obviously coming from money. She pictured his house. It was sleek and stylish, with glass walls and lifts, and a multitude of bedrooms in case he got bored of the one he was currently occupying. She pictured him returning home to a hero's welcome. She could see thousands of people lining the streets as he passed by, all waving and throwing gifts.

Teela noticed two faces in the crowd, by the side of the road, and her mind quickly shifted. Faces created entirely by her, so she could imagine them exactly how she wanted to. She stopped the procession and focused on the features. They were always the same. The man was always tall and slightly gangly, although rather handsome, and had an athletic build with a strong jaw-line and neat stubble. The woman was slightly smaller, but with an equally athletic build. Her face seemed kind and inviting, and her large emerald green eyes contrasted well with the ruby hairpin that sat proudly on her dark brown hair, tied back into a ponytail.

A sudden silence brought Teela back into the Control Room. There was a short pause.

'This is Captain Sheridan, next transmission, three hundred hours, universal time. OVER AND OUT.'

Teela looked at the time and slumped again on the desk. She tapped a discarded light-patch with the tip of her finger, and it flickered back to a bright glow before slowly dimming.

* * *

'Poppy?' Teela approached the Storage Room. 'I don't reckon I need any for the moment.' She placed her hand on a panel, and the tall door slid open.

The room was extremely narrow but, to compromise, was also extremely long. The walls were made up of rows and rows of drawers and storage containers and, pushed back against the far wall, sat a rather bulky printer, used for making tools and components. Two strip-lights ran parallel along the ceiling, providing the only source of light, below which hung a netted structure that stored support poles, extra wall panels and floor grates.

Teela squinted to the other end of the corridor-like room and could just about see the darkened figure of Poppy knelt at a drawer three quarters down.

The door shut behind her as she stepped inside, causing Poppy to look up in her direction.

'Poppy?' Teela watched as she hastily got to her feet and wiped her eyes. 'What you doing?'

'I was looking for the light-patches.' Poppy ruffled through a few nearby drawers and pulled out a fresh box, holding it towards her.

'I don't need them anymore,' said Teela, examining Poppy's face. Her eyes were red, and mottled bags had formed under her lower lids.

'Fine.' Poppy casually tossed the box back in the drawer before brushing past.

'What's up with you?' said Teela, catching up with her.

Poppy gave a detached smile before continuing. 'Nothing, just tired.'

'I'm gonna get some food,' said Teela, following her. 'Do you want anything bringing?'

Poppy shook her head. 'No.' She waited a moment, her mind somewhere else. 'Thanks.' She gave another shallow smile before disappearing round the corner.

* * *

Teela entered the Morgue and grasped the cupboard handle nearest to the sink, the brushed steel causing a shiver to run down her arm. Inside, a small silver pouch of Fruit Beads sat pathetically on the middle shelf. She rescued it quickly before hitching herself up onto the cold worktop surface and studying the packet.

Large metallic lettering on the front, in a scarlet typeface read, "FRUIT BEADS", and underneath in a smaller, less attractive style read, "Concentrated Fruit Flavour: Strawberry". On the back, in tiny black letters, hardly discernible from the silver, read the long list of ingredients.

She burst open the packet with a pop and used her finger and thumb to transfer the bright red beads individually into her mouth. A sticky, sappy substance came oozing out as she bit into the first bead. It didn't taste like how she remembered strawberries tasting.

The metal pole clicked as it passed over the leafy greens. She was on the farming ship, walking along the side of the crop, brushing the plants with a thin strip sensor she held in one hand. She reached the end of the first line and a green tick with, "95% RIPE", appeared on her monitor. She paused for a moment and bent down towards a large heart-shaped orb that hung from a bright green stem. She hesitantly poked it with her finger, and it wobbled, knocking a bit of water from the leaf above onto the back of her hand.

'What you doing?'

Teela jumped and spun round to face Mr. Gulliver, her back to the crop. 'I was just looking,' she said.

'Yeah? I don't pay you to look, do I?' Mr. Gulliver pointed to his watch.

'You don't pay me at all,' shouted Teela.

Mr. Gulliver crumpled his already crumpled face and stabbed his finger to the plants. 'If I catch you eating the profits…' He turned round and began to hobble away, muttering to himself before he could finish the threat.

Teela looked at her hand and found herself holding the large, red orb. She brought it to her mouth and took a large satisfying bite. A sticky stream of juice ran down the speckled flesh of the fruit and onto her fingers as the sweet texture burst across her tongue. She took another bite, and another, wiping her mouth with the back of her hand to dispose of the evidence.

Teela tipped the last remaining beads into her mouth and threw the empty packet down the wastage shoot before offering a small burp. She went over to the fridge and pulled out two squidgy tubes of yoghurt. She ripped the tops off with her teeth and squirted them over another packet of beads, this time blueberry in flavour. A stray red bead caught her eye as she poured the contents down her throat. She wiped her mouth and pinched the runaway, holding it to her face. It reminded her of the hairpin. The bead was slightly smaller than the ruby and more spherical, but just as intense in colour. She tried to think about why it had come into her mind, but then she remembered Poppy, and the conversation, and the high-pitched screech that had interrupted them. For a few fleeting moments she had forgotten, oblivious to everything except rubies and strawberries until, abruptly, it all came flooding back as Sheridan's voice entered her mind.

She distracted herself by making another batch of Fruit Beads and yoghurt, this time tipping the mixture in a bowl, before grabbing a spoon from a nearby drawer and leaving.

* * *

Teela climbed the ladder to the Control Room, doing her best not to spill anymore from the bowl.

Poppy was slumped in her chair. 'Don't worry,' she said. 'I'm just listening to the broadcast and then I'll be gone.'

Teela approached the desk. 'I was wondering where you were.' She held the food towards her face. 'There you go.'

'What's this?'

Teela proffered it with the tips of her fingers, imitating a posh waiter. 'Blueberry flavoured fruit concentrate beads with creamy yoghurt.' She bowed her head.

Poppy righted herself in the chair and stared at the bowl. 'But I said I didn't want anything?'

'I know,' Teela stood up straight. 'I just thought, y'know-'

'What?'

'You just seemed a bit...' She paused, trying to think of the word. 'If you don't want it...' She began to move away.

'Wait, I'm sorry.' Poppy held out her hand, and Teela passed her the bowl. She stared at the bluish mixture, which now seemed a little watery. 'I should eat it; it won't keep.'

Teela watched as she began to shovel the mixture into her mouth. 'I knew you needed something,' she said, sitting in her seat.

Poppy wiped the corner of her mouth with her thumb. 'I could've waited longer.'

Teela leant forward across the desk, trying to look down a crack where the control board didn't quite line up flush with the wall behind. 'Why? If you're hungry, you're hungry.'

Poppy looked up from the bowl, trying to work out if she was being serious or not. 'I don't wanna go over it again,' she said, resigned.

Teela turned to face her. 'What?'

They both stopped as the high-pitched tone again filled the room. Teela grabbed the receiver.

'Vitula, this is Captain Jason Sheridan from the Department of Search and Rescue. Do you read me? OVER.'

'We read you,' she said, forcefully.

Poppy stood up as if it mattered, her throat pulsing slightly faster as she waited for the inevitable.

'Vitula, this is Captain Sheridan. I've failed to read you. OVER.'

They hardly acknowledged the disappointment, Poppy sitting back down and Teela climbing back onto the desk.

'You've got a fruit bead stuck on your shoe.'

Teela looked to Poppy, and then to the sole of her right foot where a red bead had been squashed into the dark rubbery surface. She reached over and took a small round device from the toolbox. It lit up as her thumb made contact with the centre, scrolling through the list of icons until she found the right tool.

'Well?' said Poppy, as Teela picked at the bottom of her shoe with a pointed hook.

'What?'

'Are we really going to do this silly dance again?' Poppy leant back in her chair and looked towards the ceiling. 'We need to start thinking about what we're doing. I mean, really think about everything we do.' Her voice was calm yet serious. 'There's a number in that file,' she pointed to a black dossier that had been left on the desk. 'And I know you've read it.'

'What number?'

Poppy leapt up and grabbed the file, swiping her hand across the first page causing it to flash into life. 'This number.' She held it to Teela's face. 'This number.'

'Okay,' said Teela, jumping slightly as the page was forced towards her eyes, 'I can see.'

Poppy collapsed back down and looked over to the lights on the exposed desk that were brighter now they weren't enclosed in their coverings. 'It's the amount of days we have left.' She sat up in her chair. 'And that's if we hard ration, less if we don't.'

Teela stood up. 'Why would you even say that?' She accidentally placed her foot on a discarded panel, causing it to crack.

'Don't pretend it's a shock,' said Poppy. 'You knew exactly what that number meant, you just didn't want to say it out loud, so you made me say it.'

Teela looked at her with complete shock, trying to pretend

as if what Poppy had just said wasn't true. 'But the number means nothing,' she picked up the cracked panel. 'Because I'm gonna find something.'

Poppy nodded, humouring her.

'I am,' said Teela.

'There's nothing here,' said Poppy. 'You said yourself.'

Teela sat back down in her chair and softened her tone. 'Maybe not here.'

Poppy looked up at her.

'I've been thinking about this for the last week or so,' she said. 'I've made up my mind.' She dug her thumbnail into the side of her finger. 'I think it's best if… I need to go outside.'

Poppy shook her head. 'Are you being serious? Not a chance. It's too dangerous. Totally against protocol. You can't just make decisions like that. Every bit of training says we should just sit tight and wait.' The words rushed from Poppy's mouth in a wild deluge that seemed more articulate when she had formed them weeks earlier, waiting for this inevitable moment.

Teela scraped her fingers across her scalp. 'Fuck protocol. That's what I say.' She stopped to calm herself slightly. 'How long are we gonna wait? We knew this was coming, Poppy. We tried not to admit it to ourselves, but we knew it was coming.' She leant towards her. 'We need to go outside. I know it and you know it.'

Poppy stood up. 'No, it's last resort. We're not cut out for that sort of thing. We're just delivery people. We're posties, not soldiers.'

Teela joined her. 'This *is* last resort. We're in it!' She grabbed her shoulder. 'We both know it. We've both known it for a while. It's been coming since the start. We've tried to hold it off and hold it off, but we need to look it in the eyes and face it head on. I've-we've checked this room countless times and haven't found a single problem, not one. We've been all over the ship.' Her voice cracked into anger. 'Do you think one's suddenly gonna jump out for us? The only place we haven't looked is outside.'

'Captain Sheridan wi-'

'Sheridan is doing nothing and will do nothing. He doesn't care. If he did, he would've been here by now. It's down to us, and you know it is.' She stared at her resigned face. 'Well?'

Poppy sat down. 'It's such a risk... a grasp.'

Teela perched on her chair, dragging it slightly towards her. 'It's all we've got.'

Poppy looked at her straight in the face. There was silence as they both stared into each other's eyes before, slowly, her head dropped in resignation.

Chapter Six

The Other Side of the Glass

'Captain's log, on board Star Express Transit Ship – Vitula. Poppy Talib…' Poppy looked down at her watch. 'It's nine hundred hours, universal time, and it's almost-' her train of thought changed. 'I wonder what they're doing,' she said, somewhat absently. 'On Earth, I mean.' She leant forward out of view from the camera so her elbows were pressing down on her thighs. 'If it's the same time, I bet Dad's making breakfast. Mum will be proofreading her article at the table, before she uploads it… toasted seed parcels with honey. He'll be standing in front of the oven like a kid, watching them cook-I haven't had anything yet. I've told Teela I don't want anything.' She rambled. 'I can't eat. I'm hungry, but I feel a bit-she's had something, though.' Poppy straightened her back and took a deep breath. 'It's nearly time to go.' She coughed. 'It'll be okay, we'll be fine… it's got to be done.' An acknowledgement seemed to be injected into her mind. 'She's right. We need to do this. We have to try.' Poppy got out of her seat and left the booth. Her heart was pounding. She tried to remember the last time she had felt like this.

'You got everything?' said Alice, handing her the briefcase. 'You've got your notes? You know your password?'

Poppy nodded and headed towards the front door.

'Well then, you've got nothing to worry about.'

Poppy stepped outside, and the morning sun hit her face. 'But what if I fail?' She stepped back in.

Alice folded her arms and leant against the frame. 'Your father failed his first interview; look where he is now.'

'I know, but…'

'Listen, you've studied hard for this, and that's all that matters. And if, for some reason, you fail, we go again or try something else. It's simple.' She paused. 'Turn those nerves into excitement. This is the start, a new chapter in your life. You should be excited.'

Poppy turned the corner and made her way along a slightly sloped side corridor, until she reached two heavy doors at the far end. She went through and was immediately met with a stark contrast to what had gone before. The white plastic panels that had lined her route were replaced by steel supports. The bright lights and constant droning that typified the rest of the ship were deeper and transformed into a low, muffled echo, and the grated floor seemed sturdier than before, due to the lack of traffic. She thought that it was as if she had crossed a curtain between the main stage and the wings, where the inner workings of the whole production had been quietly hidden, left to get on with their job. There was a stillness here that she liked and hated simultaneously. The peaceful shade was pleasant whilst creating a certain darkness.

Eventually, she came to a door just off the central passage. It seemed no more important than any of the other unmarked doors she had passed, but this was the one.

Teela had her back to the door as Poppy entered. She was knelt down, wiping the visor on a helmet. In front of her, across the floor, lay all the equipment that she had just finished checking and triple checking.

'Neat for a change,' said Poppy, admiring the rather small and extremely square room. She clocked the thin metal bench that ran round the perimeter and sat down.

'I can be, when there's a point to it.' Teela placed the helmet down and stepped away with her hands on her hips. 'I think we're about done.'

'Need a little more than "think" if we're really going to do this.' Poppy went over and inspected her pile. Everything had been set out in the order of usage. Underwear went at the top, and then inner apparel such as perspiration vests, gloves and socks. After that, was the uni-layer – a one-piece garment that covered the entire body, providing much needed insulation. Lastly, the suit itself – a hardwearing, skin-tight costume that resembled a child's wetsuit when unworn.

She picked up the suit and ran the fabric through her fingers. The outer layer felt like the skin of a basketball, the tiny bobbles hugging her flesh as her fingers passed over, with the inside layer being covered in thousands of tiny perfectly formed dimples. At the back, was a hard mound of what seemed to be carbon fibre where the oxygen canister sat. Her fingers reached the neckline of the suit and met a circular band of metal that formed the seam of the collar. 'Where we getting changed?' she asked, turning round to find Teela already stretching the tight suit over the bridges of her boots, her clothes in a messy pile beside the bench.

'Just get on with it.'

Poppy didn't reply as she began to strip down.

'That's it,' said Kaleem, 'over your head, then arms. Clever girl.'

Poppy could remember the early morning sun streaming through her bedroom window as her dad handed her a pair of trousers.

'Here we go. You like these ones, don't you?'

Poppy nodded.

'Now, which leg are you going to start with? I always go for left, but it's your decision.'

Poppy pointed her left foot.

'A fine choice,' said Kaleem.

Poppy reached for the suit and tried to pull the hard-wearing material up her legs.

Teela watched on, already finished. 'You want some help?'

Poppy shook her head. 'You sure you haven't mixed these up?' She began to feel a slight tingling sensation in her lower calves as she worked the tight material to the top of her thighs. She swore under her breath as she spun towards Teela. 'Are you sure this is right?'

Teela couldn't contain her amusement as Poppy waddled towards her. She was sat on the bench with her helmet in her hand, just laughing. Poppy stopped. She hadn't heard laughter like that for so long; it was a wonderful sound. She fell down to the bench on her side of the room and began to laugh along. It was infectious. She felt her lungs gasping for air, empty with joy, as if the very act of laughing was going against nature and what should be. She took another breath and sucked in the jubilant energy that had escaped before repeating the cycle. Again and again, she gasped, as the sound erupted from their mouths, exploding like a firework in the room only to be replaced by another and another.

Poppy's watch bleeped.

The worries of the task jolted back into view, quickly cutting the hilarity. They slowly eased their breathing, and Poppy began to pull the suit over her hips and up towards her chest, the job easier now she was sitting down.

Teela stood as Poppy slid her arms into the respective sleeves. She bent down and picked up the helmet, waiting for her hands to appear before offering it over.

'You first?' Poppy asked, watching as Teela picked up her own helmet.

Teela nodded and placed three fingers on three black dots that ran along the side of the orb, just below the visor. The clear helmet faded to black and then to its original transparent form, with the exception of a pink strip that circled the base. She placed it on her head and allowed two red dots to track her irises. Her eyes moved rapidly to and fro across the face of the visor as the dots changed to green before dissolving entirely.

Poppy copied her actions step for step. A red strip around the base confirmed she had signed in and a distinct click told her it was correctly positioned. From the inside, the visor acted as an optical display. She wiped away a smear on the glass and a message appeared in front of her eyes, asking her to focus on a large purple oval that had stretched itself across the width of the visor. She narrowed her gaze, and the oval shrank until it formed a small circle in the middle of her face. She followed it around the room. At first in a figure-of-eight, then zigzags, before darting towards each corner of her vision. She concentrated carefully as the dot changed to green before being replaced with a fully functional display.

She gave a thumbs-up and watched as Teela's eyes started to flit back and forth before eventually coming to a halt towards her. A large icon depicting a mouth and an ear flashed up on Poppy's display. She focused her vision on the, "ACCEPT", option and waited for Teela's voice.

'Can you hear me alright?'

Poppy nodded.

'You need to speak,' said Teela, pointing to her lips. 'I need to hear you.'

Poppy coughed. 'Yes, I can hear you. Clear as a bell.'

'I'm sending you an option to access my feed, so you can see my POV. Have you got it?'

Poppy nodded as a small square appeared on her visor, showing Teela's point-of-view.

'Speak, Poppy.'

'Sorry.' Poppy tapped on the helmet with her knuckles. 'It just doesn't feel natural.' She caught sight of herself in the square.

'What?'

Poppy shook her head. 'It doesn't matter. I'll send you my feed.' She focused on a list of commands at the bottom of her display and chose the option.

'Got it,' said Teela, bouncing on her toes, psyching herself up. 'You ready?' She began to walk towards a door positioned in the centre of the far wall.

Poppy reached for her arm. 'Remember, Teela, let's just take things easy. Please.'

Teela nodded, sincerely, before opening the door and going through, leaving her behind in the room.

'Don't rush me.' Poppy stood at the top of the climbing frame, Catherine behind her. 'You promised you wouldn't rush me.'

'I'm not rushing you,' said Catherine, impatiently. 'I just want a go.'

She looked down at the slide as it curved round, dipping and diving towards the bottom. 'I'm going,' she said, edging forward.

'You said that last time.' Catherine leant forward and placed her hand on Poppy's back.

'Wait, stop.'

Poppy felt the door shut behind her as they trudged along the extremely narrow walkway, Teela leading. She could hear her fast breaths through the helmet as they marched purposely on.

'This is the one,' said Teela, as the walkway began to widen, pointing towards a large arched door extruding from the wall in front.

Poppy stared at the black number three that dominated the dark grey metal.

'We can do this, Poppy,' said Teela, as they approached the door that towered over them. 'We have to do this.' She reached over to a black control panel attached to the wall and pressed her hand onto the cool, but gritty plaque.

A curved light-tube, following the circumference of the door, awoke with a dim glow and worked its way round the crescent. By the time it had reached Poppy, the light had transformed into an intense beam. Teela slid three fingers down the length of the black panel, and five large hisses, followed by five large clunks, sounded from the door as it erupted into life.

They both stepped back as the door started to rise, the bottom seal breaking with a whip crack. Teela bent down, impatiently looking underneath. It grinded upwards like a mediaeval portcullis, causing the room to groan, before halting abruptly. Only the bottom quarter of the number three was still visible, the rest hidden in the wall above. She signalled to Poppy, and they hesitantly stepped over the large threshold to the airlock.

Inside, Airlock Three was no different to any of the other airlocks they had seen. It was a small closet of a room, probably the smallest space on the ship. Glaringly bright lights, with white walls and a spotless floor, contrasted greatly with the half-finished, backstage aesthetic they had just left. On either side, facing each other, were two light-grey seats embedded in the walls, with a jungle of straps and safety belts protruding from every corner, and in the middle, a pathetically small white ladder led to a round hatch in the ceiling, complete with porthole window.

Poppy sat down on the left seat as Teela took the right. They looked up in unison towards the hatch. A large handle covered most of the circular window, obstructing the view to nothing more than two black slits either side.

'Not much, is it?' said Poppy.

Teela didn't reply, focusing instead on getting positioned in her seat, the cradle shape of the chair and her tool bag not making the task an easy one.

'Are we going to link up now or after?' asked Poppy.

'After,' said Teela, shifting in her chair. 'We've been through this; the line will just get caught in the straps.' She reached up to the cluster of buttons and switches above her head. 'I'm shutting the door.'

Poppy watched through her feed as she slid her fingers across a black panel, similar to the one outside, causing the door to shut like a steel curtain, gradually blocking out the view of safety. A large hiss signalled that the seal was secure.

'Straps,' said Teela, bringing her hand down.

Poppy went first, meticulously untangling each belt before

locking it into its corresponding buckle. She fastened the final yellowing strap across her chest and gave a sharp tug to make sure they were in place before gesturing over. 'Now you.' She carefully supervised as Teela copied her belt for belt, cocooning herself into the morass of tough webbing. 'You sure you're in?'

'I'm not moving.' Teela gave another tug to convince her.

Poppy nodded, staring across at Teela, whilst she stared across at her, both silently acknowledging there was no more official procrastination to be done.

'You set?' said Teela.

'Ready,' said Poppy, her nods restricted by the harness. She watched as Teela reached up to a large circular dial by the left of the buttons. It seemed stiff and bulky to turn, not helped by the impeding straps.

'Turning dial and equalising pressure,' said Teela, wincing. 'Five… Four… Three…' their eyes met briefly. 'Two… One.' Teela paused. 'Pushing dial for full transition.' She firmly pressed the dial in towards its housing and held tight to the underside of the chair.

Poppy did the same as a peculiar sensation surrounded her body. Her skin suddenly felt extraordinarily heavy, whilst her innards seemed desperate to emerge from her mouth, as if her torso was pulling in the opposite direction to the rest of her. She glanced over. Teela's hands were still clasped to the seat. A small bead of sweat ran down her forehead, just missing her left eye. A breathy, plummeting ball formed in Poppy's stomach before a sudden jolt made her feel like she had just been dropped in water. She noticed the straps were now digging into her shoulders slightly, and there was a cooling sensation under her thighs as they lifted off the seat.

Poppy reached down and pulled herself towards the chair. 'You okay?'

Teela nodded. She looked flustered, slightly red, with the wispy hair around her fringe sticking to her forehead. Poppy looked at herself through her feed. She was in a similar condition.

'I'm unbuckling,' said Teela, the oxygen canister's hunch and tool case making it difficult for her to lean back.

Poppy followed her lead and began to undo her harness. It seemed easier than before, the individual lines drifting out of the way rather than getting tangled up in themselves. She released herself and floated up slightly, before planting her feet and hands between the seat and ceiling, ensuring she kept still.

'We gonna link up?' said Teela, finding it harder to wedge herself between the ceiling and chair due to her height.

Poppy nodded and began to pull the line from a dispenser on her right hip, as Teela pulled from one on her left. An indicator on Teela's visor told how much cord had been released. She focused on an option to, "Clamp Line", and immediately felt it pull at her side. She gave a yank to make sure no more cord could be released before casting the end across.

It swam through the void like a water snake hunting for prey. Poppy plucked it from near her head and held it to the end of her line. She brought the two ends together and felt the attraction pulling in her palms like a magnet. She let go, and they rapidly surged towards each other through the small space between her hands. She pulled them apart and repeated the process. They flew towards each other again. She held the bonded ends to her face and concentrated on the connection. "Secure Tie", appeared above the cord, and she focused on the letters until they turned green. She grabbed the bonded line and tried to separate the two ends. 'Secure,' said Poppy, failing to pull them apart. 'You're stuck with me, I'm afraid.'

They both took a moment, just floating gently between the seats and ceiling. Teela's face seemed a little less self-assured now it was really happening.

'I know this was my idea and everything,' she paused. 'But I'm a little...'

'Me too,' said Poppy. She racked her brains for something

comforting. 'It'll be alright when we get out there. The doctor's Waiting Room is the scariest part of the building.' She smiled to herself, thinking of the time her father had said the same thing. Teela nodded. There was a short stillness as they listened to each other's breaths through the helmets.

'I reckon this is the bit where we close our eyes and jump?' said Teela, after a moment.

'I reckon so.'

Poppy kicked off from the wall and glided towards her, using the ladder to halt herself halfway across the room. In the breaststroke position, and with one hand on the middle rung of the ladder, she held out her hand. Teela copied Poppy's kickoff and flew towards her, landing quite comfortably in her grasp. Poppy waited patiently as she worked her way down and found a space on the ladder below, her body parallel and only a step from the floor.

Teela ducked her head under her torso and looked back at the airlock threshold, taking in every detail, painting the door with her eyes, making sure none of it went unnoticed.

Poppy watched through her feed. 'We'll be back in no time.'

'I know,' said Teela, her words overly confident for their tone.

Poppy pushed her legs back and walked her hands up the ladder. She reached the top and clamped her palms round the hatch's thick handle. She jammed her left foot firmly between two rungs and wrapped her right leg round the side of the ladder. 'Opening hatch.' She looked down towards Teela. 'Good luck.' With all her strength, she pulled back on the handle and turned it anticlockwise. A large vibration stormed through her fingers and ran up into her arms. She let go as the hatch began to open. 'I'm moving up, watch out.' She tried to kick back, but her foot had become lodged between the tiny rungs. Swearing, she pressed down on her thigh, trying to force it out of the hole.

Teela seized the back of her ankle and began to coax her foot out of the gap. 'Kick,' she shouted, and Poppy kicked hard, as hard as she could. 'Nearly,' she said, slightly prematurely.

A small icon of an oxygen canister in the corner of her visor, ticked down to, "99.9%".

Poppy rocked her foot side to side, and it slowly came loose from the ladder. She worked her way up, opening the hatch as she went, before poking her head out of the ship for the first time since the start of the route. She felt like a tiny beetle, crawling out from a crevice on the side of a great oak tree. Teela watched through her feed. Outside, the small ladder continued and ran like a rail down the whole length of the ship. Poppy lowered her head and stared down the rails, walking her eyes along to the place in the far distance where it seemed like the two parallel rails came to a point.

'How come you can draw so well?'

Alice took her paper and showed it to Poppy. 'Because I use that thing we talked about. Do you remember what it was called?'

'It begins with, "P",' said Catherine.

Alice nodded. 'Can you remember? Perspec-'

'We have to tie ourselves to that rail,' said Teela. 'We're gonna have to uncouple our line.'

Poppy brought her head back in and looked down towards her. 'We'll wait until we're both out. It's hard enough getting through the door.'

Teela nodded.

'You stay here until I'm out and tight to the rail. Follow only after I say.' She stuck her head back out of the hatch. 'Ready?'

Teela held the inside ladder hard. 'Ready.'

Poppy closed her eyes and held her breath, her lips moving slightly as she counted down from five. She grabbed hold of the rail in front of her, each hand on either side of the ladder, and tentatively shuffled further and further down the track until she felt a tug at her waist. 'Can you move up a bit?' She watched through her feed as Teela slowly worked her way up the ladder to where she had just been. 'That's fine,' she said, before edging further down the rail and out of the ship, the paranoia forcing her to double and triple check her grip with each movement.

'You're out.'

Poppy's legs cleared the gateway, and she swung them round, moving both hands to the left rail of the ladder. She was flush to the ship and could feel her stomach and toe caps brush against the surface. 'I'm in position,' she shouted, raising her voice, as if it were necessary now she could no longer see her.

Teela swore as the words screamed into her helmet before stepping up the ladder. Poppy could just see the top of her head as she began to rise from the ship, then her face, and finally the pink hoop of her helmet. She watched as Teela's eyes drifted around the bluish-black blanket that enveloped them.

'It's something,' said Teela, soaking up the outside firsthand. 'It definitely is.'

They paused for a moment, allowing the first hurdle to pass them by as the next one came into view.

'You ready?'

Poppy's eyes darted from Teela's hands to her own, obsessively checking they were still holding on as Teela pulled herself from the safety of the ship. She hadn't held anything so tight in her life. She could feel the underside of her knuckles contracted to the rail, the thin skin kneading hard against the metal, her gloves providing little relief.

Teela pulled her chest close to her forearms in order to fit the tool bag under the rim of the hatch. Poppy could see the concentration in her eyes. She looked down again at her own shaking hands, no longer feeling the rail. She couldn't tell if she was gripping or not, even though her eyes told her she was.

Teela's feet passed through the opening of the hatch, completely free of the ship.

Poppy edged towards her and grabbedat her waist. She pulled her bottom half close to the rail before letting go and seizing the line that bobbed beside her. 'Grab onto the ladder.'

'I am.' Teela wrapped her arms even tighter round the metal bars.

'You on? Secure? I'm going to uncouple us and re-couple us to the rail. Hold tight.'

Teela nodded and hugged the rail with all her might as Poppy concentrated on the centre coupling. "Release Tie", appeared on her display. She accepted, and the line gently drifted apart without any spectacle, as if it had never been attached. She gripped the cord at her hip and ran it between her fingers, to make sure it wasn't tangled, before passing it under the rail. 'You got it?'

Teela was already waiting with her cord. She brought the two ends together and secured the bond, tugging at the tie to make sure it was united, before letting it free from her grasp. It didn't move as she pulled her hand away, remaining completely still between the gap.

She looked at Poppy, and they both hesitantly began to loosen their grip on the rail. Slowly, they brought their bodies up and tucked their legs underneath to a kneeling position. It was the first real opportunity to survey the surroundings. They stared through a mixture of awe and fear. Poppy turned round. The large neck-like tower of the Control Room rose into the air, looking down on the right-angled torso of the ship below. She could just make out the tiny black slit of the window running horizontally across the top. She turned her head to follow its gaze across the front of the ship, trying to match the view inside to the view she now saw. It felt strange, similar to viewing the street from a neighbour's window. She knew the landmarks, the lampposts, the distinct road markings, the other houses, and yet something felt skewed.

'It's bizarre,' she said, her eyes flitting momentarily towards Teela who was still drinking in the colossal view, 'I can't take my eyes off it. It's a different world.'

Teela looked back at her, but stayed silent.

Poppy gestured to the pipes and cubicle cells, like small

buildings that sat either side of the rail, travelling down the length of the ship. 'They looked so insignificant up there, but down here they look…'

Teela nodded slowly, indicating she knew what she meant even if Poppy couldn't find the words to say it. 'They're like veins,' she said.

Poppy paused a moment, which felt like hours. 'When was the last time you saw something new, something that wasn't the inside of the ship?'

'Can't remember.' Teela's eyes shot across the scene, devouring more and more until they almost choked, not wanting to miss a thing.

* * *

The oxygen icon on their visors dropped a point, and they awoke from the semi-paralysed state the universe had induced in them.

Teela tried to stand, but the ladder was too low to keep hold of. 'We can let out more line, but I think it'd be easier to just swim down,' she said, clambering back to the kneeling position. She grabbed the rail and leant forward so her body kissed the ground. Poppy did the same as Teela began to count down. 'Slowly on three,' she said, making sure she was ready. 'One… Two… Three.'

They both pushed off, propelling themselves forward at a moderate speed through the blocks and pipes that rose beside them, forming a predetermined gully to glide down, their eyes poring over the worn cubicle blocks as if the boxy structures were the greatest things they had ever seen.

'I feel so small,' said Poppy.

Teela nodded.

Poppy's eyes drifted down the rail, counting the cubicles on each side. 'But these aren't important?'

'No,' said Teela, pausing to let Poppy catch up, 'there's nothing in these that would affect the transmission. It's the far end, that's where the business is.'

They both silently pushed off, the line hanging effortlessly between them under the rail.

* * *

'Just stop a second,' said Teela, as they reached the end of a particularly large block.

They turned their heads sideways and looked down the narrow passageway that sat before the next row of cubicles. The thin ginnel was like a rib, protruding from the spine on which they drifted.

Poppy glanced back at the old block and then to the new. The thin, web-like scratches they had seen previously had turned to deep, dented lacerations, and the streamline edges were now warped, as if melted. She noted a look of worry on Teela's face. 'I suppose it's good, in a way,' she said.

Teela gave a half-hearted nod and propelled herself down the rail. Poppy copied her, catching up before the line had time to snag.

* * *

A droplet of sweat hung from the tip of Poppy's nose. She shook her head, but it danced, as if mocking her.

'There's something ahead,' said Teela.

Poppy looked down the track. In the distance, a greyish heap lay to the side of the rail. They moved closer and the heap slowly began to reveal itself as a flattened cubicle block, the metal twisted and contorted.

'What's inside?'

Teela shook her head, pulling her body closer to the ladder

and sitting up on her knees. She looked back towards the tower. 'I told you. Nothing. It's empty.' She began to move forward. 'They're just shells where…' Her voice trailed off as she looked past the wreckage.

'What's the matter?' said Poppy, trying to see past a large section of grate that was blocking her view. She clambered over to Teela's side of the rail to get a better look. She could see the framework of the transmitter pole in the near distance. They were closer than she thought. It rose up from the ship's surface and pierced the blackness above them like a single needle in a pincushion. The fragile beginnings of a smile formed on her lips before quickly dissolving as her gaze sank from the tip of the mast to where Teela looked.

They both stared quietly, showing no obvious signs of emotion. Nothing needed to be said. A perfectly scalloped crater had punched into their path, creating a deep bowl filled with debris.

'Well, we were definitely hit,' said Teela. 'Probably only a cluster. Just grazed us, too. Could've easily gone right through, but it was just a clip.'

Poppy's eyes followed the ladder as it rolled flat down under the awaiting rubble before emerging on the other side.

Teela could see Poppy's mind racing. She grasped the rail and stared ahead. 'It's like somebody, somewhere, has the specific job of pulling the rope tight for people to trip over,' she said, beginning to rant. She turned to face Poppy. 'We're gonna have to uncouple from the ship.' Poppy began to speak, but Teela ignored her. 'We'll edge across using the side of that.' She pointed behind Poppy's head to where a cubicle cell formed a tempting ledge to climb across. She paused. 'We'll have to jump.'

Poppy sized it up. 'It's too risky. We promised we wouldn't take risks. There's nothing to grab hold of.'

'It's all we've got.' Teela kept herself tight to the ladder, trying to give Poppy as much of the line as possible without uncoupling. 'We don't have time for doubts, Poppy,' she said, trying her best to look for an alternative. 'You've got nothing to lose. If you miss, I'll just reel you back in.' She pointed to the cord.

'But then you have to…'

Teela leant forward. 'We both knew there'd be risks. Don't lie to yourself.'

'But not like this. No, we can't. We can't. It's too much of a risk. You'll be flying through the air not attached to anything.'

'I'll be attached to you.'

'But I'll just be holding onto that ledge.' Poppy took a breath to calm down. 'What if I can't hold on?'

'So we just go back then?' said Teela.

'No, of course not.' Poppy looked around, but found nothing. 'Of course not.'

Teela softened her tone. 'It needs to be done. You know it does.'

The oxygen icon ticked down again, forcing the hand.

'I'm not turning back,' said Teela.

'No.' Poppy nodded in resigned agreement and reluctantly eyed up the target. 'Just give me a moment.' She edged into position the best she could and slowly counted to three. She took a breath. 'I'm ready,' she said. 'I…' She paused, closing her eyes momentarily. 'I'm going!' Poppy kicked off, flinging herself across the gap towards the steel ledge, her mind and heart racing, but her body drifting considerably slower. She lifted her arms above her head and gripped the rim as hard as she could. 'I'm on.'

'Okay. I'm about to uncouple the tie.' Teela straddled her legs across the ladder. 'Uncoupling in three, two, one.' She uncoupled the tie and pulled both lines out from underneath the rail and re-coupled them above. 'We're bonded, but no longer secure to ship,' she said, holding on to the ladder.

Poppy watched through her feed. 'Be careful, Teela, I'm not sure how stable I am.'

Teela swung her legs round and positioned herself. 'I'm going!' She counted down in her head before stopping, hesitant without the insurance of the ship.

'I don't know how long I can hold,' said Poppy, feeling like her torso was pushing her away from the very ledge she wanted so much to keep flush to. 'You need to go!' She started to count. 'Three... two-'

'Wait,' said Teela. 'Wait!'

Poppy's fingers shook in their crimped position above her head. 'Go. If you're going, you need to go now, or re-couple us to the ship. Now!'

Teela kicked off and flew towards her. Poppy could see the back of her head growing larger and larger in the feed as she approached. She braced as Teela clashed into the back of her, knocking her foot off its perch and into a small gap between the wall grates. Teela scrambled for a spot on the ledge, pushing on her body. Poppy moved, grimacing as her ankle twisted, jarring it between the grates.

'I can't reach,' said Teela, hanging from her arms, but kicking with her feet. 'I'm too small!'

Poppy closed her eyes trying to gain a state of control. She pulled her foot from the gap and let it dangle, the pain too strong to use it. 'Wrap your leg round my right.' She shimmied closer to Teela. 'Don't knock my foot.'

Teela guided her leg towards Poppy's body and anchored herself, using her as a platform for her feet.

'Slowly,' said Poppy, as she began to edge awkwardly across, like a lifeguard dragging someone back to land.

Teela held on with just her hands, walking them across the rim of the cubicle cell, with Poppy guiding her on where best to place them, the instructions and replies given in grunts and nods rather than words.

* * *

'Nearly.'

Poppy stopped as they approached the bank. Sweat dripped down from her forehead, accumulating in her brow, before trickling down to her cheeks. Her arms had become stiff and rigid, and her neck was aching. 'You're going to have to move to my other side.'

Teela tilted her head and looked for the best position to switch her hands to. She reached out and planted one on Poppy's left shoulder before quickly gripping the opposite side of her neck. 'Okay, letting go of the cell,' she said, as she slowly clambered around, the protruding mound of the oxygen canister on Poppy's back making it difficult to keep tight.

'Slowly,' said Poppy, as Teela reached the other side and moved her hands back onto the rim of the cubicle cell.

'I think I can plant my foot,' said Teela. 'Just edge along a little more.' She dangled her right foot over the edge of the crater as they moved, her tiptoes just catching onto the rubbled exterior of the hole. 'Keep going,' she looked down at her foot. 'I'm almost there-'

'I can't,' said Poppy, her voice dry. She tilted her head back. 'There's no more ledge for us.' Her body trembled from the pressure. 'You need to jump.'

Teela shook her head. 'I can't jump sideways. There's nothing to aim for.' She looked down the small gap between the two cells. It was too narrow to fit through. 'I might be able...' She pulled at the tool bag on her back. 'I could jam this in.' She pulled a light-tube, about a metre long, from the bag.

'Will it fit?'

'I'll force it.' Teela swung the bag round and reached for the gap between the two cells. With brute force, she awkwardly managed to ram the light-tube into the space, creating a makeshift handlebar. Tramline scuffs on the metal walls showed where she had scraped the ends into position. She placed her hand in the middle and gave it a yank to test its strength. 'It seems okay.'

'Make sure,' said Poppy.

Teela gave it another test before carefully beginning to untangle herself from Poppy's grasp. She placed her hand on the tube and let her feet take flight as she crossed the border – the bar, for a moment, the only thing supporting her. She grabbed the ledge on the other side and managed to plant her legs on the rubble that mounted up against the cell, giving her a platform to ground her feet. She turned to face Poppy, her cheeks flushed, as the safety line floated between the two sections like a rope-bridge linking the two cells. 'Now you.'

Poppy edged herself closer to the corner of the cell, her ankle feeling like a balloon in her suit. She saw the bar stuck fast in the gap and clutched it, releasing the ledge she had been dependent on for so long. She felt her legs begin to rise, but managed to control them enough to catch a piece of rubble on the other side where Teela had been standing moments before. She winced as her foot made contact with the uneven ground. 'I'm on,' she shouted, as a bead of sweat ran down her cheek.

Teela didn't reply as they both took a moment to inspect the new territory. It was the same size as the last cubicle, but had deeper corrugations in its walls, useful for anchorage.

'Take your time,' said Poppy, as they tentatively began to move along the cell, grasping tight to the ledge with their hands whilst using the rubble as a walkway.

'Look, Mummy!' Catherine was standing on the edge of the kerb, her trainers flashing with each step. She held out her arms for balance and made it to the lamppost before swiveling on the spot.

'Be careful,' said Alice.

Poppy could feel the heat of the late afternoon sun as she sat on the driveway eating the ice cream. She watched as a large drip melted down the side of the cornet and onto her fingers. The cold liquid burnt her skin, dripping over her knuckles like candle wax.

'We should get back on.' Poppy pointed to the newly emerged rail as they cleared the crater. Her hands were shaking.

Teela looked up at the transmitter pole, now almost directly above. 'But we're nearly there. I reckon we just carry on? We'll only have to get back off again when we reach the mast.'

The lack of a reply confirmed she was right, and they both continued on, Poppy lumbering behind, her leg becoming tighter and tighter in the unforgiving suit.

* * *

Sweat poured off the both of them as they travelled the relatively short distance. Teela reached the end of the cubicle and waited for Poppy to catch up. The transmitter cell was larger than the others, protruding out, narrowing the gully, and an intelligently placed ladder meant they had a clear object to aim for.

'I'll go first,' said Teela. 'Move nearer.'

Poppy moved along the ledge, shadowing her closely.

'Okay, I'm going.' Teela readied herself. 'Hold the rail. One... Two... Three.' She hopped across, catching the ladder comfortably with a hooked arm. 'I'm on. Now you.'

'Brace the rail tight, Teela,' said Poppy, as she readied herself for her turn. 'You may have to reel me in.' She gestured fleetingly towards her foot, not wanting to draw too much concern. 'Okay, I'm going. One... Two... Three.' She bent her knees and pushed off, her left leg doing the majority of the work.

Teela held out an arm and caught her as Poppy clumsily drifted towards the ladder in an awkward parade of outstretched arms and legs. She waited until Poppy found a place on the ladder before propelling herself up.

'Slow down,' said Poppy following, her bad foot dangling

beside the rail all the way.

Teela waited until she had caught up before scrambling over the top, searching for the new ladder that continued along the surface.

'Ready?' said Poppy.

'Ready,' said Teela, clutching the rail.

Poppy swore as she pulled herself over, her foot catching the edge of the cell. She found the new ladder and kept tight hold of the rail.

'I'll tie us down,' said Teela. 'One... Two... Three.' She uncoupled the link and bonded it under the rail.

Poppy tugged at the coupling. 'Secure?'

'Secure,' said Teela, letting go.

Poppy exhaled deeply and slumped onto the ladder, her arms outstretched and her legs nearly crossed. She looked over to Teela who was watching her every grimace.

'What happened?'

'Nothing,' she said, trying to hide the pain. 'Just my ankle. I twisted it between a grate.'

'Let me take a look.'

Poppy shook her head. 'There's nothing you can do.' She uncrossed her legs and compared them. Her right ankle was considerably bigger than the left. 'Look at it.' She elevated her leg on the rail. 'We'll take a breather.'

Teela reluctantly slumped on the rail, and they once again took in the new surroundings, the novelty of which had not worn off.

The triangular transmitter dominated their view and filled about a third of the cubicle cell, which acted as a plinth, raising it high above everything else. A small fence, no taller than a knee, ran round the large framed legs, acting as a superficial boundary to the inside, where a small cell unit about the size of a wardrobe, sat directly under the mast.

Teela scoured the area for any obvious signs of damage. She noted a bit of debris near the boundary line, and a few small dents and scratches that covered the floor, but it was nothing compared to previous cell cubicles. Her eyes climbed the mast, hoping for something distinctive to focus on.

* * *

They sat there for what seemed like days, not wanting their fears to be confirmed or to acknowledge the reality,, but the silence between them said all that needed to be said. The whole thing was a daze. The weightlessness felt strangely comforting, and yet at the same time menacing, as the safety line drifted calmly from their hips.

Poppy's oxygen ticked past the sixty mark. Her eyes twitched towards the icon. She turned her head slowly towards Teela who had twined the cord through her fingers. 'What now?'

Teela pointed to the unit in the middle. 'That's the thing I talked about. I need to check inside that.' Her voice had a false sense of pragmatism. 'Can you move?' She watched as Poppy bent her leg and winced as the pain shot around her ankle. 'I'll need to detach, then,' she said, holding the cord.

'No, I… I can move.' Poppy tried again, pushing herself along the rail.

'How are you meant to help like that? You're gonna have to let me do it,' said Teela, the statement hanging awkwardly between them.

'It was the one rule.' Poppy drooped her head in resignation. 'We'd never detach from each other.'

'Yeah, but-' Teela reached for the cord. 'We weren't to know.' She gestured to Poppy's ballooned leg. 'You'll be able to see everything I can,' she knocked on the helmet. 'And we'll still talk. You'll virtually be with me.'

'But I won't.'

'No,' she quietened her tone, 'you won't. But what else is there?' Poppy looked into her face. 'You won't be stopped, will you?' Teela didn't reply.

'Just take your time and…' Her words tailed off, not needing to state the obvious.

Teela nodded. 'Keep hold of the ladder whilst I detach.' With her legs clamped tight, Teela gave Poppy's half of the safety line back to her, before fastening herself solely to the rail using cord from her other hip. She reached over and helped Poppy do the same. 'Right.' She tried her best to remain casual. 'I won't be long.'

Poppy forced a smile and watched as she drifted off down the ladder, away from her.

'Seems bigger in here,' said Teela, as the ladder guided her through a small gap in the fence to the under section of the transmitter. She looked up at the skeletal innards of the mast, the framework growing narrower as it reached the point, as if trapping her in. 'I don't like it.'

'Can you see anything?'

She shook her head. 'No, there's nothing.' She reached the unit and examined a small box fixed to the side. Poppy squinted at the feed as Teela carefully unlocked the covering plate with the multitool, making sure not to lose any of the small components that held it in place.

Inside, there was a monitor, similar to the ones in the Control Room, only more bulky and robust. She positioned her helmet closer to the box. A layer of chalky dust speckled the screen and collected in the corners of the outer housing. She tapped firmly on the gritty surface, and the screen slowly illuminated.

'What's the reading?'

Teela examined the bar charts, intricate and detailed, each light flickering and dancing like a fragile flame.

'Teela?'

There was a long pause.

'I don't get it.'

Poppy watched through her feed as Teela brought out a long metal wrench-like instrument from her bag. She locked it onto a small nodule at the base of the main unit causing a click, and the door gradually rose like a flap. She stepped back and peered in, the thick, light-grey door now forming a shelter overhead.

Inside, were hundreds of tightly packed transparent sheets hanging neatly in separate slots, each one veined with perfect circuitry.

Teela studied them intently. 'It's all… perfect. There's nothing.' Her voice had a slight crack. 'No damage, no faults. I don't get it.'

Poppy chewed on the peeling skin of her bottom lip. 'Are you sure?'

Teela meticulously showed the helmet's camera every portion of the unit, scanning her head up and down so she could see. 'Nothing. It's like new. Completely new.'

There was a short silence as they both stared into the ordered unit, the copper circuitry glistening as it caught the various lights dotted around the cubicle's surface.

'There must be something you can do?' said Poppy.

'Like what?'

Poppy hesitated. 'I don't know. This was your idea. Why don't you try opening the tool bag?'

'What do you expect me to do?' Teela's voice broke, shocked at the sudden attack. 'I can't fix something if it's not there to fix? There's nothing here, Poppy. There's nothing fucking here!' Tears began to meander their way down her cheek, leaving behind streams that mirrored the copper circuitry. More and more followed the trail, accumulating under her chin before dropping into the bottom of her helmet. 'There's nothing here.'

Poppy listened as she tried to disguise her weeping, unsure of what had just happened.

* * *

There was a long break before either of them spoke, the peace alone a comforting thing, with the stars serving as a pleasant accompaniment. The level in their canisters dropped past the halfway mark.

'I'm sorry, Teela,' said Poppy, eventually. 'Let's go back.'

Chapter Seven

The Relatable Fact

Poppy finished her breakfast and pushed her plate towards the middle of the table. Alice collected it and placed it on the side without a word, clattering it absentmindedly against the worktop.

Poppy looked towards the window. The sun was shining through the kitchen blinds, the rays breaking in at the edges providing spotlights in which the dust could dance. Outside, she could hear the noise of life, the odd shouts of neighbours and strangers going about their morning routines.

She climbed down from her chair and lumbered towards the hall. Her oversized pyjama bottoms wrapped themselves round her small bare feet, the soft material comforting her against the hard tiled floor.

'Pull your joggers up,' said Alice.

'They're too big.'

Alice wiped away the crumbs from Poppy's place at the table. 'You'll grow. We're not made of money.'

Poppy gathered a large roll of white fabric from around her waist and tried to hoist them up, pointing her toes in a half-hearted attempt. It lasted a few steps to the hall before the sea of excess material sank back, drowning her feet once again.

'Don't run on them stairs.' Alice's voice travelled down the hall to Poppy's spot at the foot of the first step.

She crumpled her face in her mother's general direction. She wasn't going to anyway, not today. She thought about it for a moment. She didn't know why; she just knew that today was not the day for running upstairs. There was a quietness to the house. Everyone was up, but nobody was making any great sounds. She began to climb the stairs, awkwardly clenching a fistful of material around her belly button. It felt like something was going on that she didn't know about. It seemed like her family weren't going to take part in life today.

She entered her bedroom and sat on the bed that filled most of the floor space. She grasped the smooth metal of the bed's frame and brought her knees onto the mattress. Climbing up, she peered out of the perfectly square window above her bed. She'd always wondered if she could fit through the opening. The first floor wasn't that high off the ground. If she ever needed to escape, she was sure she could squeeze through the gap and use the wall to scuttle down.

Until then. Poppy closed her eyes and began to imagine. She reached over and grabbed a captain's hat Grandma Lehrer had made for her. It was a deep scarlet with a shiny black brim. She was now in charge, and this whole room was her ship. She looked out of the window and tried to remember the rocky planet with molten lava she had dreamt up the day before. She squinted her eyes and tried to turn the nearby road back into the fiery lake.

A car sped past the house, distracting her from her efforts. She took off the cap and tossed it aside. She wasn't bothered. The house was too quiet for spaceships.

She slumped down so her bottom was resting on the tops of her heels, before leaning back just enough in order to flop upside down across the duvet. Her toes pressed against the smooth glass of the window, which had now returned to just being her bedroom window. The hard surface felt cool against her slightly clammy soles. The sun, although bright in the morning sky, had not yet warmed her side of the house.

Poppy jumped as her father's voice boomed in from the landing.

'I hope you're getting dressed?'

'Yeah,' she scrambled down and pressed a pad on the wall that caused her wardrobe door to shoot up out of view. 'I'm nearly ready,' she said, staring inside at the neatly ordered shelves.

'Put your best on today,' said the deep voice.

Poppy waited until her father's steps had left the landing before fishing out her favourite pink top and a pair of trousers. She put them on and compared the difference by seeing how much of her feet were visible. They were a tighter fit than her loose pyjamas, but she preferred it. She pressed the pad on the wall, staring at herself in the glossy wardrobe door, before commencing her usual game of trying to trick the reflection. She jerked her head quickly to the left, then to the right, before rapidly opening and closing her eyes in a bid to see herself with her lids closed. She did a silly dance and spun round, shaking her arms and legs before disappointedly trudging back to the light of the window.

She looked out at the road again. The early morning bustle of people hurriedly going to wherever they needed to be had slowed, leaving behind a still street devoid of harsh movement. She watched as a small bird with bluish feathers took its opportunity to land on the partition between the house and next-door's side gate. It seemed to be studying something in the nearby shrubs. She waited as it hopped down to a small patch of abandoned dirt and began to peck triumphantly at a bug in the undergrowth. She tapped on the glass, and its head turned towards the noise before suddenly flying away as quickly as it had come.

Poppy slumped down again, slightly bored at how the day was panning out. In the next room, she could hear her mother getting Catherine out of bed.

'I hope you're ready?' Alice shouted, as if knowing she was listening.

'Yeah,' Poppy said, somewhat smugly. 'I am.' She waited to see how she would come back from that.

'Well, what are you still doing in your room? Shoes. Come on.'

Poppy wrinkled her nose in her direction and climbed off her bed. She clumsily put on her shoes and went downstairs, pulling her coat from the rack and slumping on the bottom step.

'The day doesn't need a coat, Champ,' said Kaleem, as he brushed past, tapping her lovingly on the head.

Poppy frowned and did her best to replace the coat on the high rack before sitting back down on her claimed step. She leant over and rested her shoulder against the wall.

'Poppy.' Alice came scampering down the stairs with Catherine in her arms. 'Isn't there any better places for you to sit?'

She shrugged and dragged herself into the lounge, listening as Alice began to hurriedly sort out Catherine's breakfast in the kitchen.

'What do we need that for, anyway?' she said, leaning against the arm of the settee and pointing towards a shiny red balloon that bobbed against the ceiling.

'Blue or red?' said Kaleem, bounding in, holding two thin ties up to the window's light.

'Red,' said the muffled voice from the kitchen.

Kaleem nodded and began to wrap it round his neck. He stopped halfway through. 'Have you ordered?'

'No,' said the voice after a few seconds. 'You'll have to do it.'

Kaleem placed his finger across his lips, signalling for Poppy to remain quiet, and positioned himself in front of the large black rectangular frame fixed to the wall. He touched the three small dots at the bottom, and the walls of the room changed from a peachy colour to a dark green as he signed into his account. 'I'd like to order the next available carri-car, please,' said Kaleem, talking to the, now illuminated, frame, 'from this address to Willow Hospital. Thank you.' A soft ting rang out from the screen, confirming that the request had been successful. 'I've ordered the next available.' He signed out, and the room returned to the peach colour.

'Are you fully ready?' said Alice, carrying Catherine through to the lounge.

Poppy nodded and moved over to the window.

'That's it. You keep a lookout, Champ,' said Kaleem, as Alice helped him with his tie. She tied it into a neat knot and rubbed a mucky mark from the collar before turning away as he quickly flicked a bit of fluff from her back.

'Mum,' Poppy dangled her untied shoes towards Alice.

'I thought you said you were done? Kaleem.' She pointed Kaleem, who was still fiddling with his tie, in the direction of Poppy's shoes.

He bent down and laced them up in a peculiar knot. 'No escaping from that,' he said, proudly, standing up. 'I learnt that from a video I watched when I was fourteen, and it hasn't let me down since.' He looked out the window. 'Anytime now will do,' he said, under his breath.

'But why do we need the balloon?' said Poppy, again.

'The balloon!' Kaleem spun round. 'Alice, where's the balloon?'

She pointed towards the shimmering sphere, unmissable in the corner.

'Ah,' he said. 'Where would I be without you?'

'I don't know, but you'd be balloonless,' said Alice.

Poppy scrambled at the window ledge as a faint shape in the distance came whizzing round the corner. 'It's here.' She waited a few seconds to make sure before repeating herself more loudly. 'It's here!' She watched with great delight as the rectangular capsule pulled up in front of the house. 'It's yellow!' she said, as she was shepherded out of the door. 'It's yellow!'

Kaleem raised his eyebrows marginally to acknowledge the discovery. 'Here, hold that,' he said, giving Poppy the balloon.

'What does the writing say?' Poppy gestured towards the vivid green letters scrawled across the scratched yellow surface of the car.

'"Ninety-nine percent off everything". It's just an advert.' Kaleem paused for a moment and looked back at the house. 'Now, are we sure we've got everything? Everyone's here? We're fed, we're dressed, we're happy and,' he looked at his watch. 'We're early. How on life did we manage that?' He waved his hand across a small, red sensor on the car, and it turned to green, causing the doors to part with a soft hiss.

Poppy crossed the threshold and sat down on a black padded seat next to Alice. She swung her feet, buzzing with interest, and examined the compact pod. The interior was completely white, but had lost its brilliance – the endless journeys having diminished the bright, lively gleam to a drab dullness. Advertisements on panels between the glass windows played constantly in a cycle of garish colours and bold text, and on the floor, two large green arrows boomeranged on a recorded loop, pointing the way to the exits.

A small bell chimed and Catherine began to cry.

'You take her,' said Alice, passing her over to Kaleem, 'you know how she gets when she travels backwards.'

Another small bell chimed, and Poppy lifted her feet as the carri-car cleanly pulled away from the house. She looked down to the floor, trying to shut out her peripheral vision. 'If you don't look at the windows,' she said, excitedly, 'it feels like we're not moving.' The smooth glide of the carri-car hushed as it gradually began to reach top speed.

Kaleem smiled. 'That's because of the magnets. You remember how Mummy told you about magnets and how they can float?'

Poppy nodded.

'Well,' he said, 'it's the same thing, roughly speaking.' His voice began to speed up. 'Of course, there are some differences. For example, the size and shape of the magnets and, of course, the electro asp-'

'Kaleem.' Alice pointed to a large strand of dribble swinging from Catherine's mouth.

'Yes, well,' Kaleem wiped the drool away with his finger. 'I'll tell you about it when we get home.'

Poppy turned away and pressed her face to the window. She

watched through the scratched and dirtied glass as the world flashed by in snapshots of life. She felt like it was all a show put on especially for her. Every role perfectly cast and performed. From the business people in their sharp suits, to the shoppers with their bags. From the old woman sat on the bench, fishing around in her handbag for her glasses, to the kids in their freshly washed, but newly muddied school uniforms. All playing their parts as well as they could, in the only way they knew how, totally unaware they were being studied in the process.

She placed her finger on the glass, delicately, feeling like she needed to be quiet – the fast-paced noise of buildings, pavements, streetlamps and endless reflections at odds with the still atmosphere inside the compartment. She was worried that if she made even the slightest hint of a noise, they would all realise and snap out of the act, as if she had turned the theatre lights on.

'It's green now! Light green,' said Poppy, abruptly, as the image of the car reflected quite clearly in the passing buildings.

Kaleem took the break in silence to deliver the day's code of conduct. 'Now Poppy, remember what I told you last night?'

Everyone's heads turned towards the booming voice.

'Grandad Lehrer will be sleeping when we get there, and we don't want to wake him, do we?'

Poppy shook her head with disappointment. 'He's always sleeping.'

'Well,' Kaleem moved Catherine from one knee to the other. 'You sleep when you're ill, don't you? So does Grandad.'

Poppy took the answer and rested her head against the window. 'But he's always ill.' She caught Kaleem's eyes drift towards Alice and could sense something was happening, but didn't want to look.

A couple of familiar buildings with glass fronts flashed by her eyes, marking the outskirts of the hospital, but she didn't speak. The soft hush of the carri-car slowly dissolved into nothing, and she began to pick out the details even more clearly.

'Are you ready?' said Kaleem, as Alice gathered her bags. 'Keep tight hold of that balloon.'

Poppy looked down at her hand, almost forgetting she was holding it.

They passed through the archway into the hospital grounds.

'There's the tree!' she said, pointing to a cast metal sculpture of a willow tree.

'Aye, nearly there now,' said Kaleem, lifting Catherine up as they drifted through a landscaped meadow towards the main building. The lurid green of the artificial grass seemed to corrode the melancholic faces of the hospital goers, the printed marks on their wrists separating the patients from the visitors.

'You have to wait for the bell,' said Poppy, as the car pulled into its designated taxi hut.

They obliged and waited for the small ting before standing up. The green arrows on the floor started flashing, and the doors opened, allowing the strong echoes of the enclosed parking hut to invade the compartment. Catherine burst into tears. Alice swiftly exited the car and disappeared round the corner.

'Where's Mum going?'

Kaleem, with Catherine's tears running down his shoulder, held out his remaining hand for Poppy and led her onto the platform. 'She's just getting some fresh air, I think.' He crouched down, dangling Catherine between his legs, her feet tapping against the grey tarmac. 'Look at that roof.'

Poppy followed her father's gaze out of the hut and towards the grand frosted glass ceiling that hung over the hospital's entrance hall, covering a large portion of the sky. 'What?' she said.

'It's good, isn't it?' said Kaleem.

Poppy nodded, not quite sure why her father had only just noticed it. 'Yeah.' She felt a small tap on her shoulder.

'We all ready then?' Alice stood behind them, her cheeks shinier than before and her eyes with a stylish coat of dark eyeliner. Poppy leant her head against her hip, and Alice patted her softly on the head.

'Lead the way, Champ.' said Kaleem, taking Poppy's place next to Alice before putting his arm around her shoulder and giving her a small squeeze. Poppy pretended not to notice and scuffled down the corridor, doing her best to keep a few paces ahead.

The hospital was just as it always been. Every surface, from the floor to the ceiling, seemed to shine, emitting menacingly bright reflections as if coated with a thin glaze. Poppy scrunched her nose as a waft of disinfectant penetrated her nostrils. She trudged through the main entrance and entered a large room, filled with solemn faces, which tugged at her as it always did. 'Why is everybody quiet?'

'Because they're nervous,' said Kaleem. 'You get like that when you're nervous, don't you?'

'Only when I'm scared.'

'Well, the doctor's Waiting Room is the scariest part of the building.'

'Why?'

'Because,' said Kaleem, whispering, ushering Poppy past the rows of people, 'when you're in the doctor's room, you don't have time to think. But when you're out here, your imagination runs wild.'

Poppy took the answer and lumbered on through the room and down the endless maze of long corridors until she was met with a turning she knew well.

'Keep going, Champ, not this one.'

'Why is he not in this place anymore?'

Alice gestured for her to continue. 'Because he's been moved. You remember?'

Poppy turned and began to walk backwards down the straight corridor, her feet squeaking all the way. 'Yeah, but why?'

'Because,' said Kaleem, 'Grandad's illness has changed and this new place is what's best for him.'

Poppy spun round and noticed the lift at the end of the corridor. 'Can I do it?' She hurried towards the doors and waited for them to catch up. 'Can I do it?' she repeated, as they reached the lift.

Kaleem nodded, and Poppy quickly hopped on the pressure pad in front of the glass compartment.

'Please state your desired floor,' said a friendly voice as they entered.

'Do you remember what to say?' asked Alice.

Poppy nodded, waiting until the message had looped twice before taking a deep breath. 'Floor twenty-one, Hop-Hospice Suite,' she said, in a slow, but confident voice.

'Good girl.'

Poppy leant forward as the lift began to ascend, looking down through the glass at the corridor shrinking below. Soft violin music played through the speakers. She closed her eyes and pretended to wear her captain's hat. The buttons on the lift flashed as they passed by each floor, and the sun burst through the large glass roof as they rose higher and higher. She looked up and closed her eyes, the rays pleasantly warming her face. They seemed softer than the lights downstairs, yet every bit as powerful.

'Floor twenty-one, Hospice Suite,' said the voice, interrupting her imagination.

A small chime, identical to the one in the carri-car, rang aloud, and the doors hushed apart. Poppy waited until everyone had safely alighted her ship before jumping across the threshold, making a rather large echo as her feet hit the floor.

'What did I say in the taxi, Poppy?' said Kaleem in a firm, but fair voice.

Poppy held her head down low and gave a sheepish look. 'How long we staying for?'

'A while,' said Kaleem, giving a purposely vague answer.

Poppy dragged her feet as they walked to the glass entrance of the suite. Alice held her thumb to the chunky black lock on the doors, and they swung inwards, allowing them entry. Poppy felt the doors close behind her as she slumped along the corridor. The squeaking of her feet had stopped and the chemical smell had gone.

'Hello, Mrs Lehrer,' said a warm voice from behind the reception desk, set back in a small alcove. The woman stood up, revealing a pristinely white trouser suit. 'How are you?'

Alice approached the desk. 'We're okay.'

'Good, good,' said the woman, smiling and proffering an elegant box, no bigger than a pack of cards, in her direction.

Alice held her thumb to a shallow indent on the smooth surface, and it flashed to the same peach colour present in their lounge, before turning back to black. 'Got the whole family today.' Alice turned towards Poppy who was shadowing Kaleem. 'Go on, Poppy. Say hello to Cathleen.'

'Poppy!' said Cathleen, reaching down below the desk in an excitable manner. 'I didn't see you there. What are you doing hiding behind your Dad?' She pulled out a frosted bowl filled with sweets; each one wrapped perfectly in either pink or white foil.

Poppy edged hesitantly forward and took a pink sweet that sat at the top of the heap.

'Go on,' she said, as Poppy pulled her hand away. 'Take a handful.'

Poppy reached in again and took a couple more, not wanting to be rude, but not wanting to miss out.

'There you go.' She offered the bowl to Alice and Kaleem, who politely declined, before returning it to the desk.

Poppy immediately regretted not taking more.

'Can I have your thumbs, as well, please?' said Cathleen, offering the box to Kaleem.

He pressed down, causing it to flash green.

'And Poppy.'

Poppy did the same, and the box flashed red.

'And the little one.'

Kaleem held Catherine's hand to the box.

'Plum,' said Cathleen, stroking Catherine's cheek, 'that's my colour too.'

'Is my Mum here?' asked Alice, as Cathleen placed the box back under the desk.

'Yes,' she nodded enthusiastically. 'Been here since eight. Only a few minutes after I arrived, in fact. She's such a good soul, isn't she? What a lovely woman. I was only thinking to myself the other day what a lovely woman she is. So lovely.' She paused for a moment, allowing her mouth to rest. 'Do you want me to walk you down?'

'No, we're fine.' Alice moved away from the desk. 'Thanks, Cathleen,' she said, sincerely. 'Don't know what we'd do without you.'

* * *

Poppy followed her parents down a mirrored hallway, just off the main corridor. She looked at her reflection in the intermittent glass panels that lined the way. She knew the mirrors were actually windows, allowing the occupants to see out without her seeing in, but she never fully believed it. She stared as hard as she could past her reflection, trying to see if it was possible to peek through to the room behind.

A door opened at the far end of the quiet hallway.

'Look who's there, Poppy,' said Alice, pointing to a moderately tall woman with bright pink hair, just past middle age, who looked tired, but wore a genuine smile.

Poppy peered through Kaleem's legs. 'Grandma!' She ran down the hallway and hugged at her arm.

'Poppy.' Kaleem caught up to her. 'I just told you, not five minutes ago, that you weren't to go shouting around and acting the goat.'

'Aw, leave her be,' said Grandma Lehrer, pulling Poppy to her hip. 'A bowling ball off a wardrobe couldn't wake most the people in here.'

Kaleem gave a disapproving look towards Poppy, but didn't argue.

'How's Dad doing?' Alice followed Grandma Lehrer into the room.

A whispered voice from the upright bed made her jump. 'Why don't you ask him yourself?'

'Dad, I didn't expect you to be awake.' Alice rushed towards him and gently wrapped her arms around his shoulders, being careful not to knock the transparent nosepiece pushed to his nostrils.

'Come on,' said Kaleem, as Poppy dawdled, poking her head in and out of the room, examining the one-way mirror. 'Look who's awake.'

'Why's it so dark?' said Poppy, finishing her experiment and entering the slightly dimmed room, the blinds only partly drawn. She looked around as her eyes adjusted to the contrast.

'It's just so I can get a bit of shuteye, Sunbeam,' said the voice from the bed.

'Grandad!' Poppy skipped towards Grandad Lehrer, but slowed as she reached the bedside, slightly intimidated by the nosepiece. Grandad Lehrer reached out a hand, and Poppy nestled her own inside the still firm grasp that dwarfed her fingers considerably.

She looked around the room, her eyes now accommodated to the darkened state. A box full of compressed clothes sat at the base of a doorless cupboard, and a pastel worktop, complete with sink, lined the wall behind Grandma Lehrer. On the far wall was a monitor, which she had never seen switched on, and to the left was a large window covered by a drooping curtain.

'They've taken the machines out,' said Grandma Lehrer. She pointed to a small grey box in the corner. 'Just got the ventilator now. Looks a bit bare, doesn't it?'

'Not, "bare", Iselda,' said Kaleem, 'minimal. It's amazing how spacious a room can look after getting rid of a bit of clutter.'

'Oi, Poppy-popcorn,' said Grandad Lehrer, pulling Poppy towards him, his voice whispered and coarse, 'I haven't seen you in ages. How you doing?'

'I'm okay.' Poppy gave him a hug, making sure to examine the nosepiece carefully as her head rested momentarily at eye level to it.

'And what colour was it this time?'

Poppy stood up, excitedly. 'Well, at first it was yellow with lime green writing on the side, which Dad said was an advert, but then I saw it in the reflection of a building and it was light green with orange writing.'

Grandad Lehrer widened his eyes in amazement. 'Lime green, ey?'

'Yeah!' Poppy opened her hand and revealed two remaining sweets. 'Do you want one?'

Grandad Lehrer shook his head. 'Better not,' he tapped her on the wrist. 'You eat 'em for me.'

'Hey, Poppy.' Kaleem gestured towards the balloon.

'Oh yeah, this is for you.' She handed the balloon over to Grandad Lehrer who took great delight in examining it.

'Thanks, mate,' he said at last, handing it back. 'Do you think you can put it with the others for me?' He pointed behind his head to where at least half a dozen balloons, of reds and whites and pinks and mint greens, bobbed gently above his headrest.

Poppy nodded and wrapped the string round the frame before moving away and leaning against Kaleem's chair.

'Well done,' said Kaleem, as Poppy began to quietly observe her Grandad.

He too seemed different. Like the room, he looked bare. His skinny limbs and torso formed deep shadows that looked like they were being drowned by the waves of his blanket, saved only by the gust of air forced into his nose by the ventilator, which pumped up his lungs before letting them droop quickly back down.

* * *

'Well, put a smile on your faces,' said Grandad Lehrer to the room, breaking the stillness. 'You look like a row of cabbages. I know I don't look up to much, but it doesn't mean you have to as well.'

'You're right,' said Kaleem, looking around for a topic of conversation. 'Say Richard, how's James doing? It was James, wasn't it? You two were having quite the riot the last time we came.'

'He's dead,' said Grandma Lehrer. 'Fell asleep whilst watching History Plus and never woke up.'

The room fell silent. A smile formed on Grandad Lehrer's lips; it grew to a chuckle before transforming to a fully-grown laugh. It passed to Kaleem, and his shoulders slowly began to rock, before landing on Alice and then Grandma Lehrer.

'I'm sorry,' said Kaleem, wiping the tears from his eyes.

'Don't be,' said Grandad Lehrer between exhales. 'The old fella had a good run. Three hundred, wasn't he, Iselda?'

Grandma Lehrer struggled to reply through the giggles. 'Not quite.'

'Well, he seemed that old.'

Poppy tugged on Kaleem's shirt. 'Why are you laughing?'

Kaleem paused, taking his time to think of an answer between remnant chuckles. 'Because we can,' he said, finally, his bellows dominating the room. 'If you can laugh, it's best to go ahead and laugh.'

The ventilator in the corner bleeped.

It cut through the joyful sounds as Grandad Lehrer's chuckles mutated to a throaty cough. He looked towards Alice and Grandma Lehrer, trying to comfort them by hiding his discomfort.

'Why don't you play with Poppy on the floor?' said Kaleem to Catherine, as he lifted her down to a small foam mat by the window. 'Be a good girl.' He tapped Poppy on the back and nudged her in Catherine's direction.

Alice fished a brightly coloured ball from her bag and gave it to her as she went by.

'What's this?' said Poppy, showing Catherine the ball. 'Who's that?' She pointed to a face on the side.

Catherine stretched out her arms as she rolled it to her, the face changing expression with each rotation.

Poppy gave a surprised look, as if she had never seen it before. 'Clever girl!' she said, trying to sound as grown-up as she could as Catherine rolled it back, shaking her hands with excitement.

Behind her, Poppy could hear her Grandad coughing. She had her back to the room, but sensed something more was happening. She thought she heard someone come into the room and debated turning round, but the whispered tones of the adults put her off.

* * *

The ball nestled at the shins of her crossed legs again. She picked it up, but Catherine had turned her back. 'Catherine,' said Poppy, trying to gain her attention. 'Cathy, look what I've got.'

Catherine ignored her, more interested in her surroundings. Poppy watched as she used the base of the sink unit as leverage, trying to lift herself up onto her feet. Poppy thought about stopping her, but was interested to see if she would succeed. Her hands worked their way up the pearl white compartment, her fingertips turning the same shade as they pressed against it. She brought her legs underneath her torso and slowly began to rise. She wobbled as her legs straightened, taking a small step backwards to establish her balance. Poppy crawled quickly towards her, but it was too late. Her small bowed legs buckled beneath her and she fell straight down, hitting the mat with a muffled thud.

Poppy smiled at her reassuringly as Catherine stared back, shocked, before screwing up her face and erupting a loud wail from her gaping mouth, her face turning blotchy, with tears trickling down her cheeks, soaking the neckline of her top. Poppy tried to lift her up, but she was too big for her arms to handle.

Kaleem approached from behind. 'What have we here then?' he said, lifting her above her head.

'She fell over.' Poppy turned round to face the room. Grandad Lehrer was asleep in bed, and Grandma Lehrer was folding up the shirt he had just been wearing. It had a small patch of red staining near the sleeve. She turned her back, trying to hide it, before shoving it into a bin by the cupboard.

'Why don't you take the kids home, Kaleem?' said Alice, who had positioned her chair nearer the bedside.

'If you're sure?'

She nodded. 'Yeah, I'll stay a bit with Mum. We'll share a taxi back.'

'Are we going?' Poppy stood up.

Kaleem tapped her on the head. 'Yeah, probably best, Champ. Grandad isn't feeling too well. We better let him get some sleep.' Kaleem turned her towards Grandma Lehrer who was now sitting beside Alice. 'Come on, let's say goodbye to Grandma.'

Poppy walked round the bed and sank her head into Grandma Lehrer's lap.

'There's a good girl,' she said, stroking her hair. 'Whisper goodbye to Grandad, he'll be able to hear you.'

Poppy stood on her tiptoes and leant over the bed. She stared into the sleeping face of her Grandad. The small nosepiece hissed, causing his nostrils to open and close. 'Bye,' she said, her voice a loud whisper.

Alice gave her hair a small ruffle as she went by. 'I'll see you tomorrow.'

Kaleem opened the door and waited for her to go through before gently shutting it behind. Poppy turned round and waved at her reflection, regretting not having done another experiment with the mirrored window. She hung her head low before remembering her spaceship. 'Dad, can I do the lift again?' Her eyes lit up. 'Can I do it?'

Kaleem nodded.

They reached the end of the long corridor and entered the glass compartment, with Poppy going first, to make sure everything was in order.

'Ground floor,' she said, in her best captain's voice as the doors shut. There was a brief pause before the lift began to descend, and she looked up to the glass roof. The intense light from the outside world was still streaking through, but seemed to ignore her, her ship no longer in direct sight of the sun.

* * *

'Right,' said Kaleem as they approached the large sliding doors of the main entrance. 'Do you want to pick us a taxi?'

Poppy nodded, excitedly, and dragged him outside. She left her father's side and carefully studied the row of neatly parked carri-cars, identical in everything, but advertisements. She paced up and down on the path, examining every detail. 'This one,' she said, after a good while of debate. She pointed proudly to a car in the middle with an animation on the side for, "Bubble Balloons! The sweets that go POP!" She gazed, hypnotised, as a cartoon girl bit down on a spherical sweet, no bigger than a marble, causing colourful exclamation graphics to crash and splat across the side of the otherwise black vehicle.

'You sure?'

Poppy nodded and waved her hand over the sensor, causing the doors to open. She noticed a large stain on the car's floor as she entered, but chose to ignore it, not wanting to undermine her decision. She sat beside Kaleem and Catherine, looking around at the interior. 'It's the same as the other one,' she said, disappointed, clocking the familiar promotions.

'I think-' Kaleem leant forwards and looked into the window of the next carri-car, noting the loops and animations on the walls, 'I think they're the same in every taxi,' he said, trying to make her feel better.

'Please state your chosen destination,' said a voice from the speakers.

'Home,' said Poppy, in a definite voice, and they began to move.

The taxis either side of the window seemed to retreat as they slowly pulled away from the hut. She looked back and could see them huddled together in a pack, a single empty space in the middle showing where they had just been.

* * *

Poppy left the booth.

Chapter Eight

A Rising Defiance

'Captain's log, on board Star Express Transit Ship – Vitula. Poppy Talib.' Poppy pinched the bridge of her nose. 'Days just seem to drift into another.' She brought her hand down to her mouth and gave a wheezy cough. 'It feels so quick since… it feels like we've just been asleep. Y'know, where you can't judge how long it's been? When you don't know if you've been asleep for seconds or hours?' Her mind darted back and forth, speaking thoughts. 'Teela's not…' She gave a light-hearted laugh. 'I hardly see her. We don't see each other… not anymore.' She paused. 'She says she wants to be alone but…' There was a jolt of animation as a new thought entered her mind, intensifying the rambles. 'Captain Sheridan is still here, somewhere. I feel like I know the guy.' She tilted her head back and gestured with her hand. 'I couldn't recognise him, of course, if we met. Not by his looks at least. Obviously if he spoke, I'd have a better chance…' She sat up and exhaled slowly. 'If we met…' There was a long pause as she thought, her eyes flickering left and right and yet looking at nothing. 'Teela still thinks…' Poppy stood up.

'Recording session terminated. To continue recording, please remain-'

'What's the point?' She pressed her eye right up to the camera. 'I wonder what you look like?' She knocked on the speaker. 'Hello? Anyone in?' An intense smirk slashed across her face. 'Are you even real? You're just ones and zeros. Well, look at me!' She stepped back and positioned her body in line with the camera. She lifted her shirt, revealing a fragile torso, her pasty brown skin stretched tight over her emerging ribs. 'See, living matter. Alive!' She collapsed on the chair. 'I'm alive...'

'Recording resumed.'

'Oh, fuck off.' Poppy stumbled out of the booth, and the intense light pricked at her eyes, stunning her into a more composed state as if a powerful sedative. She used her arm to shield her face for a moment before stretching her back and looking at her watch. It was twenty-six minutes past five, universal time. She ran the daily schedule through her mind between dazed blinks. She knew Teela wouldn't be where she should be.

* * *

Poppy walked down the corridor and climbed the ladder to the Control Room. A half empty bottle of water gave her a dose of false hope as she poked her head out of the shaft. She sat down on her chair and stared at the bottle. It stood bolt upright in the middle of the floor, taunting her, removed from everything. A vertical statue completely opposing the horizontal plane on which it sat, and yet, completely part of it. It was perfection.

She spun round and reached over to the intercom. 'Teela, I need a word. Can you come to the Control Room, please?' She clenched the receiver, almost strangling it, wishing it were only that easy to transmit outside. 'Please... Teela.'

She leant back in her chair and stared towards the ceiling. Her eyes felt dry, but it was too much effort to shut them. Thoughts of home and the botched mission flashed across her sightline like lenses, appearing and disappearing before appearing again. She thought of her old bedroom, the sunlight shining on the landing, toasted seed parcels with honey, the smell of her father's shaving foam, Catherine's trainers flashing as she walked, the oxygen canisters beeping down to under a quarter full, the race to get back, her foot in agony, the sweat and tears, Teela's back as she walked away from her.

Poppy's watch bleeped. 18:00 U.T. She wondered if it was the lack of anything to anticipate that caused the time to pass by so quickly. That, in order for time to drag, there has to be something to look forward to, something for it to drag towards. She stood up and leant her back against the control desk. She crossed her legs, placing the weight on her left foot and folding her arms.

Her new posture reminded her of how her mother used to wait for a latecomer in class. A whole new set of lenses slid in and out of view as she thought about her old teachers and classmates. She speculated about where they were, how many were married, how many had kids, how many had good jobs, how many were happy, how many were sad, how many had died. She stopped. She tilted her head back. She knew it was entirely possible, probable even, that at least one or two from her school days would have reached the end too quickly. A drunken fall onto the edge of a step. A traffic accident. An undiagnosed illness that reared its head only when it was too late. She wondered if any of them were having the same macabre visions about her, somewhere, that she was having about them.

An intrusive thought entered her mind as rolls of faces flashed by her eyes. It was a list. A list of people she disliked at school. A list of people she least cared about. A list of people that, if someone had to go.

'What do these people actually contribute though?'

Poppy could see the back of the young woman's head sitting proudly on the confident shoulders. Further down, the rest of the auditorium hunkered down for the habitual comments that nobody asked for.

'It's just my opinion,' she said, finishing in the same way she always did before starting again. 'I just think we need to ask, I mean…'

Poppy shook her head as a sharp stabbing pain pierced

through the base of her left calf. She swapped her weight to the other leg as a small distant clang of metal deflected her from the discomfort, the bangs and crashes growing in volume as they worked their way through the grated corridors towards her.

Teela didn't say anything as she emerged out of the shaft, choosing instead to stare in Poppy's general direction.

'It's your turn.'

Teela folded her arms. 'For what?' Her voice croaked with lack of use.

'It's your shift.'

'Why?'

Poppy gestured towards her chair.

'But why?' Teela shrugged. 'What's the point?'

Poppy didn't reply.

'There isn't one. There's nothing. We all know what Sheridan will say-'

'*Captain* Sheridan,' said Poppy, correcting her.

'We all know what *Sheridan* will say,' continued Teela, ignoring Poppy. 'He won't change. It'll be the same question, as it always is. And it'll be the same question left unanswered, as it always is.'

'But there's nothing else we can do.'

Teela raised her eyebrows, giving a casual shrug. 'If that's what you think.' She moved away from the ladder. 'Let's face it, Poppy, Sheridan-'

'*Captain* Sheridan! It's *Captain* Sheridan!'

'HE!' shouted Teela. 'HE doesn't give a shit about us. Don't you see?' She placed one hand behind her back and gestured violently with the other. 'This is a jolly for him. He's probably having the time of his life. Face it, for all we know, he's been sat on his arse, doing nothing since he arrived. If he finds us, if he's successful, what happens to him then? I'll tell you. He goes back, sat behind a desk hoping for someone else to disappear. That's all there is, really. This is the best bit of action he's had in years.' She paused. 'I mean, how hard would you look if you were searching for a ticket back to hell?'

'That makes no sense at all,' said Poppy.

'Yes, it does. It's what I'd be thinking.'

'Just because you feel like that, doesn't mean everyone else does. Some of us have people to go back to.'

The room emptied itself of noise and replaced it with a mixture of bitterness and remorse.

Poppy opened her mouth, but nothing came out.

'They're loops, Poppy.' Teela's voice was lower, as if it had just been beaten down. 'They're just recordings. Verbal sedation. He doesn't care about us. We're just a job that distracts him from something worse.'

Poppy sat down in an attempt to deflate the room. She squeezed her head between her hands, relieving some pressure. 'You just need to trust people, Teela.'

'Yeah, that'll get me far.'

'It would if you just–'

'Oh, fuck off, Poppy. They started it. They let me down first, left me swinging in a fucking flower basket.'

Poppy stood up again, her voice calmer than before. 'It's not you against the world, Teela. You can't blanket everyone.' She paused. 'Do you remember those early days? The ones where I hardly got two words out of you? We were both fairly new, but you were cold. I knew you'd had a hard time of it, but you can't judge until you've walked in their boots.'

Teela snorted. 'Well, good for you. I owe it all to you. My saviour.'

Poppy tilted her head to stretch her neck. 'I'm not saying that. Just, maybe if you'd had a different captain, it wouldn't have worked so well. For you *and* for me. I'm saying we both helped each other.'

Teela nodded, sarcastically. 'But maybe with them, I would've got someone who had some guts, at least.'

'What's that supposed to mean?'

Teela gestured with her hand. 'It's meant to mean that maybe other people wouldn't be trying to cling onto times where everything was rosy. Why don't you understand? The times of standing watch, doing reports and recording captain's logs—they're gone. The roof is falling in, and you're worried about the wallpaper. Another captain might be able to see that.' She paused. 'We're on our own.' She forcefully turned her back, bringing an end to the argument, before climbing down the ladder and disappearing from view.

Poppy stared at the space where Teela had just stood. The clangs faded down the corridor in reverse to how they had come. Her upper arms began to ache, and she realised she still had her hands firmly grasped to the side of her head. She lowered them slowly and propped herself up against the desk. Her foot caught the chair as she turned. She kicked it away, her leg shooting backwards like a spooked horse. It flew across the room with great speed, knocking over the water bottle Teela had left on the floor, before crashing into the opposite wall. The loose lid came off the bottle and rolled towards her, nuzzling at her ankle, allowing the contents to spill on the metallic flooring.

She watched as the liquid began to pool, the surface possessing an odd sheen, the reflections of the room almost red. She walked over and dipped her finger into the reddish juice, licking it – pilfered blood-orange juice.

Poppy let her knees buckle under her, sitting on the floor and resting her head against the compartment behind her. She stared at the sticky patch that had already begun to congeal around the edges. She knew she would have to clear it up, but there was no rush. She wondered if she would ever feel the need to hurry again. All the times she had wished for tomorrow, or the day after, or the next week, slowly rolled into her mind.

'When I grow up,' she said, looking directly into Grandad

Lehrer's intrigued face, 'when I grow up…' She paused, trying to finish the sentence in her mind before saying it. 'When I grow up, I want to be older.'

'Oh really,' said Grandad Lehrer. 'Well,' he smiled to himself. 'I think that can be arranged. And tell me, why do you want to be older?'

Poppy didn't need to think this time. 'So I can do whatever I want.'

'And what do you want to do?'

Poppy opened her mouth before realising she didn't have an answer.

The juice was ice cold and left a tacky residue on the fleshy part of her fingertip as she unconsciously swirled her finger in the puddle. She thought about the funeral. About the flowers on the coffin and the look on Grandma Lehrer's face. She remembered playing aeroplanes in the gardens, whizzing around with the other kids, offering a pleasant distraction for the adults who watched as they ran in and out of the trees and across the flowerbeds.

Poppy rubbed her finger and thumb together, breaking the fine layer of film that had formed. She looked down at the small puddle with apathy. She didn't have the energy to care. She didn't even really mind that Teela had taken the juice at all. It seemed trivial. A distant smile hovered over the corners of her lips.

'Now, promise me,' said Alice, 'you're not going to spill that glass of blackcurrant juice all down your top?'

Catherine shook her head as if the very thought offended her.

'Okay, fine,' said Alice, nodding to Grandma Lehrer to give her the glass.

Poppy remembered the noise as it hit the floor halfway through the meal, the remnants from the glass, draining through the planks of the picnic table. Then the silence. Then the tears as the dry white top Catherine had been wearing turned into a wet pink top that stuck to her skin.

* * *

The grinding sound of an incoming transmission rudely interrupted her lethargy, as her watch beeped 20:00 U.T. in unison. She had been there for hours, yet it seemed like Teela had only just stormed off. There had been no seven o'clock transmission, as far as she could remember. She tried to think. Maybe she had missed it.

Poppy didn't move as the recognisable voice entered the room, her tired body thankful that Teela had made incoming transmissions automatically accepted without added clearance. She closed her eyes and allowed the dry tones of Captain Sheridan to surround her. She listened intently, more intently than she had since the first weeks. She tried to establish the cadence in the voice. She wanted to find a quiver or stutter that suggested the message was heartfelt. She wanted to find minor differences, intonations, to convince herself they weren't the same loops from the very first day.

She opened her eyes. It was no use. She couldn't distinguish between actual abnormalities in the speech and abnormalities in her imagination. She thought about what Teela had said. She reasoned it entirely plausible she was right.

Her thoughts drifted to nothing as she realised the room was silent. She got up and opened the compartment doors, searching for something to clean the juice with. She placed the whole of her left arm into a holder marked, "Medical", and retrieved something that looked much like a paint roller. She squeezed the head of the soft foam material. It felt comforting against her palm, a feeling of pure luxury. She knelt down in front of the spillage and placed the roller at the banks. She pressed down and pushed it away, causing the juice to disappear, instantly soaking into the absorbent fabric.

Poppy ran her fingertips over the spot. It felt bone dry except for remnants of sticky residue. She reached back into the

Medical holder and brought out a scourer and what looked to be a deodorant can. She sprayed it liberally over the tacky floor before rubbing it away with the scouring pad in tiny jagged motions. It scraped across the metal with a horrible sound that travelled up through her fingers to the tops of her arms, leaving them weak, but she kept going as years of dark grime lifted from the single square, dissolving away within the solution as if forgotten in an instant.

She reached the middle and stopped. The tile was spotless, and the weak irritation in her arms gave way to a sense of achievement. She clambered to her feet and stepped back, causing the satisfaction to drain away as quickly as it had come. She looked down across the rest of the floor. It was like a new penny thrown into a wishing well. She watched it sink through the water before being enveloped by hundreds of faded and muddy coins as the bright patch of gleaming serenity by her feet was immediately dampened by the approaching surroundings of dull, callous squares of dark metal.

She knelt back down and sprayed more of the cleaning solution on the floor before scratching away at the grime, moving outwards, tile by tile, always starting at the border and working her way in.

* * *

Poppy sat slumped in the corner. Sweat rolled down the curls of hair, causing strands to stick to her skin, before gathering in the creases of her frowned forehead. Her eyes were red from the fumes, and her fingertips were wrinkled and raw. Six empty cans littered the otherwise spotless floor.

The episode left an unsavoury taste in her mouth. She looked at her watch, twenty-one minutes past twelve, universal time, and clambered to her feet. Her arm ached as she bent down to collect the empty cans, and a yawn gaped her mouth open, yet she didn't feel tired, just irritated. She felt like the dirt and grime she had cleaned off the floor had smeared itself over her body. She wanted to peel off her skin and emerge fresh.

She threw the cans back in the compartment and stumbled towards the ladder shaft in a distracted daze. She thought of her father prepping some potatoes. She could see his large fingers scrubbing away at the mud just before the sharp knife began to peel at the skin, ripping it away in long satisfying curls. She flung her leg carelessly off the platform and missed the rung. The weight of her limb hanging down with no support caused her lower torso to lose balance and follow it down the void. She flailed her arms, trying to find something to grab hold of, but was too slow. Her fingernails dragged across the polished floor, and she let out a painful scream before disappearing down the shaft.

There were three loud bangs, and Poppy lay motionless at the bottom of the ladder, her eyes fixed to the doorway she had been at, but moments before.

She was completely still.

In the distance, about halfway up the street, she could see her parents and Catherine. They were all holding hands, and Catherine was intermittently swinging between them, lifting her feet off the pavement and using their arms to propel herself forward, the lights on her trainers flashing each time she touched the ground.

Poppy looked down to the kerb, her hands scratched and bloodied on the gritty surface. Three ants disappeared down a crack in the paving. Up the road, the light had begun to disturb the sharp lines of the buildings, and her family were moving towards it, becoming increasingly hazy. She shouted to them, but they didn't hear as they slowly continued on towards the blur of bright-grey obscurity, Catherine's soles flashing as they went.

* * *

Poppy opened her mouth, almost manically, and shuddered.

Her body convulsed with shock, and she could hear her heartbeat in her throat. She grabbed at her neck as if trying to strangle the adrenalin, gasping three times, violently. She tried to replay the incident in her head, but struggled. A flash of the Control Room lights as she fell backwards jumped across her vision, followed by a sharp image of an orange-tinged rung as her face flew towards the ladder. The rest was just confusion.

She released the grip round her neck, and the pulsing began to drop. She pulled her hand away and felt a sharp sensation on the top of her fingertip. She held both hands in front of her face and squinted her eyes to focus. Her fingers were covered in blood, and she had lost one of her nails. She waved her hands, trying to dry the dripping wound, but the unprotected nail bed stung as the cold air-current passed over. She stopped quickly, turning her attention to the rest of her body.

She took a deep breath and used the base of the ladder to haul her tender frame up so she could assess herself more thoroughly. A sharp pain coursed through her lower half. She lifted up her right trouser leg and looked at her ankle. She tentatively tried to place some weight down, but a severe pain tweaked at the joint. She prodded the side of her foot. It had already begun to swell.

'Teela!' she shouted. Her voice echoed down the corridor before vanishing to a pathetic nothingness. 'Teela!' Still using the ladder as support, she swivelled on her good foot and faced down the long passage. 'Teela!' She waited a second for the echoes to dissolve before pushing off from the ladder and taking her first staggered steps down the corridor. She stopped immediately, spreading her legs and arching her spine. Her head was almost fully tipped back, staring at the ceiling. The lights were like a burning sun, beating down across an unforgiving desert.

She stood completely still in the arched position for an age, before abruptly setting off again along the grated floor, pausing every few metres to correct her swaying balance, the grates creaking now instead of rattling, before carrying on.

* * *

Poppy reached the bedchamber ladder and placed her left foot on the first rung. The pain shot up her right as if someone had scraped a knife along the bone. She did her best to plant her weight before lifting herself onto the ladder. She reached down to guide her bad foot onto the bar and began to heave herself upwards, sweat pouring down from her face, saturating her already damp clothes. Her arms felt like they were caving in on themselves, the muscle disappearing into nothing as the space between the rungs grew seemingly further and further apart until, eventually, they ran out and she could feel the top of the landing.

She nicked her exposed nail bed on the side of the ladder as she tried to pull herself up, the blood now congealed, but the pain every bit as sharp. She let out a small grimace and hurled herself forward, climbing up onto the landing and falling towards the black panel fixed to the wall.

Her bedchamber door juddered and scraped only half open, showing no sympathy to her condition. A knot tightened inside her stomach as she forced her way through and stumbled to the washroom. She decided the cold light was justification enough for not removing her clothes, as the uneven floor guided her halfway to the shower before leaving her to fend for herself as it sloped upwards. She placed herself under the rusty showerhead as cold drips from previous visits trickled down the back of her neck. She waved her hands frantically in front of the sensor, catching her finger again in the process, knocking off the congealed scab and reopening the flesh.

She cupped her palms, filling them with pink water as the freezing shower diluted the ruby beads flowing from her finger. She pulled them apart, and the pink sea crashed down onto her lower legs and the tops of her boots, leaving bloody trails that snaked across the floor to the drain.

'That's it, mucky pups,' said her mother leaning over the bath, 'make sure you get all nice and clean.' She watched as Catherine took a flannel and washed her face. 'Clever girl. Get all that dirt away.'

Poppy began to scrub away at any skin not protected by fabric. She was clean, but she didn't seem clean. She wanted to scrape it off and start again, but it wasn't working. She started at her face, rubbing it continuously until red, before moving on to her hands and lower arms. Her skin was raw and had started to crack in places, causing her to slow, the pain of the sores now worse than the relief gained from the cleaning. She tried for a bit longer before eventually turning off the shower.

Poppy stood motionless, soaking. Her wet clothes clung to her skin and piled more weight on her struggling leg. She tried to separate her sleeves from her arms, but everything was tight and constricted. She gave up and hobbled across the room, her boots squealing on the damp floor.

She stood in the doorway and stared at her bedchamber. It felt noisy in its order. She stumbled to her bed and threw the sheets across the floor. She staggered backwards and sent the contents of her desk flying with one sweep of her arm, before tipping over the chair with a lazy push. Panting, her eyes caught themselves in the mirrored lockers. She lurched towards them and planted a tight fist across her reflection, clumsily catching the sharp edge of the door and cutting the side of her hand as it made impact.

She collapsed backwards onto her bed and hung her head low, not knowing what she wanted. Dirt needed to be cleaned, but order left her irritated. She examined the cut. It wasn't deep, but it stung when she moved her fingers. She smudged the thin layer of blood that had surfaced into the surrounding skin, exaggerating the tidy slash, making it look like something a lot worse. She studied her fingertips. They had a rust tinge to them, as if she had been working with clay.

'What are you making?'

Catherine deliberated before giving an answer. 'A star bowl.'

'A "star bowl",' said Alice, watching Poppy carefully roll out a handle for her teapot, 'what's that?'

'It's a bowl,' said Catherine, not quite believing she had to explain it, 'but in the shape of a star.' She spread her fingers into a star shape to underline the point.

'You know,' said Alice, 'people have been doing this, what we're doing right now, for thousands of years.' She opened her eyes wide as the two children stared back at her in amazement.

The watch bleeped.

Poppy tore it off and threw it in the general direction of her bedside table, the strap clanging as it hit the metallic edge.

She leant back onto her uncovered mattress. The dry material pressed against her damp hair and she realised she was still wearing her sodden clothes. She didn't care. Her body heat had warmed the wet fabric, and she didn't possess the effort needed to change.

* * *

Poppy lay, just staring at the ceiling. Her eyes were open, but she was dreaming. Her mind segued between streaks of thought. The knot in her stomach was still present. The more she thought, the more it tightened. Sweat gathered on her skin. She could see the faces of her family. Her father, her mother, Catherine, Grandma Lehrer, Grandad Lehrer, her aunties and uncles, even her nextdoor neighbours and people from her town that she knew only in passing. They scrolled past her eyes as if passengers on a train flying through a station – with her on the platform. She looked harder, trying to pick them out individually. Their eyes were not how she knew them; they were different and they had smugness in the corner of their mouths. She found herself repulsed by them, her own loved ones. She didn't understand. They were turning on her. They were no longer the people she knew. Then it hit her, and the knot in her belly wriggled and slithered until, at one of the ends, the face of a red serpent appeared from the coils, hissing jealousy.

* * *

A noise outside her bedchamber stirred Poppy from her nightmare. Her dry eyes scraped across the room as she looked to where the sound had come from. She pulled her lids down and gently massaged them. They stung as she freed them from her touch and quickly began to water, submerging the room in a hazy blur. She wiped them with the back of her hand, forgetting the cut as the moisture rubbed into her skin, sporadically removing blots of the blood staining. She glanced at her other arm searching for the time, but was met with the unfamiliar sight of a naked wrist as she recalled the irritation that had forced her to cast the watch away. She stood up, forgetting about her other ailments, and staggered towards the suspected landing spot. It was hidden in a nook behind the bedside table. A small crack ran along the right side of the screen, but it still seemed to be working. She slipped it onto her wrist, and the loading screen slowly illuminated.

She looked back towards the bed, not knowing how long she had been laying there. It didn't feel long, but then, it never did. She patted herself down. Her clothes were still slightly damp and gave the only tangible indication to the passing of time. She thought about changing and tried to offer reasons against it, but the damp odour being secreted from the fabric won the argument.

She started to strip, clumsily, as agonising stings pricked her body. Her foot was stiff and shot painful streaks up her leg as she tugged at the boot, doing her best to relieve the pressure, before deciding to just leave it on. She placed the old clothes into the wash basket and retrieved some fresh ones from the locker, being careful not to cause any more stress to the door. She winced as she bent down to pull the trousers over her knees and up to her bony hips, the task of putting the clothes on more difficult than taking them off.

Her breath was laboured and wheezy by the time she had finished. She stood next to the lockers and inspected the damage to her room. It seemed mostly superficial. She remade her bed, dragging the sheet up from the floor, and replaced the contents of her desk, turning the chair upright as she did so.

Her head whipped round quickly as another noise came from the chamber landing. She had forgotten about the initial motive for leaving her bed. She limped towards the exit and wrestled her way through the volatile door just in time to see Teela disappear into her room.

Poppy hobbled across and knocked. 'Teela, you checked the cargo?' She waited. 'Teela? Has the cargo been logged today? What day is it?' She knocked politely, but persistently. 'I'd do it myself, but I'm not sure I'd make it down there.' She looked towards her foot. 'Had a bit of trouble.' She left her words purposely ambiguous. 'Teela?'

'What do you mean?' Teela's voice was calmer than before, but still possessed a clear annoyance.

'I'm just asking about the cargo,' said Poppy. 'Whether it's been checked? I was just wondering if you had-'

'No,' interrupted Teela, 'I didn't mean that.' She paused, her voice muffled by the door. 'I'm saying, what do you mean when you say you're, "not sure you'd make it down"?'

'Oh.' Poppy paused. 'It's nothing... I had an accident. Nothing major, just-' She knocked again. 'Can you open the door? I'd rather not have to shout through metal.' She listened for any sign of movement and heard Teela scratching around. 'Teela?'

The scratching grew louder as Teela moved closer to the door. It slid open, and Poppy was greeted with her back. She was mid-turn and already heading towards the bed.

'What's happened then?' she said, her tone apathetic.

Poppy waited at the boundary of her room, partly through politeness and partly because she wasn't sure if she could manage to clamber over the mess that lay before her. 'I just slipped off the CR ladder. No real damage done. I was almost at the bottom, anyway. Just lost my footing.' She tapped at her leg, not actually making contact. 'Twisted my ankle again. Typical it had to be the same one.' She felt Teela's eyes travel up and down her body, scanning for evidence. She sensed her gaze lingering on her bloody, scratched hand, but did nothing to hide it, deciding to let her assume it was all part of the same incident.

'But you're alright, then?' Teela's eyes finished the examination and met with hers in a rare moment of concern, lasting briefly, before being broken.

'Yeah, I'm fine. As I say, just lost my balance coming down.'

Poppy's downplaying of the incident lost Teela's attention, and she quickly turned her back, kneeling next to her bedside table where a strategically placed light-patch provided extra visibility.

'I just came to see if you've checked the cargo? I know I haven't, but was just wondering if you might have gotten round to it on your travels?'

'Yeah, you said that,' said Teela, mumbling into the corner, 'and no.'

'"No", what?'

'As in, "No, I haven't checked the cargo."' She shrugged her shoulders. 'What more do you want me to say?'

'Well, it's just, if it hasn't been done–'

Teela turned to face her. 'Look, if you want it doing, do it yourself.'

'I can't,' Poppy patted her leg again. 'You know what I was like last time going down there with a dodgy leg.'

'Yes, and as I said at the time, if you recall, you were stupid.'

Poppy leant against the doorway, taking the pressure off her leg. 'I agree, and that's why I'm asking you to do it.'

Teela arched her back at the tediousness of the conversation. 'Did you bang your head on the way down, as well? We've been through this. I've told you before, just as I'm telling you now, it's pointless.'

Poppy pinched her temples with her thumb and forefinger. 'Teela, I am asking you, please go and log the cargo. It needs to be done.'

'And I'm telling you that it doesn't, and I'm not.' Her voice was calm and resolute.

'Teela, go and log the cargo.' Poppy stood up straight the best she could. 'First Officer Teela Rose, I order you to go and log the cargo.'

An audible sneer of amusement met the command.

'Teela, failing to act on a captain's order is a direct act of defiance.'

Teela turned to face her. 'Arrest me, then.'

Poppy stabled herself against the doorframe. 'Defying protocol is–'

'Oh, fuck your protocol, Poppy,' Teela turned her back to her. 'And y'know what? Fuck you, too.'

Poppy marched towards Teela's back, her scrambling feet getting caught in all manner of restrictions. She had no plan for when she reached her. She knew she wasn't going to arrest her; she just felt she needed to do something.

An empty tool-belt flung across the mattress distracted

her as she reached the edge of the bed. She slowed her approach, the foolish stampede going unnoticed by Teela who continued to busy herself in the corner. Dark, oily stains from various instruments patched the sheets and seemed to signal the start of a work area. An oxygen canister, with various loose nuts and bolts placed on a small flat oasis within the mess, seemed to be the focus.

'What the hell are you doing?'

Teela quickly hunched across her work, not realising how far into the room Poppy had come.

'What is this?' she asked again.

Teela felt like a schoolgirl who had been caught passing notes in class.

'Let me see.'

Teela hunched over more tightly. 'It's nothing.'

'Teela.'

'Alright,' she shouted, and slowly got up from her crouched position, revealing everything. 'You're gonna find out sooner or later.' Teela perched on the edge of the mattress, accidentally sitting on the discarded tool belt. She tossed it further down the bed and waited for Poppy's reaction.

'What's it for?'

Teela didn't answer, remaining steadfast on gauging her facial response. She could see Poppy's mind ticking, trying to understand what was going on. She watched as Poppy picked up the flexible tubing cast-offs and other remnants, waiting for her to give up before stating an answer. 'It's tubing from the gas canisters.'

Poppy held it up. 'I can see that, but why?'

Teela paused, not out of fear, but to acknowledge that, once Poppy knew, it was the end of her solitude. 'I've been modifying the oxygen canisters. They now take triple; quadruple the amount they used to.' She saw the realisation spread across Poppy's face and waited for some sort of eruption, but it didn't come. 'I'm going back out,' she said, trying to force some kind of reaction. 'Poppy, you hear me?'

Poppy looked at her calmly. 'We're not going back out, Teela.'

'I never said anything about *us*.' She stood up.

Poppy tried to reposition herself into a more assertive stance, but was undermined by her ailments. 'You're deluded if you think you're going out by yourself.'

Teela leant in close, her face virtually touching Poppy's, they could smell each other's breath. 'And you're deluded if you think you can stop me,' she said, her voice calm and earnest.

Poppy threw the tubing onto the ground in protest. She stepped backwards, creating a gap between them. 'Last time was a farce, just like it will be this time.' Her voice changed to a softer tone, almost pleading. 'Our job is to deliver the parcels from A to B. We're not soldiers. We don't do spacewalks every other day. We're not cut out for it.' She turned away and started the trek towards the door.

Teela clenched her fists. 'Don't walk away from me!'

Poppy continued to walk. 'I've got nothing more to say.'

Teela let out a scream that felt like it came from both her heart and her gut and the very ground she walked on. 'I'm going. You might not be able to understand it, but I'm going!' She picked up a wrench and hurled it towards the lockers, causing one large fragment of mirror to crack and break away from the door. It landed on the floor in one piece, cushioned by the discarded clothing that lay underneath. Her voice was scratched. 'I'm not gonna be abandoned again…'

Chapter Nine

Locked In

'She's not going back out. I don't care.' Poppy held her head in her hands. 'She's not going back out. I won't let her.' She tried to convince herself that what she was saying was true, that she still had control. 'It's not going to happen.'

The monitor in the booth acted as a mirror. She used it for guidance as she felt for the small gold insignia fastened to her collar. She pulled it off and held it in her hands. 'What a waste.' She tossed it up and down, feeling the weight of the deceivingly heavy piece. 'Solid gold... worthless.' She held it up to the camera. 'What a waste.' She placed the pin badge back onto her collar. 'There, does that make me captain now? Am I better than you now?' She leant back into the chair, the bottom half of her face absent from the screen. 'She's not going out. She's not going out.' She hoped the repetition would cause her words to become fact. 'There's nothing out there; there's nothing to fix.' She hit the side of the booth with the back of her hand. 'There's nothing to fix!' She threw herself back against the seat and closed her eyes, pinching the bridge of her nose.

'It hurts...' Poppy was back outside Airlock Three, on the floor, her ankle like a balloon in the suit.

Teela draped her arm over her shoulder and slowly lifted her up. 'Just make it back to the room and we can get it off.'

Poppy hopped on one leg, doing her best not to let her bad foot drag along the floor. 'What a stupid idea,' she said to herself. 'What a waste.'

Teela didn't speak as they approached the door. They went through, and she carefully let Poppy slump down on the bench.

'What a waste.'

Teela watched as Poppy took off her helmet and pulled the suit down as far as she could before hitting the pain.

'What were we thinking?'

Teela bent down and eased the suit over Poppy's swollen ankle. 'It wasn't a waste,' she said.

'Oh yeah,' said Poppy, grimacing, 'well, what did we achieve other than injuring ourselves?'

'It has to be out there,' said Teela, ignoring the question.

'There was nothing there,' Poppy swore as her ankle was set free, 'you said it yourself.'

'I just needed more time.'

Poppy leant back on the bench, her head resting against the wall. 'Teela, we're universal postal workers. We're not cut out for this. Sure, we know our way around the inside of Vitula, but what were we thinking? Even if we had found a problem out there, we wouldn't have known how to fix it.' She untangled a clip from her drenched hair. 'It's like asking a first aider to do brain surgery.'

Teela threw her helmet across the room and collapsed on the bench on the opposite side.

* * *

Poppy sat in complete silence; a sleepwalking shadow slumped in the seat. A small sway in her posture made the chair creak, causing her to wake from the vacant state. She got up and stumbled out of the booth, continuing the tradition of leaning against the wall outside as her eyes adjusted to the lights. Hard shadows climbed across her gaunt face as she held her hand up as a shield. She looked back at the booth's entrance. She couldn't remember anything of what she had just said.

She knew she had spoken, but wasn't sure if she had actually said anything worthwhile, or even the date. She thought for a second. She didn't know what the date was. Her eyes slumped down to her watch. The small crack on the face magnified that portion of the screen, distorting the type. She stared at the warped number, the red digit melting across the screen, almost losing its form entirely whilst still being as recognisable as ever.

She rested her head against the wall and unconsciously placed the nail-less finger into her mouth. The bed had healed quite well, but she continued the habit of ceasing the dripping blood with her tongue. She debated going back into the booth to make another recording, but decided against it. She needed rest. She couldn't remember the last time she had even sat on her bed, her body now living off moments of daze and absentness.

She was in her bedroom, the window by her side creaking slightly in the wind, the moon shining through the curtains. She knew it was just the wind because her father had told her so. Her eyes closed and nearly succumbed to the darkness before quickly opening again as something outside began to tap at the glass.

Poppy slowly sat up and pushed her head close to the wall, peeling back the edge of the curtain with her tiny fingers.

Two eyes stared back at her.

Alice held her to her breast as Poppy continued to wail. Kaleem sat at the end of the bed, still half asleep, his dressing gown tied in a clumsy knot.

'It was just a dream,' she said. 'It shows how fantastically great your imagination is. Doesn't it?'

Kaleem yawned and nodded.

Poppy's arm began to ache. She looked at the booth and wondered how long she had been out for this time. She remembered looking at her watch. She guessed about thirty seconds, but couldn't be sure.

She used the wall as leverage to kick-start herself down the corridor. She had developed a hobble, but once into her stride, she was fairly mobile. It meant her walking action was faster than it had been, taking short quick steps rather than slow pronounced ones. She noticed the grates had changed too, from large clangs and clunks, to small clinks and chatters.

Her trousers fell down below her waist. She stopped and pointed her foot, allowing the boot to become visible again as she pulled the belt back up to her midriff. Her stomach gurgled as she tightened it. She did her best to ignore the feeling, but the thought of food beckoned her to dream.

She thought about the recurring notion of the perfect meal. She envisioned steam billowing up from a freshly cooked plate of something, presented to her on the most elegant of crockery. She tried to specify a single meal, but couldn't. She didn't care what it was as long as it was food. Her stomach howled again. She thought of Teela gorging herself on the next day's rations. For the smallest of moments, she debated copying her, but managed to keep the idea at arm's length.

She held her wiry torso beneath her skinny fingers. She remembered the fifth, and final, piece of meal bar waiting for her in her room. There was a skip of excitement in her heart before realising she must have already eaten the other four pieces. It didn't feel like she had. She wondered what was better, to eat her designated ration all at once, or to spread it out over the day. Originally, she had thought that it would be better to spread it out, so there was always something to look forward to, but the small quantity seemed to dilute the experience, the single piece hardly ever being recorded by her hunger. She imagined the concentrated euphoria of a whole meal bar, eaten all at once. A true feast.

* * *

Poppy reached the ladder, and her stomach gave another

grumble as if vocalising its encouragement to her, the final piece of meal bar acting as a rather disappointing incentive, dangling from a stick. She clumsily stumbled onto the ladder and began to climb, her weakened state making it difficult to garner any speed.

She reached the top and rested her head on the cold floor of the landing, her face hot and clammy. The contrast of the tile felt pleasant against her heated skin, and she dangled her leg over the side of the ledge. She envisaged herself sprawled out in a hammock on the shoreline of a tropical island she had read about, a pile of conch shells by her feet. She could hear the gentle breeze drifting through the palm trees overhead and the sea as it lapped up against the sand. In the distance, she could see a small plateau of pink rock and the dancing lights from numerous pools near the edge of the cove. She longed for such paradise; she could stay forever.

Another grumble brought her back. She dragged her leg onto the landing and peeled her face away from the grated tile. Lined marks imprinted themselves across her cheek. She stumbled through the jamming door and fell down onto her bed. She stopped for a moment and began to close her eyes, but her stomach gave another rumble, ordering her to continue. She swore in frustration and summoned up some energy, leaning over to the bedside table and grabbing the remains of the meal bar that waited for her.

For one glorious second, she thought that two pieces remained, instead of just one, but it was a cruel illusion caused by the way she had folded the wrapper. She masked the disappointment by pretending she hadn't been fooled and carefully peeled back the foil, exposing the last piece of beige meal bar. She held it between her middle finger and thumb, inspecting it for any signs of appeal.

She gave up and placed it on the end of her tongue. It stuck to the roof of her mouth like a cardboard brick as she began to chew, overwhelming the little moisture she had to begin with. She coughed, as a small dust particle latched to the back of her throat, and again, as the brittle block fractured into tiny crumbs of grain and seed. Her tongue struggled to cope as the masticated glue found its way onto her teeth and inside the joining of her gums. She managed to clump together a large enough portion to warrant a swallow and did so, sticking out her tongue after, as if to prove it had gone.

Poppy looked down disappointedly and examined the packet. A lone crumb hid solemnly in the corner of the silver foil. She reached in with her finger and pressed hard, the crumb sticking to her skin as if perfectly balanced, before holding it against her front incisor and slowly sliding it down until it reached the gap. She opened her jaw slightly and precisely crushed it with the tooth below. Her stomach gargled, asking her for more, but it was over.

She scrunched up the empty wrapper and threw it towards the bin. It missed, but she didn't care. Another growl, this time louder and angrier, demanded more, but was left disappointed as Poppy began to wish she had saved the piece. The moment it was gone was the moment she regretted letting herself eat it. She checked the time without actually letting it register in her brain, wondering how long she had to wait for the next ration as tiredness smothered her head. Twelve hours.

She stood up. She thought about bending down to pick up the wrapper as she passed, but couldn't be bothered, she didn't see any harm in it staying there. Her mother's voice danced around her ears as she left the room. She thought about what she would say. Her face appeared briefly before quickly dissolving, not letting her get a clear look.

She staggered out to the landing and immediately noticed Teela's door unlocked and wide open. 'Teela?' She walked cautiously towards the door, unable to understand how she had missed it on her way up. 'Teela?'

She entered the room. It seemed more spacious, the clutter

that had filled the floor now organised and neat. Most of the clothes had gone, as had the bedsheets and pillows. She stepped over a small bundle of socks and opened the locker doors. Her heart sank as the light illuminated the empty shelves, the walls bare except for the photograph of the two of them. She delicately removed it and swiped her finger across the paper, staring, mesmerised, as the loop played over and over. She had forgotten about those smiles; they seemed so long ago.

'Go on,' said Poppy, 'I never get a chance with you.' She held her watch up in the air, the camera showing the Control Room on the screen.

'What's the occasion?' said Teela.

'Just because. There doesn't have to be a reason.'

They both stood up, Teela slightly behind Poppy as she held the watch face up so it pointed down towards them.

'Three… Two… One!'

Teela pushed Poppy out of the way and stuck two fingers up to the camera, the two of them laughing in unrestrained bursts.

A small quiver from her right hand caused the photo to slip through her grasp and fall to the floor, breaking its charm. She thought about placing it in her pocket, but returned it to the locker. The large crack on the side of the door caught her eye as she moved away, the memories of that night sliding horribly into view. She had never seen Teela like that. Regret bubbled in her throat, wishing she had been more tactful. She looked around for the shard of glass. The pile of clothes that had cushioned its fall had gone. A terrible thought flashed across her mind. Her heart began to race. It banged hard against her chest. 'Teela!' she shouted, rushing over to the washroom. 'Teela?' It felt like a fist punching the inside of her ribcage. She held her breath as her head broke the boundary between bedroom and washroom. Her voice echoed through the empty room, and relief gushed through her. She staggered backwards towards the freezing cold wall and mopped her sweating brow just as another fist punched through her chest. The movement of her hand drew her eyes towards an unknown Figure, straight across, staring towards her. Her heart jolted. She pushed off from the wall, her clammy fingertips sticking to the smooth tiles as if trying to restrain her, and tentatively approached until she couldn't get any closer. She reached up, allowing her fingers to slowly caress the Figure's face. The skin felt tight and leathery, and the pointed cheekbones were underlined with dark, hollow basins. The mouth was dry with peeling snags hanging down from the lips and purple rings looped around the eyes like ink stains.

Poppy stared, repulsed, at the sight in front of her. And the Figure stared back. Yet, it was different. It felt like it was looking through her, past her, rather than at her. It was as if she wasn't there at all.

Poppy turned away and quickly left the chamber, seeking the safety of her own room. She pressed the panel on the inside wall, and the juddering door shut behind her. She stared at the perfectly made bed in the corner. It looked so inviting, but her mind no longer yearned for it. Instead, she just stood, her legs slightly apart and her head tilted back towards the ceiling, the space where her stomach should have been pushed out, forming a long curve from her head to her feet.

She could feel the Figure behind her. She began to run as it chased her out through the bedchambers and through the winding corridors, its bare feet hitting the grates with scratched beats, matching her heart as she reached the Control Room before turning back and heading towards the Rec. Room. She could feel its breath on her neck as she ran towards the window, its reflection growing larger in the glass as she reached out, trying to dodge its branched arms that just missed her back as she flung herself through the blackness to her street and the house she knew so well, the Figure's shadow overtaking her along the road as she burst through the front door to see Alice and Kaleem smiling at the dinner table, with Catherine beckoning them in to join them. Yet, she wasn't looking at Poppy, but the thing that was behind her. She had a birthday cake in her hand and lit the flame for the candles.

'Make a wish,' they all said in unison, as she ran through the table, extinguishing the fire, the Figure disappearing into the smoke.

Poppy opened her eyes, causing the lights to drone.

She listened for a moment until, all of a sudden, they seemed to stop and she felt the hair on her neck stand up. She turned round, and a bolt coursed through her heart as the Figure stared back at her from the locker doors. She turned again, and the Figure stared back from the washroom. She looked down at her desk, and the Figure looked up towards her, its eyes never really seeing her.

A thousand fists pummeled her insides as a thousand identical Figures invaded her room. It was everywhere. She stumbled towards the middle of the floor, trying to maintain the largest distance from each of them. She bent double and ran to the toilet, her hands clenched tight round her stomach. She leant over and tried to throw up into the metallic bowl. Again and again she retched, but she was empty.

She wiped her mouth on her sleeve and crawled over to the shower, sitting far enough away as to not get wet, but close enough to get splashed by any brave drops. She held her hand underneath the water jet and felt the tension leave her body as the stream massaged her open palm. She brought her fingers together and splashed her face, bathing her skin in what felt like silk. She cupped the water and brought it up to her straggly hair before dipping her head into the torrent. She splayed her fingers and ran them through the knots, trying her best to brush it back.

Kaleem shook his head. 'If I've told you once, I've told you a thousand times, comb your hair. You've got a tatty head.'

Alice leant over and ruffled Kaleem's hair. 'What, and you didn't when you were her age?'

Poppy smiled.

'You do know,' Alice brought Kaleem's hair down over his forehead. 'The only reason I married you was because of your tatty head.'

* * *

Poppy shivered as the warm water hit the cold air. Small pools had begun to form across the floor where drops, struggling to make the long journey to the drain, huddled together bravely.

She got up and walked across the room to where a small rusting rail struggled to hold up a stiff grey towel. She stepped back and accidentally stamped on one of the larger pools, displacing a fair amount of water in the process. For a fleeting moment, she thought she saw the Figure staring up at her, but by the time she had lifted her foot, it had gone.

Poppy pried the towel off the rail and carelessly dried the top of her head, the rough material scratching against her scalp like sandpaper. She quickly discarded it and made her way to the bedroom, sitting down on the bed with a drop. She looked around the room, trying to ignore her aching leg. She could still see the Figure, especially in the locker, but it seemed more lucid than before.

She pulled her eyes away and looked at her watch. Her mind turned back to Teela.

* * *

Poppy walked down the empty corridor and became aware that she was holding tight to a bubble in her stomach. At first, she thought it was hunger, but it wasn't; it was different to hunger. She knew she had felt it before, but couldn't place it. She combed through her mind, searching for a match. The bubble grew as she thought about the failed operation outside.

It was the feeling she got when she sat in the doctor's Waiting Room, and it seemed to grow the nearer she got to the Control Room. She could feel it from her gut, pulsating outwards towards every inch of her body as she climbed the ladder.

'Teela?' Poppy's head peered over the ledge to the empty Control Room, her face a mixture of disappointment and relief. She hauled herself up and marched purposely to the intercom. Large sweat patches had formed across her back, and drips clung to the tips of her hair like beads. 'Teela?' She held the receiver closer to her mouth. 'Teela? Answer me.' She waited a short time before trying again. 'Teela, just pick up the receiver. Just let me know you're alright... Teela!' She tried again. 'Answer me...' And again. 'Please, Teela! Just answer!' Each time, getting more and more frantic before finally collapsing on the chair.

She kicked the desk in frustration, and the sound reverberated around the room, shocking her. She leant back, and rested her head against the chair. It felt strangely pleasant. Her neck muscles loosened as she began to sink further down into the fabric and her arms slumped. The top half of the room began to disappear as her lids slowly closed until, eventually, there was only a small blurring slit of light left.

'Last chance, Poppy.'

Poppy jumped as Teela's calculated voice sliced through the peace.

She scrambled for the receiver. 'Teela? Thank Life! I thought...' Her voice trailed to a whisper. 'I thought you had done something stupid.'

A flashing marker on the monitor showed she was in the Rec. Room.

'You heard me, Poppy. I need an answer. Last chance. Make a decision.' Her voice didn't waver, the tone calculated and clinical.

'No wait, Teela, hold on.' The initial joy trickled off Poppy's face as she realised what she meant. She slammed the receiver onto the desk and raced down the ladder as fast as her body allowed, the floor grates returning to their rattled state as she bounded through the corridors, her limp amplified by the haste. She thought about how she could convince her, how she could offer ways that would perfectly articulate her point. Her father's face burnt across her eyes. He was laughing at her, mocking her for not possessing his level of articulation.

'You are pathetic,' he said. 'Worthless.' He let out a deep, bellowing laugh that seemed to vibrate through her very being. 'What is your purpose?'

Her pace slowed as she approached the Rec. Room, out of exhaustion rather than tact. She entered, and her eyes clung to the Window, as they always did, before being quickly distracted by what seemed to be a makeshift camp at the far end of the room. She stepped forward. Clothes were scattered in clumsily organised piles, and sheets hung untidily over the armrests of the settee, now seemingly her bed.

Teela froze as she saw the gaunt and grey outline approach her.

'What's… what's this?' Poppy stumbled on her words, perplexed by the situation.

'Couldn't stay in my room anymore.' Teela tried not to let the sight of Poppy distract her. 'For some reason, there was an awful stench of something. Something delicate and weak.'

Poppy reached the boundary of the imagined room. 'Come on, Teela, this is childi-'

'I'm surprised you noticed anyway,' she interrupted. 'How long did it take you to realise I was gone? Have you told Sheridan yet? I'm sure he would love to know.'

Poppy bent down to pick up a pile of clothes that seemed to form a border.

'Don't touch that.'

She dropped the clothes. 'He's cut his transmissions,' said Poppy. 'Only makes three or four a day now.'

Teela began to potter around her camp, moving piles of

clothes about, seemingly at random. 'I couldn't care, Poppy. He's dead to me, and his fucking loops.'

'They're not loops!' Poppy was shocked with the forcefulness of her reaction. She could feel her neck pulsating. 'They're not loops,' she said again, lowering her tone. 'You can hear his voice move sometimes as he-'

'You can't, Poppy. Trust me, I tried too. You're just projecting what you want to hear onto it. When are you going to learn that he's not our knight in white?'

Poppy faced the window. 'He's not out there just twiddling his thumbs, y'know?'

'Prove it.' Teela threw herself down on the settee, making Poppy jump. 'I'm not saying he's a bad person. He's just no use to us.'

'He's trying to save us.'

Teela nodded sarcastically. 'In what? A small SRV the company has deemed expendable. He's not exactly top of the saviour pyramid.'

'He's all we've got.'

'Well, I don't want him,' shouted Teela. She opened her mouth again, but stopped, as silence filled the space.

Poppy began to walk away. 'Well, it seems like you're set here. I'll leave you to it.'

'I take it that's your decision? You're still not coming?'

Poppy turned and marched towards the settee, dragging her boots across the clothes. 'Listen clearly, because for some reason you don't seem to get this.' She thrust her hand in Teela's direction, dominating over her seated position. 'I am the captain,' she pointed to the golden insignia. 'Nobody is going anywhere. That is the end. You're deluded if you think you can go out there and find something; you're deluded if you think you can then fix it; and you're deluded if you think you can do it single-handedly. Nobody is setting foot out of this ship again.'

'And you're deluded if you think you can stop me!' screamed Teela, their faces almost touching.

Poppy stepped back. 'I may not be stronger than you, but I can just shut off the airlock from the Control Room.'

Teela lurched up from the settee. She reached down behind the side of the armrest and pulled out the shard of glass. 'Go on,' she held it to her own neck. 'Do it. Try and stop me.'

Poppy jerked forward, but halted as Teela forced the tip harder against the skin. She could see the jugular throbbing in terror as the surrogate blade pressed against her flesh. 'Teela, please.' Poppy's already weak legs began to buckle. 'Teela, let's just stop and think.' A thousand words flooded through her mind, but she didn't know how to order them, and her lips didn't know how to form them.

'I've had enough, "let's justs",' said Teela, her voice not as strong as her stance portrayed. 'I gave you your last chance, and you declined.' She took a small step closer to her. 'I'm sorry, Poppy, but I don't have another choice.'

Poppy backed away slowly to maintain the distance, her eyes fixed to the shard. They reached the doorway, and she stumbled out into the corridor. 'Where are we going?'

Teela didn't reply.

They began to move slowly down the hall, the tacit agreement not to speak intensifying the sound of their footsteps as they hit the grates. Poppy listened as Teela's two purposeful clangs were echoed each time by her carefully placed backwards rattles. Her eyes ran from the shard to Teela's determined expression that refused to acknowledge her. She wondered if she had a plan or whether this was just one impulsive action she didn't know how to finish. She noticed a slight tremble running across Teela's free hand. She seemed nervous, the hand holding the shard so stiff and awkward that a pressure sore had formed on its palm.

'Teela,' she pleaded. 'Come on, let's just stop. Look at me.'

Teela's gaze darted briefly towards her.

'You don't need to do this. Please.' Poppy stumbled round the corner to the bedchambers. 'Teela!'

'We're going up,' she said, as they approached the ladder, and gestured for Poppy to start climbing. 'No, wait.' Teela studied the ladder and calculated how to go about the ordeal. 'I'll go first. You stand there and wait until I'm up.' She ushered her to the side before removing the shard from her neck and sliding it under her waistband.

Poppy could see a small red mark where the sharp point had sunk into her skin. She knew if she were going to do something, this would be the time. For a second, she thought about leaping forward and trying to tackle her, now there was no direct threat. She gauged the distance, but it was too far to make in one bound, and she didn't trust the effectiveness of her wavering legs. She looked back down the corridor and briefly thought about making a break for it, but knew she'd never outrun her.

'Don't fucking try anything, Poppy,' said Teela, as if reading her mind. 'You know I'm faster than you.'

Poppy nodded innocently, as she made her ascent.

'Right,' Teela peered over the edge with the shard back firmly against her neck. 'Your turn.'

Poppy reluctantly turned towards the ladder and began to climb, each rung feeling like a crowbar slowly battering away at any chance she had to escape, the sweat pouring off her face the higher she got. 'Teela,' she panted, as she reached the landing, holding out her hand.

Teela pulled Poppy up and showed her towards her chamber. 'Open it.'

Poppy stumbled forward and tapped at the panel repeatedly. The door clanking open with a struggle. She looked towards Teela for instruction.

'Bed.'

Poppy nodded and dragged herself through the door to the bed. 'Now what,' she said, still panting, as she perched herself on the edge of the mattress.

'Now...' Teela paused for a moment as she confirmed to herself that this truly was the course she was taking. 'Now, I'm going out,' she concluded, almost casually.

Poppy stood up, causing Teela to step back and bang into the lockers.

'Just stay there, Poppy.' She pressed the glass harder against her skin. 'Just please... stay there.' She edged towards the door as Poppy tentatively sat back down. 'I'm gonna have to lock you in.' She paused, trying to reason in her mind. 'You won't be trapped. I'll come back. To get you. After I've finished. After I've fixed it.' She spoke in short bursts of self-convincing arguments. 'I promise.'

'Teela, please!' Poppy caught her gaze for the first real time and saw a flash of the true Teela for a fraction of a moment.

'I'm sorry.' She stopped for a second before continuing. 'Don't try anything.'

Poppy watched as Teela grabbed the bin, emptied its contents, and with two short strikes, smashed the door's panel on the inside of the room.

'I'm sorry, Poppy.' She dropped the bin and left the room, frantically swiping across the panel on the landing.

Poppy stood up and staggered towards her as the door jolted across. She saw Teela's sorry eyes look back at her as the sheet of metal blocked the path, penning her in. 'Wait!'

Teela's footsteps slowly edged away from the door, and Poppy's eyes quietly dropped down to the remnants of the panel that hung from the wall, attached only by a solitary piece of casing. It looked pathetic, dangling, just waiting to fall and hit the cold, empty floor.

'You're a stupid fool!' she shouted, pounding on the wall, her voice cracked and raw. She stopped, listening. 'A hopeful fool,' she whispered, under her breath. A smirk somehow found its way to her lips. She swung her good leg round flamboyantly and sat down on the bed. She stretched back with her arms out behind her and gazed up at the ceiling. There was a small clang as Teela reached the bottom of the ladder, and Poppy began to laugh. Her body jerked up and down, but no sound came from her mouth. It started as a small gentle motion, but progressed into a violent shaking of her entire body. She couldn't understand what was happening; it just felt like the right thing to do. She wasn't even sure if it was definitely laughter, more a silent wail. Tears had formed along the bottom of her eyelids, and her throat had closed. She wanted to scream out with all her might, but couldn't, baring her teeth without a sound passing them. She tried again, and a pathetic rasp struggled to fill the room as the tears began to stream down her face, her mouth grimacing and half open.

She fell back to face the wall and began to scrape the dirt off the yellow panels, creating brilliant streaks of pure white that lined the walls like glistening slug trails. It collected under her fingernails, turning them black, before being meticulously picked out, rolled into a ball and flicked away.

'Look, snakes!' said Catherine.

Kaleem got up and walked towards the fence. 'They're not snakes,' he said. 'They're slugs. Look.' He stepped back as thousands of grey slugs suddenly began to crawl up from the muddy ground, overpowering the fence until all that could be seen was a pulsating mass of flesh. 'Look,' said Kaleem, pushing his hand into the middle of the growing mound until it reached his elbow. 'I'm hungry. Are you hungry?' He pulled out his arm and held a fistful of the slugs. 'Yummy,' he said, smiling as he forced them into his mouth, his teeth, now black, gnawing at the slimy flesh as his jaw rotated round and round.

* * *

Poppy scratched another line into the wall. She thought about how close Teela would be to the airlock. Her nail juddered as it reached the bottom, the pressure turning her fingertip a mottled white. An ache tightened in her stomach as Teela's makeshift oxygen canister flashed in front of her. She brought her legs up closer to her torso and turned over to face the lockers. Her throat cramped as the Figure stared back, its demonic eyes piercing through her.

'I'm for you,' it said, growing larger.

Poppy pushed her back against the wall, trying to keep away.

'I'm for you.' It reached out its withered claw and grabbed at the bedsheets. Poppy closed her eyes, but could smell the stench as it slowly loomed over her. 'I'm for you,' it said, as it reached, raking its fingers across the wall, scratching its white, silvery lines into the panels, outlining Poppy's form as its hand traced over her body.

She couldn't see, but she could hear the sound. 'Please,' she said, 'please leave me.'

'I'm for you,' it said.

She could feel its smile just in front of her face. 'I know.' Her voice cracked. 'I know.' She paused. 'But I am not scared of you.' She could hear the Figure stop, the shadow across her eyes shrinking as it stepped back towards the lockers. 'I am not scared of you,' she said again. The room fell still as it took one last step back and she opened her eyes to see it locked back inside the mirror. 'I'm not scared of you,' she said, staring at it.

* * *

Poppy was still on her side. A small bead of sweat trickled down her temple and jumped across to the bridge of her nose. She wiped it away, not knowing if it was sweat or a tear. The Figure didn't seem to move. She looked down towards her feet, knowing there was another lurking in the desk, and another inside the washroom. She sat up quickly, pulling her legs away from any danger, positioning herself in the corner, tight against the headboard. From here, she could see every conceivable path of attack.

Slowly, she built up the courage and began to work her way down towards the end of the bed, her back pushing up against the wall, smudging the grime and dulling the brilliant white lines she had created. She extended her arm and felt out for the edge of the bed, not wanting to break eye contact with the Figure in the locker. She took a breath. Her head slowly began to turn towards the washroom entrance, her eyes remaining fixed on the lockers. She took another breath. She needed to look; she needed to see what she knew was there. She felt out for the end of the washroom wall and sharply whipped her head round, peering directly into the room. She caught a sight of the gaunt Figure before quickly pulling her head back to the lockers.

* * *

Poppy looked at her watch and repeatedly bumped her head against the wall, causing vibrations to spread throughout the room. Everything felt grimy to the touch. She envisioned peeling back the dirt as if it were a fine film covering everything in sight. She closed her eyes and fantasised about revealing the clean, unblemished interior underneath. She would start at one end and work her way across until it had all been removed. A satisfied smile cut across her face as she studied the room, wondering where the best place to start would be. She noticed the laundry chute, but knew she wouldn't fit, and carried on until her eyes settled on the bin.

She stopped.

Abruptly, before giving enough time to talk herself out of it, she jumped up from the safety of her bed and grabbed it. The Figure did the same, bounding closer to the front of the lockers. Poppy steadied herself before hurling the bin towards its face. It bounced off the surface as a large crack ran down the centre, carving the Figure in two. She picked the bin back up and struck again and again at the Figure, sweat pouring down her face, before eventually, the locker doors shattered, causing large pieces of glass to fall from above. She watched as the Figure tried to protect itself, shielding its face with its arm as the shards rained down.

Poppy's heart raced as she tentatively knelt towards the broken, glinting mess on the floor. She picked up a piece similar in size to Teela's and held it towards the light. The glass was completely transparent. She looked at the dark, matt surface of the locker doors. The Figure was gone.

She leant back and examined her bloody and scratched knees. Small fragments had pierced through her trousers and embedded themselves in her skin. She slowly picked them out, one by one, each like a dangerous diamond in her fingers, quietly calling to her. She brushed off the excess and placed the larger pieces in a pile beside the bed before examining the bin. Numerous dents painted the sides, but it remained solid.

She edged towards the desk and quickly removed all her possessions with a swipe of her arm. She took a breath. With one great effort, she flipped the desk, scraping its surface against the wall, the legs sticking out into the room.

She stood with her hands on her hips, admiring her work, before jolting back, realising she was in direct view of the washroom. She grabbed her bed sheet and hesitantly entered the room, holding it aloft. She edged forward a couple of steps and threw the billowing fabric so it totally covered the mirror and draped down over the basin. She gave it a small tug to make sure the protection was secure before returning to her room.

Her chest puffed out triumphantly as she stood in the middle of the floor, letting out a loud victory wail, the sound thundering from her lungs. She spun around and, without thought, kicked the bin hard towards the landing door. It hit the metal and rattled the frame unexpectedly.

Poppy turned towards the noise. She moved the bin aside and held her hand to the surface of the door, inspecting it. It rocked back and forth quite easily without much persuading. Her teeth clenched with excitement as she picked up the bin and smashed it hard against the smooth metal. The door shuddered under the force. She aimed for one side and pounded hard again. A small gap developed between the frame and door. She wiped her brow and repeated the process, beating the door again and again, the metal shuddering again and again.

Her hands began to bleed as the sharp rim bit at the fleshy part of her hands with each blow. She looked around for something better suited. She grabbed a large shard of glass and tried to wedge it between the gap, but it snapped as she began to place pressure on it. Frustrated, she threw herself at the door. It wobbled on its axis as her shoulder impacted against the steel. She tried again, but recoiled as her arm began to seize, the door too heavy to continue. She rested against the lockers, her chest rising and falling as raspy pants crawled from her lungs. The newly revealed matt surface felt cool against her sweating skin. She thought about Teela; she would be outside by now.

Poppy opened the locker and peeled off the photo of her family, staring at the still image. She traced her eyes across the faces, but couldn't see their smiles, only Teela. She kept appearing in front of them, mutating across the group. The faster Poppy's gaze moved, the faster she appeared. Her face staring back, replacing even her own.

She turned the picture over and placed it back inside the locker before pausing. She stepped back and examined the door. A newfound energy rose again inside, as her eyes darted back and forth between the locker and landing doors. She retrieved the photo and placed it on her bedside table before barging all her weight against the hinges of this new hope. There was a loud snap as the worn brackets buckled under the pressure and the door fell away from the locker.

She propped it up against the bed and gauged the weight. It was lighter than she expected, no heavier than a small ladder and a similar length too. She swung the door round and held it above her head. She calculated the weakest spot on her target before launching into an attack, her bad leg slowing her down slightly. It smashed against the landing door, making it rattle, but not much more. She tried a new action as she held the locker door in front of her knees and, with both hands, swung it to and fro in a rocking motion, letting it flow freely for a few cycles before stepping towards the target and crashing it forcefully against the hard surface. The door crumpled, forging a large gap.

She quickly clambered to her creation. She pushed her face right up against the frame and peered out of the crevice. The landing that greeted her was old and normal, looking like it always did, but she thought it seemed magnificent. She got up quickly and repeated the process, each time knocking the door more and more off its axis.

* * *

Poppy braced herself. Her hands pulsed, and sweat caught in her hair. She knew this would be the final swing. She could see increasing amounts of landing with each blow. She pulled back and swung her make-do battering ram as hard as she possibly could. It hit the door with a chime, causing it to buckle and flap upwards, the senile motors of the mechanism whirring as they tried to work out what had happened.

She threw the locker door to the ground and stumbled over to the bedside table. She placed the photo in her pocket as the pile of glass gleamed at her from the floor. She picked up a large shard and tucked it under her waistband, as Teela had done, before taking it out and throwing it back down. She hesitated for a moment, debating whether to pick it back up, before leaving the pile as it was and heading towards the exit. She looked back briefly from the doorway, surveying the prison that had now returned to being her room, before pushing the mangled door out of her way and scurrying underneath. The top half, still attached to the mechanical workings, juddered as she let it crash down behind her.

She fumbled down the ladder as fast as she could and hobbled through the maze of corridors towards the two heavy doors that led to the airlock. Dread stabbed at her as she crossed the boundary between the two sides, fearing what she might find, intensifying as she reached the side room where Teela kept the equipment.

Poppy's suit was neatly spread out across the floor, like it was before, only this time alone and stripped from its partner. Regret churned in her stomach. She imagined the suit as Teela's lifeless body. It seemed to move, morphing in shape, the form contorting the fabric as her limp body filled the space.

Poppy kicked the helmet and collapsed on the bench, her head in her hands. She sat motionless, staring at the ground, before a glint behind her heel caught her eye. She bent down and picked up the shard. A smudged replica of Teela's fingerprints clouded the transparent glass. She threw it across the room, the shard violently hitting the opposing wall before breaking into two smaller pieces. The lack of noise amplified the sound as they crashed on the floor next to the helmet.

She looked across to where she thought they had landed. In the distance she could still make them out, glistening like oases across the grey-tiled floor as her gaze drifted slowly from the shards to the upturned helmet. Her eyes traced its outline, moving across the smooth rounded contours of the back before wandering towards the flattened visor at the front.

The blood began to pulse through her neck. She stood up and stumbled over to the helmet, holding her fingers across the three dots and frantically forcing it onto her head. The smell of the previous outing lined the inside, and claustrophobia pinned her body as she dropped to the bench. She took a moment to steady herself before sending a call out to Teela.

Her thumbs dug deep into her sweaty palms as the icon on the visor spun round and round without reply. She sent another call and another call, but nothing. Her chest rose and fell in installments as her body shook from terror and exhaustion. She tried again. Nothing. And again, and again, each time without reply.

Tears welled in her eyes and overflowed onto her cheeks. She tried to wipe them away, but couldn't, she didn't care. She thought about where Teela could be. She gagged. An image of a reddened helmet, the transparent walls smeared with blood, flashed in front of her eyes – the lifeless body tied to the ship as if dangling from a noose, the limbs stiff, floating inertly, as if in water.

The lips of her father hung millimeters from her ear. 'You did this,' they said.

And on the other side, her mother's. 'It was all you. Everything has been you. You did this. Look at what you have done.'

Their voices were whispered and soft, but pierced deep into her brain, gnawing at her temples from the inside.

Poppy choked as a small message on her visor brought her back. Her eyes blurred as she found herself looking at the blackness of the outside. She wasn't sure if it was real. She could see Teela's hands in front; her fingers were moving. It was happening. She could see the ship and the open airlock hatch. 'Teela! Can you hear me?' Poppy shifted to the edge of the bench; her eyes fixed to the visor. There was no reply. Teela was moving closer to the airlock. Poppy could hear her wheezy breaths as she gasped for air. The camera jolted back and forth, the airlock disappearing from view before reappearing intermittently. Vast shots of blackness filled Poppy's eyes, followed quickly by blurry close-ups of the rail as she dug her thumbnails further into her palms. She stood up and then immediately sat down, the frustration consuming her ability to think. Words formed on her lips as encouragement, but disappeared quickly in the haze of fear. She tried to estimate how far she had left to go, guessing about a hundred metres to the hatch, but couldn't be sure. The camera swung back down towards the rail. Teela's movements were slowing, the propulsions along the track becoming more and more laboured.

Poppy sat on the floor, her back to the bench. She didn't know what to do. She didn't want to watch, yet couldn't take her eyes from the feed. Her arm muscles clenched as Teela propelled herself across the halfway point, as if trying to help with the workload. 'I'm here, Teela. You're nearly there.' Her words were whispered, but their passion was loud. 'Keep going, keep swimming.' Her voice cracked. 'Please...' Tears collected under her chin. 'Just keep swimming, Teela.' She tried to laugh. 'Think of that air, that glorious air when you take your helmet off. Keep thinking of it. Keep going.' Poppy looked around for what Teela might need. She grabbed a medical bag and took the oxygen canisters out of her suit, flinging them over her shoulder. 'Keep going, Teela. I've got everything you need. It's just waiting for you.'

Teela passed the three-quarter mark.

Poppy decided to move the supplies to the airlock door. Sweat poured from her face as she hobbled down the walkway carrying the heavy luggage, all the time hardly taking her eyes off the feed. She set up camp underneath the control panel, her back pushed firmly against the wall and her legs bent upwards to form a platform for her elbows to rest on. 'Come on, Teela. You're nearly there. I'm out here waiting for you.' She froze, as the camera drooped towards the rail, giving a prolonged dark and fuzzy close-up that painted itself across the whole of her visor. It remained for dayish seconds before a light from the ship flared into the lens, causing Poppy to close her eyes. 'You're there, Teela! You're practically there! Just one more.'

The clarity of the feed increased as Teela moved closer to the inside lights, and the detail on the airlock's hatch became visible.

'Come on!'

Teela stopped. She was at the threshold, but the camera kept drooping to the rail before being slowly brought back as her head lifted.

'Come on, Teela! Last push!' Poppy's loud shouts pierced through the helmet and seemed to work as Teela began to move again, reaching up to the rim of the hatch, pulling herself forwards before stopping, abruptly, wrestling with something off camera, appearing to be caught. Poppy watched as she slowly detached her safety line from the rail, her hand gripping tightly to the rung whilst the other fiddled with the cord. 'Come on, Teela! Head up, stay awake.'

Teela's head drooped again.

A close-up of her hand filled the screen. It trembled as she clamped onto the rail, her thumb and fingers twitching and flexing.

'Move, Teela! Get in!' Poppy banged on the door with both her fists as Teela's second hand came into view, taking over the role. She leant her helmet forwards against the door as Teela awkwardly shuffled along the rail and deeper into the airlock, just managing to close the hatch before drifting to her seat. 'Come on, please!'

Teela reached for the first floating strap and fastened it across herself before her head dropped again.

Poppy banged on the door. All she could see was Teela's lap as loose straps wafted into shot, her knees growing across her visor as her head drooped further. 'Wake up, Teela! Come on!' she shouted, but Teela's head remained down. 'Come on! Lift your head!'

Teela's hand entered into frame as her head bobbed upwards. She lifted her hand to the circular dial and twisted it as far as it could go before letting herself flop back down.

Poppy pulled the helmet off and threw it aside. Fresh air smacked her face and cooled the sweat. She stumbled to the control plaque and waited as the lights lit up the circumference of the crescent door. It hissed and began to rise. She slid the medical bag into the airlock and crawled under, carrying the canisters the best she could.

Teela was slumped in her seat, the single belt stopping her from falling completely to the floor.

Poppy rushed to her side and removed her helmet. 'Come on, Teela.' She sat her up and placed the oxygen mask over her face before carefully loosening the canister's valve. 'Come on. Wake up. Wake up!' She shook her gently. 'You made it. You're back!'

Teela's head drooped forwards.

Poppy lifted it up and supported her neck, pulling the makeshift canisters out of her backpack with the other arm. 'I've got you.'

Teela's eyes slowly drifted open, and she began to speak half words.

'It's alright,' said Poppy, comforting her, 'just breathe.'

Muffled whispers came from Teela's lips. She reached up and pulled the mask away from her face. 'I'm sorry, Poppy,' her eyes widened. 'I had t…'

Poppy placed the mask back onto her face. 'Just breathe, Teela.'

Chapter Ten

The Tomatoes Taste of Rubies

'It's just through here.'

Teela followed the old man up the narrow stairs, her bag slung clumsily across her back, and down a small corridor that smelled like nobody had walked there for years.

A large skylight, running down from one end to the other, lit up the place and exposed the grime that had crept in at the corners.

'Old fella. Young mother. Young person, just a bit older than you. Three kids. Family of six. Young couple. Trio.' The man pointed with his finger as he passed each coloured door, his voice loud and proud as if he was doing them a favour.

Teela imagined their faces listening on the other side of the thin walls as she wafted past, their ears fixed to the man's voice as he listed them off like he was doing a stock check.

'Listen,' said the man, turning to face her in an almost accusatory fashion, 'I don't ask questions. Just make sure the pix are there each month and keep yourself to yourself and that'll be the end of it. I really don't care what goes on, or what you're into, as long as it stays behind the door.'

'I'm not into anything-'

'Yeah,' said the man, interrupting, 'that's what they all say. But if you weren't, you wouldn't be living here. I don't care about your story, just your pix. If you have them, great. If you don't, there's always another coming along on the ol' conveyor belt.' He carried on for a few more steps before reaching the dark grey door, second from the end. 'This is you.' The man nodded his head towards a small black box no bigger than a doorbell.

Teela placed three fingers on the strip sensor, and the door changed colour to a light pink.

'Pink,' said the man, looking down at the other coloured doors. 'Been a while since we had a pink. We had a peach not so long ago, but not a pink.'

'It's just a colour,' said Teela.

The man shrugged and waited for her to open the door before going in first.

'What's your colour?'

'Mustard,' said the man, apathetically.

'You can always change it.'

The man shook his head. 'I'm not wasting my money. It's just a colour,' he said, as he led her into the tiny living area.

Teela looked around at the cracked panels of the bare walls that did their best to shine her colour around the room.

'Not much to show you,' said the man, pointing with his arm. 'Kitchen is through there. Toilet and shower in there. And the bed is in there.' He smiled. 'Notice how I said, "bed", and not, "bedroom", you'll find out why when it comes to it.'

Teela looked up to another skylight that covered most of the ceiling, letting in the precious sun.

'Perks of being on the top floor,' said the man. 'You should see the ones below.' He paused, smiling. 'Then again,' he let out a bellowing laugh. 'Means you can see where you're living.'

'I'm not gonna be here for long,' said Teela.

The man's face dropped, his laughter lines smoothing out before wrinkling again in curiosity. 'Oh yeah?'

Teela nodded.

'And how you gonna afford that?' said the man, his voice low and hushed.

'I thought you said you didn't ask questions?'

'Completely right.' His face leapt up again along with his tone. 'Doesn't bother me if you're here for a month or ten years. As long as…' He held his mouth open for Teela to finish his sentence.

'…as long as the pix are there,' she said.

The man nodded and rubbed his hands together. 'Well, I think that's about it. My details are on your account but, I'll be honest, you probably won't see me again.' He shrugged innocently. 'It is what it is.' He paused, leaning in, responding to a criticism that hadn't come. 'And what it is, is a roof over your head for a decent price. I'll let myself out,' he said, squeezing past.

Teela waited for the door to click shut before letting her bag slide down off her shoulder and onto the floor. It hit the hard tiles with an empty thud. She abandoned the bag and headed towards the far wall and the tiny square window that was so small it wasn't really worth the effort. She craned her neck and looked out to the city. Just below her, she could see the battered roofs of the different tenement buildings, varying in size, but all rammed like a jigsaw that had been made from different sets, the pieces forced together with the brute end of a hammer. She looked over the different colours, all glowing in their own way, fighting against the sun, some reds, some blues, some greens, but each droning at the one next to it, as if competing to be the most separate within the puzzle.

Teela bent her head down. In the distance, she could just make out the tops of the port buildings, glinting and silver in the summer sun, each of their structures like large pinecones touching the highest blue of the sky. She imagined the ships on each of the protruding platforms, and how they would wait quite comfortably on the ledge before suddenly rising up and disappearing into the worlds above, thousands of them, like tiny bubbles in a drink, each following the one above until they reached the rim of the glass, disappearing, without noise, to somewhere else beyond.

Teela sat down on the settee and dragged her bag closer. She pulled out a scrap of paper from an inside pocket and slid her finger across the edge, bringing it to life.

'Hello and welcome to Green Shoots – Where brightness comes from darkness. What will you grow?' An animation at the top of the page repeated itself over and over as three green stems emerged from a base of dark soil.

Teela scrolled down the various pages until she found the farming ships, their sizes measured in numbers too great to visualise. She gazed quietly at the colossal forms, the domed roofs curving across like whole planets, the rows and rows of crops going on seemingly forever underneath. At the bottom of the page, she found the smallest one. It was secondhand and just a pebble compared to the others, but she looked at it the way a parent would a newborn baby. She zoomed in and ran her eyes around the circular base, and then to transparent walls and ceiling that arched overhead like a crystal crown, creating a terrarium for the skies.

'If you can't find what you are looking for, please contact us direc-'

Teela folded the paper in half and shoved it back in the bag. She leant back against the hard settee and gently unbuttoned the left breast pocket of her jacket. For a terrifying second, she thought it had gone, but it had just managed to hide itself behind the thin seam that held the fabric together. She fished it out with the tips of her fingers and held it in the palm of her hand, the hairpin resting on a small callous at the base of her thumb. She lifted it up to the skylight and let the sun hit the sharply cut sides, illuminating the gem with fantastic flashes of red, before bringing it back down, her hand shaking as if the very act of holding it might cause it to break.

A noise in the corridor outside forced her to put it back in the pocket as she stood to attention, as if being caught out. She went over to the two doors either side of the front door and peeked inside. The kitchen was tiny and dark with no windows, the drawers struggling to open fully without banging into the opposite wall. She turned around and walked across to the other door, smiling to herself as she saw the bedroom. It was just a bed, rammed into what seemed to be a closet, the floor space taken up so completely she had to climb onto the bed just to get inside.

Teela ripped off the sheets and pillows and threw them in the general direction of the settee, revealing a stained mattress. She closed the door, shutting it away, before collecting the bedclothes and arranging them into a makeshift camp in the living area, covering most of the floor, using the front of the settee as a headboard.

She collapsed down and settled herself in. 'Play sunrise and sunset times for the next month,' she said, aloud to the room, as she took a handful of Jellystars from her bag and rammed them into her mouth.

The pink-coloured panels of the walls dimmed slightly as the friendly voice started to speak. 'Today, the sun rose at six fifty-nine, and will set at seventeen forty-eight. Tomorrow, the sun will rise at six fifty-six, and will set at seventeen forty-nine. The day after tomorrow, the sun will rise…'

Teela didn't really listen as the voice continued reeling off the various numbers. She sprawled herself out and glanced at her watch before staring straight up at the blue sky above, the sun no longer beating down like it had, as if it had just stepped into the wings, preparing for its final bow.

* * *

Footsteps outside caused Teela's eye to twitch. She knew she had watched the sky turn dark, but it had happened so slowly that she couldn't remember it. In the skylight above, she could see herself reflected in the glass. It was as if she was swimming in the blackness, caught somewhere between the real world and that place beyond this planet. She imagined herself up there, alone in her little space garden. 'Turn off the lights,' she said to the room.

The wall panels quietly faded.

She watched herself dissolve into nothing, revealing the sky above completely unmarked. She couldn't see the stars, just a rectangular piece of black, but she knew they were there. She looked across to her jacket, folded loosely on the settee behind, and the pocket, which she knew held everything.

* * *

Teela yawned as the carri-bus glided to a stop in front of her. A flashing advertisement on the side spoke of, "everlasting friendships", "unrivaled work environments", "rich experiences", and, "adventure to last a lifetime". The last one caught her eye as the bold white type expanded across the whole two decks before scattering into a thousand tiny stars. She waited a moment for it to loop round again, before climbing on board.

It was early, but already there was hardly a seat left. She slowly shuffled down the aisle, glancing at the faces as she passed by. Their expressions were blank, their eyes half closed due to tiredness, and half due to the early morning sun that hung low in the sky and pierced through the glass. It hit their faces with a bright yellow light that was difficult to avoid no matter how much they squinted, as if to purposely torment.

'Is anyone sat there?' said Teela, to a middle-aged woman who had chosen to sit on the aisle seat and leave the window seat free.

'No,' said the woman, giving a slight shake of her head.

Teela stepped over and sat down, grabbing her jacket pocket as it lingered in front of the woman's face for a fraction.

'Haven't seen you get on this stop before,' said the woman.

Teela nodded. 'No, I'm new.'

The woman smiled as if she had solved a great puzzle. 'I thought so,' she said, nodding proudly. 'Always good to see new faces, I suppose.'

Teela smiled and turned to the window, not realising they had already set off and were halfway down the road. She rested her temple against the glass and watched as the streets drifted by the window in a golden blur, the world already awake with the pounding of hundreds and thousands of sets of feet on its pavements and high walkways.

The carri-bus glided to a smooth stop as a voice overhead announced the street name. Across the road, high up on the third floor of a dilapidated building, covered with various multi-coloured light panels, a young woman planted a paper windmill into a window box. Teela watched as the pink blades caught the soft breeze and started to turn, the sudden movement making it seem like it had come to life, like its very existence in the city hinged on simply being present. It spun round and round, stopping ever so often as the breeze fell away before starting up again to finish its journey back to the beginning. Teela squinted. In a certain light, the paper windmill could almost be mistaken for the hairpin, with the pink blades quite easily taking the place of the rounded cut of the red ruby, and the wooden dowel a perfect substitute for the silver stem.

The carri-bus set off again, but Teela didn't notice. She was thinking about her ship. She imagined planting the hairpin into the dark soil. How she would carefully pat it down at the base to make sure it was compacted into the earth, before sprinkling it gently with water, watching the rainbow as the light hit the curved stream. Then, waking up the next day to see a thousand ruby hairpins, all in perfectly neat rows like roses.

For a second, she thought about all the ships she could buy with her harvest, a fleet of as many as she wanted, of all different kinds, growing all different things. She could hire people to work for her. Before long, she wouldn't have to work at all. She could see herself behind a sleek desk, with a queue of people handing over documents to sign, like a controlled stampede of bureaucracy. She could feel her heart speed as every eye looked at her, waiting for her to do something, her feet in tight shoes instead of free upon the soft mounds of earth.

Teela held onto her jacket pocket and felt the single hairpin inside. The fleet disappearing as quickly as it had come, as well as the army of people in front of her desk, leaving behind her single ship and her single crop. She peeled her head away from the window and found the middle-aged woman gone from her seat, lost at one of the many stops they had passed since the paper windmills.

She stayed alert as they began to slow.

'Next stop, Vale Walkway. That is, Vale Walkway, next stop.'

Teela stood up, fully aware that it wasn't the closest stop, but she needed some air. She made her way to the front and waited for the red lights to turn green as the doors swiftly opened, letting the sounds of the outside world in, as she stepped the opposite way. Her watched vibrated on her wrist as it crossed the threshold, announcing through a quick flash on the screen that four pix had been subtracted from her account. She glanced down and noted the number, doing the maths in her head as she left the main road and entered the maze of pedestrian walkways.

It was dark at first, as she passed through the link tunnel, before coming out at a large square, filled with people and surrounded by either entrances to buildings or lifts. A floppy haired man pushed past a slow-moving couple and entered a nearby lift. The glass cubicle rising up after a few moments to the platform above. Teela's eyes lifted to the web of gangways and connecting bridges above her head, each one offering an anchor to a building that rose up further than she could see.

Her watch vibrated again. It was an appointment reminder for Peele Antiques. She tapped on the small screen and brought up a map, followed by a bullet-pointed list of directions. She matched the numbers with the signs and embarked on the long journey to the other side of the square.

She could feel the heat as she walked, the sun now fully awake and reflecting off the buildings, bouncing down through the web of walkways to the bottom, its rays channelled down to a fine point as if through a giant magnifying glass. In the middle was a huge fountain, styled into three loose human forms that occasionally took pity on the people below and let the breeze blow their cooling mists across the square.

Teela felt a couple of drops hit her face, but nothing more as she walked round the large base and crossed over to the edge. She double-checked her directions and headed over to a lift marked, "Delor Way". It was slightly smaller than the other lifts, but seemed to be a little cleaner, the glass spotless and the large panels reflecting the rest of the square like a mirror. She stepped inside and waited for a moment, the camera on the front making sure nobody else was approaching before the lift quietly shut its doors and ascended to a gangway three stories up.

'Delor Way,' said a professional voice from a speaker in the corner. 'Please, mind how you go.'

Teela stepped out and looked over the side to the square she had just been. It seemed smaller from her new vantage point, the three human forms of the fountain now nothing more than dolls, their intermittent relief overtaken by the fast gusts of cooling air that pushed through the large gaps higher up, rushing between the buildings as they tapered to points at their tops.

She walked across the bridge, turning left as it split in two, before following the new route straight across to the entrance. Large branding grew across at least two stories of the building as she approached, before disappearing as the doors slid open, beckoning her into the shaded foyer.

'Welcome to Peele Antiques,' said a voice overhead as her

watch vibrated, telling her that she had arrived.

The white floors gleamed as the sun shone through the curved glass windows that rose up from ground to ceiling, following the whole circumference of the building, and in the middle, an old-fashioned chandelier dramatically hung down, reflecting tiny shards across a display of various artefacts that seemed better placed in a museum.

Teela wandered around, gazing across the seemingly random assortment of objects, from beautifully ostentatious hats with glorious feathers, to music players and various computers and monitors. She watched as a video game character leapt from one screen to another, before circling back around in an endless parade of garish colours as it led her on to a neat collection of swords, and then walking sticks, and then walking sticks that had swords built inside. In the middle, a rectangular glass box preserved a beautiful ebony cane like a coffin. Teela read the small sign next to it and admired the stick's sleek and polished finish, topped with a weighty sunflower that had been formed with its petals curved down for a smooth fit in the palm.

She bent and studied the head, and the hundreds of peppered dimples that made up the centre, before noticing a pair of eyes watching from a desk at the far side of the room. They looked at her as if she was in the wrong place, as if the slightly lived-in clothes she was wearing weren't meant to be in the company of polished floors. Teela stood up, fully aware of the thoughts that were going through the clerk's mind. She tugged at her collar, standing it upright as if pulling on a bit of armour, before walking over to the desk.

'Hello, welcome to Peele Antiques,' said the man behind the desk, smiling. 'How can I assist you today?'

Now face-to-face, he was actually younger than his demeanour first showed from across the room.

Teela placed her hand on the reflective surface of the desk and noted his eyes quickly flick down to her fingers before returning to her face. She was tempted to smear a handprint across the whole counter, smudging great trails against the cool panel as if a creature from the time of the relics behind her had somehow come back to life. 'I have an appointment,' she said, trying to sound as if she belonged.

'Of course.' The man gestured to a small black strip hardly noticeable on the desk. 'Do you mind signing in?'

Teela pressed her thumb against the sensor, and it glowed pink before fading back to the reflective black.

'You are Teela Rose, currently residing at Oakwood Flats?'

Teela nodded.

'Okay, you have an appointment in ten minutes with one of our valuators, is that right?'

Teela nodded again as the man glanced over her body, trying to discern what could possibly be worth getting valued.

'Do you buy?' Teela said, as the man fiddled with his monitor.

'Pardon?'

'The valuation. You get something valued and then what if you want to sell it? What happens then?'

'Oh, we don't usually buy directly from people off the streets. Not usually, at least. There's a process.' The man swiped the screen clear and pointed Teela in the direction of a lift. 'I'm sure the valuator will talk you through everything that you need to know.'

Teela realised the conversation was over and walked over to the lift. It was a lot smaller than the other, with only a few people being able to fit in at once, but it felt bigger due to the large glass window at the back that looked out over the city, through the gaps between the buildings and walkways, all the way to the single-storey dwellings at the edge of the main district, lost somewhere between the haze of the glaring sun and distance.

'Valuation Suites,' said a voice, as the doors opened, revealing a long room, with various partitioned booths lining either side of the main aisle.

'You must be Teela Rose?' A short man with a receding hairline and a kind smile scurried around from behind a dark wooden desk that contrasted quite strongly with the glass monitors on top of it. He held out his fist. 'I'm Wendell,' he said quite happily as Teela tapped his knuckles with hers. 'I know our appointment isn't for a few minutes,' he looked at his watch. 'But shall we just get started?'

Teela nodded, and he led her down the aisle, bobbing his head slightly to check for free booths behind the frosted glass windows.

'This one will do,' he said, opening the doors to an empty compartment halfway down the room before stepping inside. 'It is a bit odd, I know,' he said, noting Teela's expression as she followed him into the tiny space and took a seat. 'It's just for privacy. We value a lot of things here.' He paused, leaning forward with a cheeky grin on his face. 'Some worth more than others.' He leant back and brushed away some dust on the desk, accidentally turning on the screen embedded into the wood. 'I always find it's best to be modest about these things. Wouldn't want to stand in the Northway intersection and shout that your bedside table is pre-illimitable wood.' He smiled. 'Not that we'd fit that in here; we have a special room for larger objects.'

Teela stared blankly back at him.

'Whereas,' he said, cheerily darting his eyes back and forth around the booth, 'this is for handheld object valuations which, if I'm not mistaken, is why you're here today, Teela.' He looked at her earnestly. 'You don't mind if I call you Teela?'

Teela shook her head.

'Good,' said Wendell, stretching his fingers across the desk, enlarging the screen and turning it a bright white. He flipped up a small monitor to his left and nodded to himself. 'So, shall we begin?'

Teela tentatively fished inside her jacket pocket and brought out the hairpin, pinched delicately between her index and middle finger.

'May I?' said Wendell, holding out his hand.

Teela dropped it carefully into his slightly clammy palm, trying to gauge any subtle movements of his face as he began to examine the piece. She watched as his eyes quickly travelled over the silver stem, and then up to the twisted knot and the ruby that somehow sat quite modestly at the top.

'And how long have you had it?'

'Not long,' said Teela.

Wendell held it up to the light and twisted it in his fingers, letting the ruby shine. 'It is very beautiful. Can I enquire into how it came into your possession?'

Teela hesitated for a fraction. 'I was left it.'

Wendell took his eyes off the hairpin for the first time. 'Oh, I am sorry,' he said.

'Don't be.'

He nodded diplomatically. 'I understand. It is never easy.' He paused, allowing himself to be slightly forward now he knew she didn't care. 'Though, it does help, doesn't it? The inheritance. Sweetens the lemon, so to speak.'

'There wasn't a lemon to sweeten,' said Teela.

'Oh, I see,' said Wendell, not really understanding what she meant. 'Well, it is beautiful, as I say, whatever circumstances it arrived in.'

'I looked it up,' said Teela, wanting to get back to the object itself rather than how she had acquired it. 'I found a place that said ones like these can go for ten thousand pix, some of them.'

'Well now,' said Wendell, 'let's not get ahead of ourselves. It's my job to do the valuations. There are so many variables to consider.' He nodded to himself and placed the hairpin on the bright screen of the desk. There was a small flash and a thin outline quickly traced itself around the form. 'Right, let's see.' He leant in towards the small monitor and tapped on the screen. 'Let, us, see,' he said again, in a whisper, pronouncing every word as if it were its own sentence. 'So, you're right; pieces such as this do go for around seven to ten thousand.'

Teela's heart began to beat so loudly she was worried he might hear it in the small proximity.

'What I'll do now is to try and date the piece, and look for any discrepancies.' He swiped on the screen, and a number of labels appeared on the desk, all with thin arrows pointing to a different place on the hairpin.

Teela watched the small percentage signs at the corner of each blank box. 'How long does it normally take?'

'Oh, not long. This Loupe Deck is one of the latest models.' Wendell smiled. 'It's just running the background on the various metals, making sure they are what we think they are, and the stone of course. Then, it'll look for any damage.' He saw Teela's confused eyes scurry across the hairpin. 'Obviously, yours is in fair to mint condition, like it hasn't been touched for twenty years, but as well as any everyday wear and tear, it'll take into account any micro-scratches or structural damage.'

The numbers moved up to seventy-five percent.

'It can even take into account the future, any possible problems that may arise, etcetera. We had a beautiful, ornate doll's house the other day that lost a chunk of its value because it had real glass windows, which is what you want of course, but it said the likelihood of the windows breaking and then the house being damaged during the replacement process, due to the style of this particular house, was far too great to warrant the value.' Wendell smiled to himself. 'It's a heartbreaking paradox. We make beautiful and delicate things because we want them in our lives, knowing full well it's the very delicacy that will take them from us, and yet we carry on making them. We have to make them,' he added.

The numbers moved up to ninety-eight percent, and then to ninety-nine. Teela bit the skin on her bottom lip as they paused for a moment, before finally ticking over to one hundred percent as the blank labels were quickly filled with various words and diagrams.

'Okay,' said Wendell, leaning forward to read his screen, 'we have liftoff.'

Teela tried to read the upside-down letters of the label that branched off from the red stone at the top. She tried to pick out any reference to ruby, or mineral, or chromium, or to any of the other words she had learnt during her research. She looked up to Wendell and noticed his expression had changed; his fluffy eyebrows that had often bounced around his forehead, now solemn and stuck tight to the bridge of his nose. 'Well?'

'I'm very sorry,' said Wendell.

The beating excitement that Teela was worried about him hearing pinched itself shut, transforming into a heavy weight.

'It's just imitation, a very good imitation, I'll say. We wouldn't have noticed if we hadn't put it through,' he tapped softly on the edge of the monitor, as if patting a dog that had warned him of danger. 'But it is just imitation, I'm afraid.'

The weight toppled down from Teela's chest and landed somewhere in the pit of her stomach, before spreading out from her gut to her extremities, as her arms and legs began to weaken and shake under the pressure. 'I don't get what you mean?' she said.

'I mean,' Wendell's eyebrows finally rose, doing his best to comfort her. 'I mean... it's not real.'

'No,' said Teela, coughing to hide the crack in her voice, 'no, it is. I checked. It's definitely real. It's exactly like all the others. The seven to ten thousand pix ones. It's exactly like all of them.'

'In looks,' said Wendell, 'yes, I completely agree. But see,' he twisted his fingers across the desk, turning all the labels towards her so she could read them. 'This isn't ruby. It's synthetic. As synthetics go, this is one of the better examples, but that stone has never been underground. And the stem...'

Teela followed his finger and read the label that had a name of a metal she had never heard of before.

'Those numbers and that word I can't even pronounce is the makeup of the most common form of imitation metals. It looks beautiful, it feels beautiful, that's why it's used so much, but it's not platinum or silver.' He paused, trying to find the right words. 'We're very much herd creatures. We want the real thing because that's what everyone says is desirable, regardless of what it looks like. We've been making diamonds in labs for centuries, all without impurities, all absolutely perfect. Yet, they still don't sell for as much as the ones dug up on quarry planets.'

'Okay, so it's not the real thing,' said Teela, 'but it still must be worth something.' Her voice was rushed and panicked. 'You said they're popular so someone must be buying them. They must be worth something.'

'They're popular because they're so cheap,' said Wendell.

'But how much?'

Wendell recoiled slightly at her bark. 'I can see you're upset, let's just-'

'Please,' said Teela, her tone flipping between anger and hopelessness. 'How much?'

Wendell shook his head. 'You can buy these in bulk. A version of this will be in every decent jewellery shop you can find.'

'But how much?'

'For a single one?' Wendell thought. 'Probably not much more than ten to twenty pix.'

Teela stood bolt upright, pointing down towards him. 'No, no because I looked,' she said, her voice breaking. 'It said ten thousand. It said ten thousand!'

'Yes, for one made with actual materials. This is just costume jewellery. Beautiful, but ultimately worthless. Monetarily, at least.'

Teela looked directly into his eyes. She wanted to lurch across the table and squeeze the very life out of him as compensation for him squeezing the life from her dream, but she could see the look of terror in his kind eyes and knew he wasn't to blame. 'I want to see someone else,' she said, grabbing the hairpin, causing the labels on the desk to fade away.

'What do you mean?'

Teela clumsily opened the door and barged out into the main aisle. A woman, dressed in a neat suit, was just about to lead a client into a booth at the far end.

'Wait,' shouted Teela.

The two halted in their tracks, looking down at Teela as she strode towards them.

'It's okay, Penny,' called Wendell from behind, following Teela with short, quick steps, doing everything he could not to break into an unprofessional run. 'It's absolutely fine.' He waved his hands in the air and made a jokey face to try and diffuse the situation.

'I want you to check this,' said Teela, brandishing the hairpin into the woman's face.

'We've had a bit of bad news,' said Wendell to Penny. He tried to lead Teela away, but she shrugged him off.

'Please,' said Teela, forcing the hairpin into Penny's hand. 'Please. Just check it again and then I'll be gone.'

Penny looked at Wendell with a slightly dazed expression as she just began to realise what was happening, and Wendell replied with an expression that told her it was entirely her choice.

'I don't mind,' said the client, stepping back to allow Teela to go inside. 'I don't mind waiting.'

'If you're absolutely sure?' said Penny.

The client nodded and cleared the passageway even further to allow Wendell to follow.

'It's all the same system,' said Penny, leading the three of them into the booth. 'It'll read exactly the same way as it did on Wendell's.'

'Please,' said Teela, 'I just have to know. Maybe his desk is broken, or there was a glitch in the software or something.'

Penny walked round and flipped up the small monitor before tapping on the desk and stretching the now illuminated surface to the desired size. The labels reappeared as she carefully placed the hairpin down, the percentages rising faster than they did the first time.

They all stood in silence as the numbers reached past the ninety mark, then ninety-five, before jumping to one hundred.

Teela scanned frantically across the labels as they began to fill in the exact same way they had before, with every word, number and diagram copied perfectly from Wendell's desk. 'Thank you,' she said, not needing any confirmation. She bent down and took the hairpin before seeing herself out. The client, who was pretending to watch a poster about the art of cutting gemstones, smiled at her as she went by, and she smiled back, trying her best to walk in a straight line, something which had suddenly become difficult.

'It was a pleasure to meet you,' shouted Wendell, as Teela reached the lift.

'You too,' she replied, in a quieter tone, as the lift doors shut, allowing the booths to disappear into the ceiling as she sank down to the floor below.

The main foyer was brighter than she had remembered, the chandelier like a second sun that seemed too proud of itself. She ignored the clerk behind the desk, who she could sense was watching her, and marched as fast as she could past the exhibit of old antiques, which no longer interested her, to the main entrance and the sliding doors. She stepped over the threshold, and the warm breeze met her face, comforting her a little before stinging slightly as it veiled over her eyes.

Her watch vibrated, flashing up that fifty pix had been subtracted from her account before fading back as if nothing had happened.

* * *

A single leaf fluttered down from a window box overhead. Teela stood at the bus stop wondering where the afternoon had gone. She remembered aimlessly wandering around the various squares and across the tangle of bridges, not really caring what the destination was. In the sun, just faded from its zenith so it was bearable, she felt oddly free. It was like all her responsibility had left along with her dreams, as if, now that she had no control, she would simply close her eyes and lean into the wind, seeing where it took her.

The carri-bus pulled up, and with it another advertisement for the Star Express Postal Service. She watched as stylised animations of various ships took off from the pinecone port buildings before shooting away, leaving the atmosphere and entering the navy-blackness of space. She watched as stars flashed by in fantastic streaks, as well as planets in balls of bright colours, before transforming into thousands of tiny parcels. "Star Express Postal Service", appeared in bold letters, "Removing The Space Between Us".

Teela stepped on the carri-bus and recognised most of the same faces that had been there before. She found the middle-aged woman and sat down next to her in the same spot.

'Did you have a good day?' said the woman, with a smile.

'Not really.'

'Oh, I'm sorry to hear that.' The woman twiddled her thumbs. 'There's always tomorrow.' She leant her head back against the seat. 'Always tomorrow,' she said again.

* * *

Teela stared up at the blackness through the skylight, the hairpin firmly in her hand, pushing hard against her skin. She brought it up to her face and noticed a small indent in her skin where the sharp point had dug in. For a moment, she thought about throwing it away, as hard as she could, in any direction, not caring where it landed.

Yet, as the hours slowly passed by, she realised it was still in her hand, glinting through the gaps in her fingers.

Chapter Eleven

Same Voice, Different Words

Poppy was slumped on the floor outside the booth. Her eyes followed a small groove in the grating until it dissolved in the distance, a far way down the corridor. She turned her head and repeated the process, from right to left, following the same warped groove until it faded to grey. Her eyes felt dry as they scratched under her drooping lids. She moved a little, and her arm brushed against the wall, now slightly warm from her body heat. The unfamiliar comfort brought her back.

She looked around for landmarks, uncertain of where exactly she was, and felt the booth next to her. She wasn't sure how long she had been sat there, but could've guessed that this was where she would be, having developed a habit of drifting towards this spot for no apparent reason. She tried to think. She couldn't remember if this was her resting before a recording, or resting because she had made one. She thought about it for a moment, trying to remember what she would've said, or was going to say, before realising she didn't care.

She rested her head against the side of the booth, and her eyes began to close.

* * *

Poppy's foot slipped from its position and jumped her awake. She rubbed her eyes and slowly stood, disappearing into her baggy clothes as they tried to find a sturdy piece of her to hang to. She looked at her watch, but didn't acknowledge the time, its place on her arm moving further and further towards her elbow with each passing day. She splayed her hand to insure it didn't fall off completely.

* * *

Poppy approached the Rec. Room and slowed her already lethargic steps. She peered in and noted the subtle outline of Teela asleep on the settee. She stopped and watched the glorious sight of life as her duvet lifted and fell with each breath.

She entered and carefully made her way towards the makeshift bed. The strands of Teela's hair that overhung the armrest wafted in the breeze as she sat down on the floor underneath her head. They danced in a synchronised wave, as she pushed her body flat against the side of the settee, before quickly nestling back down. She straightened her back and leant against the outer armrest. Her eyes began to drift again as if she was asleep, yet she knew she wasn't, she never was, not really. She could feel the settee against her spine, and the hard floor as her bony backside pierced through the loose clothes pile she was sitting on.

She knew she was awake, and yet she dreamt. She dreamt as if she was asleep. She dreamt of food, of fluffy white bread and salted butter, of creamy peppercorn sauce and golden potatoes – of home. She was there; she could see her father and mother and Catherine. The table looked perfect. Alice got up and returned with four small cubes of chocolate. The sweet brownish gold melted on Poppy's tongue in a warm glow as she shaved a tiny curl with the corner of her tooth. There was smiling and laughter.

She dreamt of Teela. She dreamt of her childhood. She recreated the events of that night, the shard of glass and the broken door, the Figure that had been locked up, somewhere, and the shallow breaths as she gasped for air. Poppy's hands clenched as she remembered the effort of dragging her through the ship. She could see herself as she pulled and tugged at the limp and listless body. How she entered the Rec. Room sweating and panting. How she lifted her onto the settee. How she woke up beside her after having collapsed at the last.

* * *

Teela shifted.

Poppy opened her eyes, curious towards the movement above her. 'Did you sleep?'

There was no reply. Poppy closed her eyes as the time between question and answer grew greater and greater.

'No,' Teela said eventually.

'Me neither.' Poppy kept her eyes closed. There was an equally long and tired pause. 'Do you want anything? How's your breathing?'

'What are you doing here, Poppy?' said Teela, after a while, not answering the question.

'I'm here,' Poppy opened her eyes. 'I'm here because you're here. There's nothing more to it.' She felt a few strands of caught hair tug from behind her head as Teela sat up. She could sense her staring at the part of her crown that poked up over the armrest.

Teela opened her mouth in readiness of a reply, but couldn't think of one that warranted the effort. She lay back down forcibly, this time with her feet temptingly close to Poppy's head.

She coughed violently.

'I went to the booth just now,' said Poppy, rubbing her brow. 'Can you remember how long I was gone?'

Teela coughed again in such a way that told her she didn't.

'I can't remember if I left a recording… I think I did,' she said to herself, before a short silence. 'Listen,' she squeezed the bridge of her nose. 'I know it's only meant to be a captain's log, but if you wanted to use it, you could.' She stretched the skin around her eyes.

'Sometimes I go there and just sit, you know, without talking.'

'What difference does it make?'

Poppy shrugged and moved to a larger pile of clothes so she could see Teela's face. 'I don't know. Sometimes it's nice to think you're being listened to.'

Teela looked out the Window. 'Even if you're not?'

'I don't claim to understand it.'

'What about Sheridan? Is he not a good listener? You spend just as much time up there as you do in the booth.'

Poppy sighed. 'We both know why it's me spending all my time up there.'

Teela repositioned her head on the armrest and focused back towards the Window. Poppy stood up, her weakened state needing the side of the settee as an aid. She wanted to leave before her alarm bleeped and underlined Teela's sentiments.

* * *

Poppy languished at the entrance, her hollow stomach scraping along the ledge as she hauled herself up. The effort needed to climb the Control Room ladder had become excruciating, with every rung feeling like a mountain.

She sat on the floor, the receiver resting on the unused chair. Her watch bleeped. It too seemed weak, the sound not piercing the air like it once had. She leant against the cold wall of the entrance and felt almost satisfied that she had arrived with time to spare. Her watch bleeped again, dragging her from the bliss that was a rare happy moment as the unmistakable, high-pitched sound screeched through the speakers, burning her ears.

'Vitula, this is Captain Jason Sheridan from the Department of Search and Rescue. OVER.'

Poppy reached over to the chair and picked up the receiver. 'Vitula speaking, we read-' Her finger slipped off the sensor. She noticed, but did nothing. 'We read you...' Her words dissolved before they reached the end.

Sheridan's voice sounded in the background as a hazy mumble. Poppy waited for it to clear before placing her finger back on the sensor. She kept it there this time, but didn't speak, her body just going through the motions.

'Vitula, this is Captain Sheridan. I've failed to read you. OVER.'

Another high-pitched sound stabbed the room as the transmission ended, but Poppy didn't hear it. Her mind had wandered to that place she didn't like, but couldn't help visiting. Her grip loosened on the receiver, and she began to think. She worked her way up, through her earliest memories, to the present day. She tried to remember everybody she had ever met, no matter how inconsequential. The neighbours, her first teacher, the dentist that used to give her stickers, the school cook, the barber, even the old woman she once helped out of a carri-car. She couldn't see their faces, but she could picture the moment, the memory, that small fragment in time where their lives linked together. She thought about the cheerful Cathleen and her bowl of sweets, she could see the red, and white wrappers as if they were actually in front of her.

The hollow feeling inside emptied further as she thought about her mother and father, with Catherine by their side, Grandad and Grandma Lehrer too, along with the rest of her family. She tried to hold onto them for as long as she could. Their very essence swelled through her and glowed from within.

She thought about how she would never see any one of these people again, or even hear their voices. If she possessed the energy she could have cried, but she didn't. Her dry eyes couldn't muster a single tear. She felt the receiver slowly roll down her stomach and cushion itself onto her lap, her fingers loosening further, as her arms finally gave way along with her legs.

She just sat there, staring across the room, her lids getting heavier and heavier, as she drifted, once again, into her state of semi-consciousness.

* * *

Poppy's head shot up as she looked around in panic. Her heart cannoned against her ribs as the loud, screeching noise once again filled the room. Her mind raced as she tried to work out what was happening. It seemed ludicrous to her that she had been fixed to that spot for a whole day, and yet the sounds of another transmission said otherwise.

She looked at her watch, accidentally knocking the receiver off her lap as she came to terms with where she was. The small square screen illuminated her face as she peered down towards her arm, the sharp red numbers confirming she had been out for minutes rather than hours. She shuffled in her position as the screeching started to wane, and picked up the receiver.

'Vitula, this is Captain Jason Sheridan from the Department of Search and Rescue. OVER.'

Poppy's heart dropped against her stomach as the captain's voice entered the room. It seemed different, yet she couldn't pinpoint why. It was like he was standing right next to her – the difference between her reading a letter and him reading the letter to her, directly. All the scripted repetition had gone. Words that were usually so sterile seemed to be awash with emotion. She listened as the message repeated, noticing how Captain Sheridan seemed to force the sounds to the back of his throat, as if trying to suppress them and regain control.

Poppy's finger shook on the sensor. 'Captain Sheridan, this is Vitula. We read you. We read you!' She waited, her fingers struggling to hold the receiver, staring at the speakers, as if trying to see a reply before hearing it.

'Vitula, this is Captain Jason Sheridan from the Department of Search...'

Poppy didn't move as the heartbreak enveloped itself around her. Her ears dissected every syllable as they passed from Sheridan's lips to the Control Room. She noticed how the cracks and rasps seemed to be more prominent as the message repeated, as if the words were beating her, breaking free from her hold.

'...*OVER.*'

The last word hardly made an impact as it travelled down the speakers. Poppy clawed her way up to the chair, using the wall as leverage. She placed the receiver on the desk. 'We hear you. This is Vitula, we hear you!' She coughed as the words caught in her throat too. 'We hear you,' she said, quietly, as if to herself.

The room fell momentarily into silence as she tightly held the receiver in her hand.

'*To Captain Poppy Talib and First Officer Teela Rose of Star Express Transit Ship – Vitula.*'

Poppy's stomach clenched as she heard someone else, other than Teela, say her name. It had been so long she had forgotten how to react. She reached over and turned on the intercom so Teela could hear.

'*I... I don't quite know how...*' Captain Sheridan's voice echoed through the ship. '*In all honesty, I hope you can't hear my words, but deep down I know that you can... at least, I have to assume you can.*'

Poppy stayed quite still, paralyzed, just staring at the speakers.

'*For the last, life knows how many months, I've tried everything to find you and bring you home. I have,*' Captain Sheridan coughed, changing the tone of his voice to one that resembled responsibility. '*I have failed. I have failed you both.*'

Tiny, pathetic droplets, exiled by Poppy's barren eyes, rolled down either cheek, drying before they even reached her mouth.

'*And so, after a period of intense search, I... I regret to inform you that I've been instructed to call off the mission.*' He paused. '*I have also been told to inform you that your current status has changed from, "Missing", to, "Missing: Assumed De..."*' Sheridan couldn't finish, his voice abandoning all formality as his words seemed to burst through the dam. '*I tried to protest, but I've exceeded my time. I've reached the limit of how far I can go. My fuel and supplies... if*

I search any deeper, I won't make it back home.' He halted himself. *'I don't know what else I can say.'* There was a small silence. *'Not as employee to employee, but as person to person, I'm sorry there isn't anything more I can do. I've tried everything to find you and bring you back, but I just... I don't know where you are.*

'It says, in my brief, that I should let it be known that if, for some reason, you can hear this,' his tone changed back to one of formality as he read. *'"Star Express Postal Services offers its deepest regrets and sympathy that you should pay the heaviest price in the performance of your route, and that, without brave people like you, the universe would be a much larger and lonely place."'* Captain Sheridan cleared his throat, and his voice changed again. *'I would just like to add that I hope you can find some kind of peace, wherever you are and wherever you may go. I know it's not enough, but there are no words... or if there are, I don't know them.'* A long pause followed. *'I shall make my final transmission three days from now, at seventeen hundred hours, universal.'* There was another pause. *'Captain Jason Sheridan.'*

The Control Room fell silent.

'Poppy, can you come here, please?'

She could hear her mother calling from the lounge. She knew something was bad from the way she tried to hide it in her voice. 'Yes?' said Poppy, stepping off the last stair. She entered the lounge and saw her father huddled close to her mother on the settee, with Catherine between them playing with the brightly coloured ball, the face on its side flickering between expressions.

'Come and sit down here,' said Alice, patting the cushion next to her.

Poppy did as she was told. Now closer, she could see the shining streaks on her mother's cheeks that caught the light whenever she moved her head.

'I've got some really sad news,' Alice said, her voice strong, but wavering slightly at the edges. 'You know how Grandad

Lehrer had been really sick?' She took a breath. 'Well, you know last night when I had to go to the hospital when we were all in bed? It's because Grandad was dying.' The tears followed the well-trodden path down her cheek. 'But,' she said, smiling, 'it was okay… it really was,' her voice changed to one filled with hope. 'Because me and Grandma Lehrer were there, and we held his hand, and he felt no pain, and it was really peaceful. And do you know what? The last thing he saw were all your balloons above his bed, and it was magical.'

* * *

Poppy stared at the speakers, hoping there was more to follow. That another bit of information would travel down through the maze of circuitry and burst out, making it all okay. That Captain Sheridan would continue to speak and say how he'd got it all wrong. That he'd misread his orders. That his fuel was fine, that his Supply Room was fully stocked. That he'd located exactly where they were and that he was already there, beside them. That Captain Jason Sheridan was their saviour, their knight in white. That he was the man who could cure all their problems. Yet, the longer she stared, the more she knew that what she hoped for wasn't going to be.

Her eyes slowly drooped and settled on a spot across the room, just above the floor. She felt a nagging pain in her forearm, her hand still gripping onto the receiver, frozen from when haste and optimism consumed her. A knot formed in her stomach. She lurched forward and fell to the ground, her weak arms not offering much support against the solid floor. She lifted herself onto her knees and violently gagged. Her body shook and convulsed, as each empty motion left no evidence, her stomach too stark to oblige.

She sat in a heap on the floor and wiped the invisible remnants from her lips. She wanted to stay exactly where she was and never move from that spot, but the thought of Teela, alone, tormented her from doing so. She scratched her nails against the tiles, hoping that the discomfort would wake her from the horror. The exposed nail bed began to bleed, forming a ruby head on her fingertip. It collected to a bulbous point before trickling down her finger, colouring her hand with a copper trail.

She let out a cry that her throat struggled to translate. It seemed to come from the pulsing depths of her stomach rather than her voice. A strand of drying spit hung down from her mouth as she tried again, using every inch of strength to make the sound heard, but couldn't. She closed her eyes and pictured her family, her mother, father and sister. Their faces seemed to appear in the blue-green shapes that formed in the fuzzy darkness of her eyelids. She blinked fast, trying to recapture them, but they were loose and vague, taunting her by dispersing the more she tried to pin them down.

She rubbed her eyes and tried again. She pictured the three of them in the family home, all sitting around the table. Plates of food filled every space, and cutlery glistened, the shooting reflections dancing bright streaks across the glass surface. She observed the glorious scene from a distance, before noticing the table seemed smaller than normal. She edged forward, trying to find her seat. She reached the middle of the room and found herself shrinking, the table dominating over her. She slowly moved around to get a better look, but the backs of her family seemed to follow her position, never allowing her to see their fronts.

She watched from behind as elbows rocked back and forth, cutting and devouring the meal. Forkful after forkful seemed to disappear into glimpses of black holes where faces should have been. She could hear laughing and ran round the edge of the table, trying to see. Faster and faster she ran, but struggled to see past their hunched shoulders. She chased a gap she thought existed, but was disappointed each time when she found it wasn't there. The harder she raced, the bigger everything seemed to grow and the smaller she felt.

She tripped on a chair and tumbled down, finding herself underneath the table. Human legs surrounded her, too many than there should have been, and yet all belonged to the three. They twitched and fidgeted on the balls of their feet as they scoffed and laughed at the meal. She lay back and stared up through the glass. She could see the body of another person neatly spread across the table, lying with its back to the cold surface. She gagged as the bladed hands of her family cut and sliced into the flesh. They worked their way down the arms, removing the skin from the bone before placing it between their, now visible, teeth.

The open palms of the body pushed against the glass as they reached the hands. Poppy became numb. She recognised them. They were hers. She held her hands up to her face for confirmation, comparing each line with the set above. She gagged again and shook uncontrollably. Alice handed Kaleem a large cleaver, and her father began to chop at the fingers, one by one, from just below the knuckle, leaving behind only stubby and bloodied remnants.

Poppy reached out and touched the underside of the table. It cracked and splintered, causing shards to fall towards her. She raised her arm to shield herself as the body dropped down, disappearing into herself.

* * *

Poppy gasped and was met with the apathetic ceiling of the Control Room. Damp patches of sweat matted her hairline. She loosened her boots, letting the air hit the sides of her feet, and shuffled towards the open shaft, her body too heavy to lift properly. She wiped her brow and swung her legs over the threshold, feeling the comfort in letting them dangle freely.

She was back. They were back. The faces of her family just like they should be, their blackened shadows disappearing as the light from a triggered memory illuminated their beautiful features. The cool air blew across her soles. The sensation reminded her of her mother's trips to the coast and the paddling they used to do in the large rock pools that formed there. She remembered how she would teach them about the hermit crabs and goggle-eyed rock gobies that made it their home. A ghost of a smile ran to the corners of her mouth. She thought about Catherine and how she used to burst out laughing whenever a goggle-eyed rock goby was mentioned. Her mind wandered to the very first trip, the one where the whole family came. She remembered the grass and sprinkling it onto her Grandad's toes.

A succession of crashes echoed through the shaft as her right boot slipped off, hitting the floor far below with a solid purpose. She was impressed by how its progress was halted most definitively, as the floor stamped through any sense of freedom that gravity and open space had momentarily given it.

She turned around and rested her abdomen against the hard corner of the threshold. She lowered herself onto the ladder, her ribs dragging against the floor lip, and began the descent. The ice-cold metal stung her right foot on first contact, but eased with each passing rung as the skin began to numb, her sock providing little protection. She reached the bottom and quickly retrieved her boot, struggling to contort her stiffened foot into the worn opening.

* * *

Poppy stopped outside the Rec. Room door, partly to gather her breath, but also to piece together what had just happened. She looked at her watch and gave way to the nagging weight, permitting herself to slide down the wall, her legs bent double and her knees almost touching her chin. She dropped her head and studied the small section of grated floor between her feet.

Five minutes soon passed by, as did the sixth and the seventh. She had never noticed how fast a minute was until now.

'What's that?'

Kaleem looked down to the rectangular ornament on his wrist. He held it to her face so she could see properly, the gold frame glinting in the light as he moved. 'It's just a watch, like yours,' he said. 'Except this is really old, and it only tells the time.'

Poppy's eyes jumped from number to number around the face, the sharp black type contrasting with the pearl-white enamel that sometimes revealed streaks of purples, pinks and greens from certain angles.

'It's very special, and it doesn't really work anymore,' said Kaleem, 'but I like to wear it on special occasions.'

'Like funerals?'

Kaleem nodded.

* * *

The watch flicked over to fifty minutes, ending the procrastination, as Poppy slowly began to make the first tentative movements. She used the wall as leverage and climbed her hand up, pushing through her stiffened knees until she became almost upright. The soles of her feet tingled as the newfound weight forced them to spread out in her boots. She pulled her lower spine from the wall and relieved the pressure. Her hand fumbled to the spot on her back where it had been pressed hard, and felt the bone as it stuck out, protected only by paper skin. She pinched her nose and stood for a moment as the blood rushed to her head, not knowing what she was going to say or if she could even say anything. Words and phrases flickered in her mind before disappearing like sparks from a flame.

Poppy inhaled deeply and crossed the threshold. She squinted her gaze and tried to position her face into a comforting expression. 'Teela?' She waited for some sort of movement at the far end, but it didn't come. She moved forward and tried to locate the curled silhouette usually present there, but she was gone. 'Teela?'

She crossed the room and sat down in her usual spot, the anticlimax causing her breaths to become looser. She looked at her watch, out of habit, and adopted the pose of a waiting person, with her legs a suitable width apart, her feet perfectly in line with her hips, and her arms tucked in, perching on the top of her thighs with her fingers spread, not wanting to use the armrest and risk being casual.

She could see the rows of solemn faces in the hospital Waiting Room. She couldn't remember their features, but she could remember their forms and what she imagined they looked like, all hushed and sat exactly how she was sitting.

'Why is everybody quiet?'

'Because they're nervous,' said Kaleem. 'You get like that when you're nervous, don't you?'

Poppy shuffled deeper into the seat as the soft material against her shoulder blades began to massage the formality out of her posture. She looked at her watch again and slowly leant her neck backwards to the cushioned support. She tried to resist, sitting up momentarily before slumping back down, falling even further into the seat. Her head lifted for a few seconds before fully surrendering to the comfort.

* * *

Poppy felt a tapping sensation on her right foot. It was a nuisance, but not enough of one for her to open her eyes. She listened carefully. The tapping seemed to set off a chain of other annoyances as she became increasingly aware of her surroundings. A series of small clangs stabbed at her ears, followed promptly by what seemed to be footsteps through sodden leaves. She studied the sounds intently, trying to determine their source. Eight seconds were counted between cycles. First a clang, before one large wet crunch, and then several, barely audible squelches.

She peeled open her eyes to find Teela towering over her, a bowl of Fibre Flakes and Milk-Repro in one hand and a white spoon, with a disproportionately small handle, in the other. She stared back quite alarmed, her eyes wide, as she tried to make sense of it all.

'You were out,' said Teela, her words mumbled by a mouthful of food.

Poppy looked at her watch. No more than ten minutes had gone by. 'You okay?' she said, her voice claggy. She shuffled along the settee as Teela perched in her usual spot.

They sat in relative silence, their eyes both attached to the neutral ground of the Window, the sounds of eating providing the only animation.

'I know what you're thinking,' said Teela, the break in procedure causing Poppy to turn her head rapidly towards her before turning it as quickly back, 'but I only filled it halfway.' She placed her thumb and index finger against the lower half of the bowl, but Poppy didn't look.

'Teela.'

'Poppy, I swear. I didn't take that much.' Her lungs hurt.

'Teela…' Poppy's voice was calm and soft.

'I didn't fully fill it-' She coughed as her voice began to break. 'I swear.'

'Teela.' Poppy moved to the edge of her seat, her head hanging low and her forearm pressing against her knees. 'It's okay.' She could feel Teela staring at the small portion of her face not blocked by her arms. 'Teela.' She tried to speak, but couldn't, yet the words she wanted to say formed articulate pools along her lower eyelids. They broke the barrier and streamed down her face. She turned her head, making sure Teela could see each word as they dripped off the edge of her jaw.

Teela replied in return, as glistening lines ran down her

innocent pink cheeks, eloquent in their silence. She stood up and approached the Window, her face clearly visible in the reflection. Poppy rose, but didn't move, watching as Teela stared at herself in the mirrored room, seemingly outside. She waited a moment before wiping her eyes and walking towards her.

They both stood for a while, watching themselves.

'You see,' said Grandma Lehrer, standing in the threshold of the hospital room, 'we can see out,' she walked Poppy into the corridor. 'But people can't see in.'

Poppy bobbed her head back and forth, in and out of the room, experimenting with the one-way window before a smudge on the glass brought her back.

Teela howled and hit the Window with the sides of her fist, punching the blackness and her reflection as hard as she could. She screamed again, and Poppy grabbed her, trying to stop her flailing limbs as she battered against the Window, using her whole body in a succession of fists, kicks, and screams.

'Teela!' cried Poppy, the words still running down her face, as she struggled to hold on. 'Stop!'

Teela broke herself free and turned away, falling down on an array of cushions and blankets at the border of the camp.

Poppy wiped her face and followed her. She reached out a hand and tried to pick her up, but couldn't. 'It's okay,' she said, collapsing down beside her in a soft heap, 'it's okay.'

Teela twisted onto her side, her back to the Window, and sobbed. Her body shook in violent bursts until the tiredness soon softened the movements to a quiver, and then eventually, stillness. Poppy began to get up, but Teela tugged at her side, and she fell back down without much persuasion.

'Just stay here for now, please? Poppy?'

Poppy nodded and reached around for a couple of pillows. She placed one under Teela's head and one under her own arm to lean on, before taking off her watch and tossing it to the side. She dropped her head on the soft fabric as they both melted into a mixture of warmth and unspoken words.

* * *

The minutes turned into hours as they rested, and the constant drone of the lights eventually faded, overtaken by the comforting sounds of each other's breathing, their chests rising and falling in complete unison.

* * *

A small muffled bleep from Poppy's watch, now buried in a heap of clothes and pillows, broke the hypnosis.

Teela tilted her head up slightly. 'Three days?'

Poppy patiently watched the back of Teela's head, trying not to interrupt her thinking. She could almost hear the thoughts whirling around in her mind.

'There's nothing we can do, is there?' said Teela, breaking the silence at last.

'We can just lie here.' Poppy's voice was soft. She could see the slight shadow of a concurring nod coming from the cushion. She moved the pillow from under her arm and stretched out her legs. Teela reached out her hand and pulled her in closer. Poppy hugged her waist, propping her head up with her free arm, peering over so she could just see the side of Teela's face.

For a long time, she watched as Teela's eyes became more and more laboured, until finally after some resistance, they shut. Poppy waited a moment, to make sure Teela was definitely asleep, before slowly moving her left arm and letting her head sink down onto the pillow. The soft fabric cradled the side of her face as wisps of Teela's hair persuaded her eyes to close.

Chapter Twelve

A Modest Plan

Poppy woke to find her arm draped over a cushion Teela had swapped as an understudy for herself. Her white knuckles cracked as she began to stretch out her hand for the first time in hours, the tips of her fingers tingling as she moved, releasing a grip that had set to form a crumpled fist. She brought it to her face. Her skin was embellished with a red crease pattern, transferred from one of the fabrics somewhere in the mess of cushions and blankets.

'You awake, then?'

Poppy rubbed her eyes and lifted her head to find Teela, complete with bowl and spoon. 'I was like a log,' she said, looking towards her bare wrist. 'What's the time?'

Teela shrugged her shoulders. 'Does it matter?'

'No,' Poppy stretched her face and yawned. 'I suppose not.' She clambered to her feet and awkwardly stumbled towards Teela; her legs caught in the tangle of sheets.

'This is for you, Poppy.' Teela handed her the bowl, full to the brim of cereal and Milk-Repro. 'Eat it slow.'

Poppy cupped it in her hands as if it were a sacred teacup, staring in at the oddly mesmeric swirling contents. 'I haven't slept like that since... I can't remember the last time.'

'Me neither.' Teela gestured towards the food. 'Go on then.' She coughed, violently, covering her spluttering mouth with one hand and pointing with the other. 'Go on.'

Poppy followed Teela's finger back to the bowl and was surprised to find it in her own hands, the drowsiness and eddied hypnotism wiping it from her memory. 'This is too much, Teela,' she said, offering it back.

Teela picked the spoon out of the bowl and handed it to her. 'Shut up and get it down you. I think you've earnt it.'

Poppy looked at her, but didn't reply.

'I mean,' Teela looked down. 'You're more than in credit.'

Poppy tried to think of a reason to disagree, but couldn't, so took the spoon, plunged it deep into the bowl and fished out the first batch of sodden nibs. As if proof to her lack of practice, a large splash of milk spilt from the overloaded spoon and dribbled down her chin. She ignored it and guided the rest of the spoon's contents into her mouth. The cold milk burnt slightly as it trickled down her dry throat and the fibrous pellets stuck to the walls of her mouth, but the sensation of her empty stomach filling up stripped these annoyances of any substance. She licked her cracked lips as they bathed in the delights, her trembling arm easing with each new journey as her muscles began to remember the routine of feeding. Each spoonful provided more and more enjoyment, until finally, after emptying over a third, she reached her limit.

Her full spoon hovered in the air expectantly, but after a small period of consideration, was returned back to the bowl, the caught nibs breaking free from their captor and floating away to mingle with the rest.

'You okay?'

'I'm gonna be sick.' Poppy leant over the side of the armrest and wretched, just managing to retain the meal.

'I told you to eat slow.' Teela took the bowl. 'You're not used to it. You've got to build yourself up.'

Poppy nodded, wiping the back of her hand across her lips to reveal a small smirk. 'Since when were you the boring one?'

Teela gave a sarcastic smile before dumping the spoon into the bowl and helping herself. 'I probably shouldn't be eating this,' she mumbled, after the third mouthful.

'If you're hungry, eat it,' said Poppy casually.

Teela looked towards the Window. 'It's a waste though, isn't it? I'm not even that hungry.' She tried to persuade her stomach that the words she was saying were true. 'I'll wait. I'll wait until I'm really hungry.'

'But you *are* really hungry.'

'Yeah, but,' she paused as her stomach ached. 'Even more hungry.'

Poppy reclined in her seat and rested one arm behind her head, her gaze now not on the Window, but the ceiling. 'Eat it, Teela. It's okay.'

Teela looked down at the bowl, torn between her stomach and her conscience. 'But why now?'

Poppy paused as she thought of a reason. 'You've done your bit, Teela. You really have. I don't want you thinking that because I didn't eat a few meals, it makes me right and you wrong.'

Teela looked at her.

'We were both right,' said Poppy. 'We were just right in different ways.' She used her finger to trace a pattern on the ceiling. 'You needed that food. Thanks to you, we've tried everything. Thanks to you, we've exhausted every possible option. There's not one thing we haven't done to fix this – and that's all on you. You never gave up.' Poppy nudged her with her knee.

'You too,' said Teela, tapping her with her foot.

'So, that's why I think you should eat it. You've earned it.'

Teela rubbed her temple and looked down towards the floor, her smile straightening. 'Why us, Poppy? It could've been anyone.'

There was a long pause as Poppy thought. 'Exactly,' she said, at last. 'So, why not us?' She stretched her arm towards the ceiling. 'What makes us so special compared to everyone else?'

Teela shrugged. 'It's just all a big mess, isn't it? Why does everything have to be so complicated? It's like there's this big, I don't know… like there's this big bull or something chasing us all the time, with these huge sharp horns, and we're just trying to run away.' She subconsciously dabbed her finger in the milk and brought it to her mouth. 'We're just trying to run away all the fucking time,' she said quieter, almost to herself.

Poppy shifted back in her seat. 'They used to actually do that, you know?'

'What?'

'Get chased by bulls. My Dad told me about it. Said it was a tradition that went on for hundreds of years in Spain.' Poppy tried to remember how Kaleem had described it. 'Apparently, a crowd would form in the morning around eight, dressed in white with red scarves and handkerchiefs on their waists and their necks. Then, there would be a rocket, and the crowd would start running. Then, another rocket and the bulls would be released, chasing the crowd through the city streets until they reached the bullring.'

'I don't know who I feel more sorry for, the bulls or the people.'

Poppy rubbed her nose and smiled. 'I can picture Dad telling me. He used to have this huge volume of books that documented historical practices and traditions. He'd spend hours reading them in his study when he should've been working.' Poppy relaxed as the warmth from speaking about her father gushed through her insides.

'Your Dad must have *been* a clever man.'

'And my Mum, she was the real brains.' Poppy closed her eyes momentarily as the happiness quickly syphoned from her body. '"Been",' she said solemnly. '"Been". You said he, "Must have been a clever man", as if…'

'I didn't mean anything.'

Poppy gave a reassuring smile. 'Don't worry.' She inhaled deeply. 'It's just the realisation that, for me, it's like he has gone. They all have. They've all kinda gone… at least from where I am.' She traced the ceiling panels as her mind whirled softly.

'No,' said Teela, 'I didn't mean it like that. I just phrased it badly.'

'No, it's okay,' said Poppy. 'I've never really thought about it like that before, but I suppose you're right. When Grandad died, he lost us just as much as we lost him.' She stopped herself, catching a melancholic expression dash across Teela's face. 'I'm sorry. What right have I got to go on about my-'

'I quite like it,' said Teela, interrupting. 'The more you talk, the more I feel like I know them. Like they're part of mine.' She looked down at the bowl.

'Listen,' said Poppy, 'how many boxes are left?'

'I dunno,' Teela shook her head. 'About fourteen, fifteen?'

Poppy continued to gaze at the ceiling.

'I should save it,' said Teela, 'shouldn't I? Wait until later?' She forcefully placed the bowl on the floor and nudged it away with her foot.

'Please,' said Poppy, 'just eat it.' She scratched the back of her head. 'There's no reason in worrying anymore.' She squinted her eyes, blurring the ceiling tiles. 'You eating that bowl of cereal isn't going to help or hinder us. So please, if you're hungry, eat.'

Teela reached down and guiltily picked the bowl back up. She wavered with the spoon momentarily before finally tucking into the food. The room fell silent, except for the incidental sounds of eating. Poppy listened to the satisfying splashes as the spoon broke the milk's surface, before the clinks as it hit the bowl. She closed her eyes and focused. The longer she listened, the more the noises grew until, eventually, they chimed and rang like a drum roll, and Teela stopped.

'What are we gonna do, Poppy?'

Poppy opened her eyes. There was a short pause before she finally spoke. 'Why don't we just have a party?'

The room filled again with silence. Teela's face didn't move.

'Just a party. Why not?' Poppy leant forwards. 'There's this phrase Dad once told me about. I think it was Dutch or Belgian, or something, I don't remember how to say it, but it's literal translation is, "Green laughing", and it means just to laugh, even though everything says you shouldn't, even though we have absolutely no right to. Laughing through it all, sort of thing?' She moved to the edge of her seat. 'I'd need to build myself up to it, but why not?' Her eyes smiled as the plan formed in her mind. 'How long do you think it'll take for us to get through those boxes, no rationing?'

'I don't know,' said Teela, 'I reckon a few weeks, maybe a month, two months. I don't know. It depends how much we stuff our faces.'

'And then when we get down to the last few boxes, that's when we'll do it, that's when we'll make the most of them.' Poppy stood up and faced Teela. 'We'll eat, smile, cry, laugh. Can you remember what that feels like?'

Teela tried to digest the words that had come firing out. 'You mean like a final, "Fuck you and thank you"?'

Poppy laughed. 'Yeah, a beautiful two fingers to it all, just because we can. The greatest reason of all. Just because.' She sat down slightly out of breath, turning to face Teela head on. 'We have a choice to make. We either dilute the paint and fill four canvases or concentrate it and paint a masterpiece?'

There was another short silence as Teela thought. Poppy could see her mind racing, weighing up all the pros and cons and ramifications.

'I,' a huge smile spread across Teela's face, bigger than any Poppy could remember. 'I say we do it.' She punched the settee with her hand in jubilation. 'Let's bloody do it! It'll be a laugh.'

A muted bleep from beneath a body of cushions cut her off and sedated the energy. Their eyes came together as a guilty look spread across Poppy's face. She searched desperately under the cushions, frantically trying to find the watch before the second bleep.

'It's Sheridan, isn't it?'

'I don't have to go,' said Poppy, 'if you don't want me to. It won't make any difference.'

Teela shook her head. 'I don't mind.' She leant back. 'To be honest, for some reason, I feel like I wanna go myself.'

'Really?' said Poppy. 'Are you sure?'

Teela nodded.

Poppy stood up with her back to the window and held out a hand. 'Let's go then.'

* * *

The grates shook as they walked down the corridors at a faster pace than usual. It felt strange to the both of them to walk with somebody other than their own shadow. The lonely echo of a single pair of boots gone, replaced by the comfort of companionship.

'You sure you want to do this?' said Poppy, again, as they approached the ladder.

Teela stretched her leg and placed her foot high up on the metal frame, missing the first few rungs entirely. 'Yeah, it feels good. It wouldn't feel right if I didn't.'

Poppy waited until she was a fair distance up before copying her, only not quite managing to lift her leg as high. She followed her up, the struggle increasing with each rung as the pain and fatigue moved from her core to the outer extremities of her body. She clambered into the Control Room as Teela stood, panting, in the middle of the floor, absorbing the surroundings.

'It feels different, doesn't it?' said Teela, wheezing, turning to help Poppy scramble to her feet. 'The room, I mean.'

Poppy subconsciously adopted Teela's stance, her hands relaxed on her hips. 'Yeah, I suppose it does.' She knew what she meant. The place seemed lighter, both in colour and weight. She stood, quite in amazement as the new room took hold, only for it to be broken by Teela who shoved a chair in her direction. It slid across the floor and nudged the side of her calf.

Poppy glanced down briefly at the spot in the doorway

where her hollow skeleton had once lurked, but opted this time for the chair. 'It was only yesterday I was down there, alone.' She pointed to the spot. 'Was it yesterday? I honestly can't remember what's real anymore.' She tried to think. 'Feels like a lifetime ago.' She stopped as the high-pitched scratch they had come to know so well took hostage of the room.

They both looked towards the speakers in the corner. The noise continued to emanate for a couple more cycles before falling silent, as if succumbing to the pressure of their stares.

'To anyone who can hear me, this is Captain Jason Sheridan from the Department of Search and Rescue. Do you read me? OVER.'

They both listened as the last voice of someone other than themselves walked into their room. Poppy reached for the receiver. She held it in her hand and looked towards Teela, whose eyes drifted up to meet her.

'Don't,' said Teela, a shadow of a head shake backing up her lack of words.

Poppy took her finger off the receiver and sat back in her chair.

'I don't really know why I'm doing this, or what benefit it has to you but, if you're listening, I just thought I'd tell you a little…' His voice waned as he searched for the right words. *'I feel like I've got to know you over the time I've spent drifting beside you in this dark corner, even if it hasn't been reciprocal.'*

The two listened as his words drifted through the room, both making sure to soak up every syllable they could.

'I only have the pictures in your profile to go on, but I just want it to be known that every time I spoke, even now, I'm looking directly into your faces, with the utmost respect and sincerity. If you're listening and both,' he paused. *'All right, I just hope you're looking after each other as best you can.'*

Poppy stared towards the ceiling as Teela focused on the point where the far wall met the floor, but they weren't really looking. They could hear the muffled sounds of Sheridan pulling the receiver away from his mouth, composing himself before continuing.

'I'm sorry, I truly am.' He coughed, trying to hide his emotion. *'Even if I found you… even if you popped up on my screen right now. I just wouldn't be able to get to you in time.'* He coughed again. *'There's nothing more I can do. There's nothing more I can say. I wish I knew…'* He paused for what seemed like a lifetime. *'I'll check in on you again tomorrow. Goodbye. – OVER.'*

Poppy held her finger to the receiver. 'Goodbye,' she said, before slowly placing it on the floor beside her.

A loud silence killed the fizzing sounds of the transmission. Poppy looked over for some sort of reaction, her eyebrows raised as if Sheridan belonged to her and she was proudly showing him off.

Teela stood up and leant with her back to the desk. 'Never heard him like that. He seems real now, at least.' She brought her hand up to her mouth and coughed. 'I hope he gets home safe.'

Poppy rubbed the bridge of her nose. 'This whole thing is just a heartbreak.'

'Running from a bull.'

Poppy nodded and leant back in her chair.

Teela looked down at the desk. A faint glow from the screens illuminated her face. She picked up the receiver and held it to her face as if she had never seen it before. 'It's weird. We're always just one step away from the edge of the crowd, and we never know it.' She seemed to stare through the receiver, through her hand, through the desk and the ship, and out towards somewhere she could not see. 'I mean, we're running along, everything seems manageable, not great, but there's still plenty of people behind you… and then one tiny thing happens,' she tossed the receiver from one hand to another. 'Your shoe comes off, you trip on a kerb, a transmitter fails… and all of a sudden you're at the back and those bloody big horns are getting closer and closer.'

'Running on the edge,' said Poppy. 'That's pretty much it.'

Teela smiled and trudged towards the files and charts at the other side of the room. 'Look at all of this shite. What a waste of time all this was,' she said, rummaging and muttering. 'Cargo reports, bloody cargo reports. I can't believe we thought this meant something.'

Poppy lifted her shoulders and let them flop back down. 'We weren't to know.'

Teela looked at her with a mischievous glint in her eye. 'You want to go down and check on them for one final time?'

Poppy smiled; it was like she had lifted the thought directly from her mind. 'It'll be like locking up,' she said. 'One final check to make sure the place is alright before it all.'

Teela headed for the ladder. 'Yeah, a final sweep of the surroundings.'

Poppy stood and followed her to the threshold before halting, staring at a pile of messy storage boxes in the corner.

'Just leave them,' said Teela. 'They're not gonna do much good now.'

'I...' Poppy looked around the Control Room, making sure to take in every surface. The control desk dominated over everything, the largest monitor in the middle casting out a glow that filled the room, surrounded by smaller screens that offered subtle support. 'I don't think we're going to come back here, are we?' she said.

Teela scrunched her nose slightly and began to climb down the ladder. 'We've got no real reason to.'

'I think I'll...' Poppy walked towards the desk and tidied the receiver into the nearest cupboard before placing her hand on the largest monitor and looking over to Teela. A subtle nod gave her the approval, and she slid three fingers down the screen until the bright white light gave way to a dusty shade of matte black. The keyboard panels began to glisten softly, no longer impeded by their beast of a sun. 'Gives them a chance,' she said.

Teela, only her upper half still visible, folded her arms and rested her head against the landing ledge. 'Looks kinda nice.'

Poppy gave an agreeing smile. 'It's got a beauty, hasn't it? Like stars. Although…' She took off her watch and carefully draped it across the lambent keys. She stepped back and admired the addition briefly, before turning to Teela. 'You ready?'

* * *

A bizarre tension weaved its way through their stomachs as they moved down through the corridors. It was one of excitement, cut with an ingredient the two of them couldn't decipher, but which Poppy suspected was fear.

Teela walked a couple of steps ahead as the long hallway ended in a rather disappointing climax, the small door of the lift looking battered and extremely sorry for itself in the far reaches of the ship. She waved her hand over the panel, and it opened with a judder, causing the stale conditions in the lift shaft to break free and invade the corridor.

Poppy clenched her nostrils and stepped onto the platform, waiting for Teela to follow. The customary jolt as the lift descended met them with a friendly punch and brought anxious smiles to their faces, their eyes jumping across the familiar scratches and marks on the shaft wall they knew so well.

'You should've brought another layer,' said Teela, as Poppy folded her arms, clouds of condensation gushing from her mouth.

'I'm alright.'

Her words were lost to the distraction of the wall as it retreated, allowing the cargo hold to crawl into view, the cold air nipping at their cheeks as they took it in.

'It feels like two minutes since…' Teela stepped off the platform.

Poppy nodded, following the narrow walkway and dripping floor pipes that ushered them down towards the hold. 'Well, there they are,' she said, as the pipes dispersed, allowing them to marvel at the three black containers that stood like great, proud beasts, mysteriously concealed behind the dirty plastic sheets. 'They're still here.'

Teela approached the one furthest to the right and bashed on its side with her fist. 'Vehicle parts? Can you actually believe it? All this trouble for a few engines and whatever else.' The beast dwarfed her body as the flesh of her clenched hand failed to make any audible impact on the ridged metal flank. 'Imagine,' she said, 'imagine if there could be anything in these containers, anything in the world, what would you want?'

'Oh, I dunno,' said Poppy. 'Some more food probably.'

'No,' said Teela, tapping on the metal of the next one, 'I mean something stupid, something ludicrous. This could be a treasury. We could be carrying some trillionaire's priceless possessions. And they're shipping them out because they have to leave Earth quickly due to some conspiracy or something?'

Poppy veered left and approached the sole container they hadn't yet examined. She sat down with her back to the cold metal. 'I watched a programme once that documented how smugglers used to hide all manner of things inside the tyres of cars, when every car had them. Maybe there's stuff hidden in these parts? Maybe they are just a front, concocted by this trillionaire so they don't get caught?'

Teela reached the final container and sat down beside her. 'That's it, then,' she said. 'It's settled, we're rich!' She coughed and softly bumped her head against the towering support. 'What would you do with it? What would you spend it on, if you had all the world's money?'

Poppy shook her head. 'I don't know. Buy a moon.' She turned to Teela, but Teela wasn't listening, already thinking of her own answer.

'I've always wanted to buy a farming ship,' said Teela. 'Nothing big; it doesn't have to be big. Just my little space, and I'd go floating around the world selling whatever I grew, probably tomatoes or something, I don't know.'

'A greenhouse in the sky,' said Poppy. 'Sounds perfect.'

Teela pictured the rows and rows of tomato plants, with a high rectangular dome of glass above, softly curving over the orchard and forming the body of the ship. She closed her eyes and imagined herself walking down the narrow, high-rise, leafy walkways as if purposely lost in a hedge-maze, the sprinklers creating a welcome mist of fine, cool water and her feet bare upon the damp, but warm tiles. She could see herself wandering to the edge of the crop, staring out at Earth that seemed so big and so close, and yet so fantastically far away. 'I've always wanted one,' she said, opening her eyes. 'My own patch up there, to get away from it all, y'know?'

Poppy nodded.

'You'd be more than welcome on board as well, Poppy. I wouldn't leave you out. I'd find a job for you. You could paint the mouldy ones red?'

Smiles spread across their faces.

'I'll most definitely think about it,' said Poppy.

The smiles lingered for a few moments until their lips grew tired. Poppy bent her legs, relaxing her elbows on her knees, and Teela finally settled her head, the soft agitated tapping surrendering to the rest.

'It's different here,' said Poppy. 'The silence, I mean. It's different to the silence up there. It's more,' she thought of the right word. 'Empty.'

Teela swivelled her head towards her. 'I know what you mean.' She stomped her leg on the floor. 'I think it's because this is the last layer before nothing. Just one thin bit of ship between in here, and out there.'

'You ever been on a skywalk?' asked Poppy. 'I once went on one. It was in the summer holidays. We went on a day trip, and one of the attractions was this huge building.' Her eyes lit up as she recounted the memory. 'There wasn't much there, but at the top you had this walkway that was made completely of glass, so you could look straight down at the people below.' She began to laugh. 'There was this ant on our side of the glass, and if you got right above it, the thing looked like it was running around on the streets below causing havoc.' She turned for a reaction, but Teela wasn't listening. Poppy watched for a moment as she drifted through a thought, her eyebrows softly rising and falling. 'What you thinking about?' said Poppy, eventually, in a softer tone.

Teela straightened her head. 'It's not real, y'know?' She paused. 'Remember that hairpin you found? It's not real.' She gave a small, but deep sigh, her damaged lungs rattling slightly. 'I thought it was for a bit, but it's not.' She coughed. 'I thought I could sell it and actually buy myself a ship. Alright, not a huge farm, but a small, one-person, little cart thing I could grow something in, just to have my own tiny plot up there, y'know?, but it's not. It's fake. Just coloured glass or whatever it is they use.' She looked down at her knees. 'But it's the only thing I have of hers. They found it in an envelope when they found me, in that stupid flower basket. I didn't even know it existed until I was checking out and it was there, written in the list of items I came in with.' She gave a wistful smile. 'I think the guy behind the desk was hoping I wouldn't notice. He never brought it out until I asked. I don't think I would've got it otherwise. I guess he thought it was real too.'

They both stared out at the vista of grey in front of them, relieved only by odd sparkles of condensation that collected on the pipes.

'Well, you got your wish,' said Poppy, breaking the silence. 'You can't say you're not away from it all here.'

Teela raised her eyebrows. 'It's not exactly how I pictured it.' She leant forward and felt her hair damp from the metal container. 'Come on. Let's go back.' She stood up and helped Poppy to her feet. 'There's no point in dwelling.'

Chapter Thirteen

Last Laugh is Ours

Teela did her best to neatly arrange the bedclothes in her, now permanent, living area. On her knees, she used an open palm to smooth out any large folds and creases, giving special attention to the joins, overlapping them and pressing them down so they wouldn't come apart. She noted the different fabrics under her skin as her hand passed over. Rough, smooth, soft, stiff. The noise sounded like distant waves, lapping at the sand.

'What you doing?'

Teela jumped.

'I said, what are you doing?'

Teela looked into the old man's face. 'Nothing. What's it got to do with you anyway?'

'Nothing.' The old man walked up to the barrier that overlooked the beach and the hazy sea beyond. 'Just don't get many lingerers here. Can be dangerous when the tide comes in.'

'I'm just looking,' said Teela. 'One last look, before I leave.'

'You're not a jumper, are you?'

Teela shook her head. 'I'm joining Star Express, long-haul division.'

'Trying to get away?'

Teela shrugged.

'It's just as bad up there as it is down here, y'know?'

'But it's quieter,' said Teela.

The old man snorted a laugh.

'I was fostered by this family who had a farm up there, just off-planet. It was horrible, but it was quieter.'

Teela stood up and admired her work. It was smart enough for a semi-rural campsite. She went over to the settee and unfolded a corner of the crushed draped blanket, only for it to curl back up as soon as it was released. She tried again, but it rolled back, bringing with it a fringe of annoyance. A small expletive, followed by a cough, crept from her lips as she reached for a cushion, strategically placing it over the crease before sitting down gently, making sure not to ruin the fine work she had done.

She looked briefly at the Window before drifting away, its spell not as entrancing as it once had been. Her gaze settled on two soft impressions in the sheets where she and Poppy had developed the habit of sleeping, their backs turned away from the glass as if it wasn't there.

To her left, a large crate, brought down from the Storage Room, waved at her from the corner of her eye. She walked over and slid off the lid, revealing a menagerie of flexi-plastic off-cuts, paper rolls and anything else they thought had potential. She reached in and grabbed a handful of sticky strips before meandering back and removing a few of the excess sheets and blankets that covered the edges of the camp. Like wallpaper, she began to plaster them across the Window, running the adhesive strips around the edge of the material, providing a tight bond to the glass, whilst trapping a small cushion of air that made the sheets billow out ever so slightly. The fifth and final sheet was the largest, and seemed to droop in the middle, the excess fabric pulling down hard on the strips.

She stepped back. The additions hardly made an impact on the vast Window that stood obtrusively across the length of the room, and yet, the blot that she had made on the single section of otherwise perfect glass was the thing that drew the eye.

* * *

The grates clanged as she walked down the corridor, her

lungs no longer allowing her to run as she once had. She had forgotten how fantastic it felt to almost fly, cutting through and disturbing the static air that had been hanging in the same place for days. She smiled. All the races she had won against the older kids in the Home came steaming through her mind. She remembered how she would peel ahead from the rest of the group, her heels narrowly escaping their last ditch attempts to kick and trip her. How she would keep on running, even after she had crossed the line, going on for what seemed like miles and miles just for the sake of running, and how, when she returned, she could still beat them again and again.

The clangs fell relatively silent as she reached the kitchen. She could see Poppy bent over a box of food with her back to her. She picked up a nearby water bottle that had been handily left on the worktop and crept up. 'Why shouldn't I?' she said, aiming it at her back.

Poppy jumped, scrambling up the worktop to her feet. 'Life, Teela! I didn't hear you.' She took a moment to catch her breath before noticing the bottle. 'Oh, I see.' Poppy's hand slowly edged towards a tube of cultured meat paste. She grabbed it in a flash and held it in turn towards Teela. 'Seems we have somewhat of a standoff,' she said, a cocky expression dancing in her eyes. 'Now, of course, if we were adults, we would be able to resolve this without anyone getting hurt.'

'Poppy,' a mischievous smile spread across Teela's face. 'You do know that tube of paste is new? Meaning you have to break the seal on the lid and remove the covering before it squirts. Do you reckon you'll have time to do that before I squeeze this?'

The cocky expression transferred from Poppy's face to Teela's.

'Why don't we just slowly lower our weapons and call a truce?' said Poppy. 'After all, this is only getting in the way of the main event.' She gestured to a small pile of boxes in the doorway. 'It won't eat itself. Look at it, just sitting there. It's just pleading for someone to eat it, and here we are.' Poppy began to move. 'Let's just...' She slowly brought her hand down and placed the meat paste on the floor, kicking it towards the boxes with her foot. 'There. Isn't that better? Now, your turn.'

Teela tentatively bent her outstretched arms and brought the bottle to her lips before taking a large swig of its contents. 'Lucky,' she said. 'Food is probably the only thing that seems more appealing.'

Poppy waited for Teela to take another swig before sidestepping past her. 'It wasn't luck,' she bent down and examined a box. 'It was tactical nous. In a negotiation, you have to offer the illusion of giving them what they want,' she piled two of the boxes on top of each other and confidently picked them up. 'Whilst actually getting exactly what you want.'

Poppy flinched as a jet of cold water landed perfectly in the space between her shoulder blades.

Teela laughed as she arched her body, trying her best to simultaneously keep the dripping fabric from her skin whilst maintaining a grip on the boxes. 'Tactical nous?' said Teela. 'Probably wait until the situation has been totally neutralised before you start bragging about your negotiating skills.' She picked up the remaining boxes and set off down the corridor.

* * *

Poppy entered the Rec. Room behind Teela and set the boxes on the table. She gestured towards the partially covered Window. 'I see you've started already.'

Teela shrugged and began to unpack the boxes. 'It was annoying me. Just wanted to shut the blinds, sort of.'

Poppy nodded, placing her hand against one of the sheets. 'It was a bit of a taunt, wasn't it?' She splayed her fingers. The thin fabric dulled the cold glass slightly as it tried to penetrate through to her palm. 'I say you did the right thing. Shame we don't have enough blankets for the whole window.'

Teela didn't reply, choosing instead to arrange the food into different categories on the table. First, all the small packets, along with any miscellaneous tubes. Then, the medium-sized boxes and cartons. Before finally, the liquids that huddled at the back, apologetically looking down on the rest.

She stared at the items, in a daze, focusing on the shapes without really looking, all meaning removed from the objects.

'I'm stuffed,' said Mr. Gulliver, rocking slightly in his chair whilst massaging his belly. 'Couldn't eat another thing.'

'Are you sure, Harold? What about those potatoes?' Mrs. Gulliver pointed to a tray in the middle with four small jackets, their skins rusty red and glistening.

'Honestly, Aida, I couldn't eat a pea.'

'I think I'll have one,' she said, helping herself. 'Harold Jnr? Ed? Teela? Can you fit another one in?'

The two boys nodded and reached over, grabbing their steals. Teela stared at the last potato still in the tray. She could easily manage it. The remnants of the hot steam wafted towards her, beckoning her to grab it. She looked up and caught Mr. Gulliver's eye.

'I think,' he said, slowly, taking great delight and relishing every word, 'I think I *will* be able to manage a potato after all.' He reached forward and dropped the potato on his plate, his eyes fixed to Teela, before leaning back in his chair and ignoring the addition.

'You okay?' said Poppy, leaving the Window and adding a few extra items to the hastily formed groupings.

'Yeah, I was just thinking.'

Poppy gave a comforting smile and emptied the last box before placing it under the table. The two of them looked down at the less than bountiful assortment that sat, pathetic, on the glossy surface.

'That's got to be the most pitiful spread I've ever seen,' said

Teela, fixing her hands to her hips.

'Well,' Poppy produced a small rectangle of paper from her pocket. 'It's not a traditional feast, I admit.' She swiped up with her finger and looked down the scribbled list. 'We have-drum roll, please.'

Teela bent down and tapped her fingers on the table.

'We have, five medium-sized bars of, "dust-paste", otherwise known as Meal Bars. Eight small sachets of Choco Powder. Ten bars of solidified milk, in various flavours. Two, "large", packets of Fibre Flakes. Six small packets of Concentrated Fruit Beads, in various flavours. Half a packet of cardboard, sorry, flatbread. Five bottles of Milk-Repro. The ol' favourite H2O and that bottle,' she pointed to a white bottle with a yellow and green flash on its neck. 'Is Lemon and Lime Evaporation Juice.' She paused for a moment to catch her breath before scrolling further down the list. 'And then odd bits and bobs, like a couple of cultured meat paste tubes, two triangles of rubbery cheese and last, and most definitely least, this,' she pulled out a small can from her pocket. 'A tin of unset raspberry jelly, which I've just tried to set in the freezer with minimal success.' She tossed it to Teela who caught it brilliantly with one hand.

'Now what?' said Teela, adding the can to the pile of miscellaneous items.

Poppy looked around the room. 'Well, a party isn't a party without proper decorations.'

Teela watched as Poppy strolled confidently towards the crate of potential. She reached in with both hands and rummaged, pulling out various rolls of paper, light-patches, sticky strips and anything else that could possibly be put to use. She unravelled a roll of pale pink paper, cut a piece about the length of her arm span, and laid it on the floor.

'What are you doing?' asked Teela earnestly.

Poppy tapped twice on the paper and began to write with her finger before quickly stopping. 'What shall we call it?

What actually *is* this?'

Teela shrugged. 'I dunno, I've never really done a party before.'

Poppy, on her knees, turned towards Teela with a mischievous look before turning back, scrawling her finger across the paper with large, definite movements. 'That'll do.' She grabbed two sticky strips and stuck the banner up on the nearest wall to the table. 'Teela's First Party!'

Teela admired the jet black letters as they cut through the innocent pink of the paper. 'Now what?' she said again. 'Eat?'

Poppy was already back in the box, looking for more ideas. 'No,' she shook her head adamantly. 'If we're having a party, we're having a party. There's no point going in half-arsed.'

Teela pulled out the chair she was leaning on and sat down. 'But isn't it all a bit, y'know, pointless?'

Poppy lifted her head from the box. 'Pointless frivolity is what makes it all worthwhile. It's what makes it so powerful.' Her voice was soft and sincere. 'Now, if I give you those,' she handed Teela a pair of scissors. 'And this sheet of paper. You can cut it into thin strips and then, if you wrap the strips around the scissors and sort of slide the blade down, you can create curly things.'

'Curly things?'

A smile formed at the corners of Poppy's mouth. 'Now, listen, curly things are the cornerstone of any decent pointless party. Don't let me down.'

Teela managed to straighten her face. 'If you want curly things, we will have curly things.' She gave a mock salute before examining the sheet Poppy had given her.

* * *

Teela slid the blade down the strip and watched as the paper curled up after it. She absentmindedly placed it with the rest before picking up another strip and repeating the process. Her eyes focused on the paper, its charm therapeutic, as the scissors made another pass. She tilted her head and drifted across a dreamland of decorations and parties. In her periphery, she was aware of Poppy ferreting away with whatever new assignment her imagination had given her. Teela placed the strip with the rest and lifted her head to see how far she had progressed since the last time, the otherwise grey room slowly being painted with colour.

She took another strip and ran the blade down towards the end before placing it with the rest, grabbing another and repeating the process.

* * *

'We've run out.'

Teela jumped from her daze and looked down at her hands. She was still holding the scissors, but in a way that suggested they hadn't moved for a while. 'What?' she said, coughing, looking over at Poppy as she put the lid back on the crate.

'Of stuff, there's nothing left.' Poppy tapped on the crate before focusing on the table where Teela was working. 'How are the curly things coming?'

'Yeah,' Teela looked at the small pile of curls next to her. 'I think I'm done.' She picked them up and made her way towards Poppy, trying to give the impression of being fully awake.

'I thought you had drifted off?'

'Nah, I was just, y'know? I don't know where you get the energy from.'

Poppy took the curls and smiled, holding up each strip, inspecting them in an excessively elaborate and pompous fashion.

'Do these curly things conform with your levels of artistry?' asked Teela.

Poppy dangled one from a paper chain she had just hung. 'Yes,' she held another two curls up to the sides of her head and hooked them to her ears. 'Yes, they'll do nicely.' She brushed past Teela and went about dotting the curls around the room before offering over the last one. Teela spent a moment considering where to hang it before choosing the spot above the door, one of the few areas that hadn't yet been touched with colour. She nudged it with her finger, and it slowly rotated in the doorway like a wind chime, causing beautifully pink reflections to flicker on nearby surfaces like sparks from a flame. She looked back at Poppy, who concurred with an approving nod.

Teela's gaze drifted to the surroundings that suddenly seemed to open up like a bud, dwarfing Poppy where she stood with flowers of pastel colour blooming from every nook and cranny. Paper chains piped their way around the room like looped icing, streamers carpeted random sections of the floor with tangled excitement, and light-patches, filtered with pink and mint green paper, battled against any bare patches of grey still left intact.

'What do you think?' said Poppy, as Teela walked back towards her, making sure to take in every little detail.

'It's,' she paused, mesmerised. 'It's fantastic. It really is.'

Poppy beamed with pride as they both let themselves sink into the colourful new world they had created.

'Now what?' said Teela, raising her eyebrows.

'*Now,*' said Poppy, 'we eat.' She led the way to the table, and they both sat down on the corner closest to the food. 'Shall we separate it out exactly or just dive in?'

Teela raised her eyebrows again. 'Life's too short. Let's just dive in,' she said, her words undermined by an unusual shyness that had befallen them both.

Poppy nodded. 'Do you want to go first?'

Teela scanned the assortment in front of her, pondering what to go for. 'Is there anything you want?'

'I'm easy.' Poppy paused, inspecting the items. 'I suppose I could…' Her hand tentatively moved towards the pile. 'Oh, sack it,' she said, abruptly, grabbing a random hand-swipe of food, signaling for Teela to do the same who obliged with little persuasion. 'Get stuck in, that's what I say!'

'If you say so.'

Poppy looked down at her pile and picked up a Meal Bar. A small dust-cloud formed as she opened the packet. She broke half of it into her hand and popped it into her mouth.

'How is it?' asked Teela. 'As disappointing as the others?'

Poppy nodded, struggling to swallow the gritty pulp that had formed on her tongue.

Teela smirked and opened one of her own. 'I don't think I've ever wanted something so much that I hate so much. Does that make sense?'

Poppy examined the other half before carefully placing it onto her tongue. 'It's like somebody has taken the compacted dust and dirt from a vacuum cleaner, sliced it into manageable bars and then shoved it into a neat wrapper.' She paused. 'It's brilliant!' She swallowed the final dregs that stuck to the sides of her mouth and reached for a bottle of water, gulping two thirds of it down without even stopping for breath. A fine layer of sediment floated within the remaining liquid before slowly settling at the bottom. She wiped her mouth and looked for her next mouthful. 'It's nice though, isn't it, eating together? Even if the food is less than savoury.'

Teela nodded, her mouth full of mush. 'You're such a captain.'

Poppy laughed defensively. 'How?'

'Saying stuff like that.' Teela paused. 'I agree though; it's nice.' She swallowed her food and tried to keep a straight face. 'At least, as nice as it can be in a situation like this, with a person like you, in a place like this.'

The comment produced a chuckle from Poppy, causing a proud smile to spread across Teela's face as they selected another item from their piles.

* * *

'Can I ask you a question?' said Teela, after squeezing the last leavings from a tube of cultured meat paste into her mouth.

Poppy looked up. 'Yeah?'

'What's your favourite memory?' Her tone was as if it were an everyday thing to ask.

'My favourite memory of what?'

Teela leant back and shrugged. 'Y'know, highlights, precious things. Of it all. Of everything.'

'Oh,' said Poppy. 'I'm not sure.' She looked down at the overly yellow triangle of rubbery cheese she held in her hand.

'Go on, you must have something.' Teela rolled up the meat paste tube, neatly from one end, to form a tight spiral before throwing it to the side.

Poppy took a bite of the cheese, her teeth creating a satisfying scalloped edge on the cross-section as she thought. 'I think it's always the small stuff, isn't it?'

Teela squeezed another tube of meat paste onto a small square of flatbread as she listened.

'Like when I used to come home from school to find my favourite meal on the table. Or going on daytrips to the coast. Or just a rainy day inside, joking around with Catherine.' She rubbed the waxy cheese substance from her fingers. 'What about you?'

'Well,' said Teela, coughing as a crumb from the flatbread hit the back of her throat. 'I quite liked it at the farm, just before harvesting, where you could look across and see all the food waiting to be picked.'

Poppy took a careful swig from her bottle, trying not to swallow any of the meal bar silt. 'I can imagine it, with all the tufts of green sprouting from the soil?'

'Yeah, and the midday break when I used to cool off next to the water sprinklers.'

Poppy took another gulp. 'Heaven.'

Teela finished the flatbread and opened the bottle of evaporation juice, pouring half a packet's worth of Fruit Beads into her hand. 'It's been pretty decent here as well, sometimes.' She shoved the beads into her mouth and took a swig from the bottle before stopping abruptly.

'What is it?' asked Poppy.

Teela looked down at the table. 'Sorry if I was ever,' she tried to think of the right term. 'Less than helpful at times, especially early on.'

Poppy shook her head and grabbed a random packet from her pile, resigned to the fact that whatever she picked would have the same empty taste. 'Don't you dare apologise. I think we complimented each other nicely.' She smiled. 'I think we've done alright for two kids straight out of training, still wet behind the ears.' She rubbed the bridge of her nose. 'I mean, really, what business did we have gallivanting around, delivering parcels across the whole known universe?'

'We had every business,' said Teela, her mouth stuffed with the remaining Fruit Beads. 'And it was great until it wasn't, and even then, there are still great bits buried within that.'

Poppy nodded. 'You're right.'

'I usually am.' Teela swallowed the beads and looked over to Poppy who had begun to giggle, slow at first before culminating in an uncontrollable howl. A smirk formed on Teela's lips, ready to join in as soon as she found out what was so funny.

'Do you remember when…' Poppy struggled to get her words out.

Teela started to chuckle along, her expectant laugh prematurely escaping from her mouth.

Poppy composed herself briefly. 'Do you remember when we realised the ship didn't have a laundry shoot and we would have to transfer everything with that bloody trolley?'

Teela nodded enthusiastically. 'I hate that bloody thing.'

Poppy wiped her eyes. 'Do you remember your first washing run, and how you couldn't get the trolley through the Utility Room door?'

Teela laughed as Poppy's shoulders bobbed up and down.

'You know there's still scuff marks on that frame?'

Teela leant across and pointed to the small scar on her cheek. 'There's still a scuff mark on me!'

'It's healed nicely,' said Poppy, examining the cut. 'I can still picture you upside down in that cart. That'll never leave me.'

She began to howl, and Teela joined in. They both laughed until they couldn't remember what they were laughing about, and the loud energy slowly dissolved into chuckles, then smirks, before finally, a hushed silence as Teela's lungs wheezed slightly.

'Come on,' said Poppy, standing up and offering her hand out to Teela.

'What?'

'Just come on,' she said again, taking Teela's hand and dragging her to her feet. She walked over to the monitor by the settee and signed into her account.

'What you doing?'

'Just wait.' Poppy turned round and began to walk towards her as beautiful music came flowing out of the speakers. 'You can't have a party without music.' She took Teela's hand in her own and wrapped her arm around her waist as they began to slowly sway side to side.

'What are we doing?' said Teela.

Poppy held her closer, and they began to drift around the room. 'Dancing.'

'Why?' she laughed.

'I dunno... because we can.'

Teela rested her head on Poppy's shoulder, and the two softly floated together, their feet occasionally getting tangled in paper decorations and loose sheets from the campsite.

The song finished and began to play again as Teela opened

her eyes. 'What is this? I've never heard it before.'

'It's old,' said Poppy. 'French, but I forget the singer.'

Teela tilted her head so her chin was on Poppy's shoulder. 'What does it mean?'

Poppy held her arms out towards the filtered light. 'Life in pink,' she said.

* * *

Teela looked down at the empty wrappers and packets that lay strewn across the table. 'That didn't take long.'

Poppy shook her head in agreement.

Teela gave a melancholic smile. 'I don't know whether to be happy or sad.'

'You can be both,' said Poppy. 'It's quite possible. You don't have to choose.'

Teela looked up, but not directly into her eyes. 'It's strange,' she gestured around the room. 'This makes me happy but, y'know…' she said, struggling to find the words.

Poppy folded a meal bar wrapper in two. The silver foil caught the light and briefly cast a pinkish streak across her face.

'And, then I do feel sad but… this brings me back up.' Teela stretched her eyes and pointed to the remaining food hidden amongst empty packaging. 'What's left?'

Poppy cobbled together a tiny pile containing a few meal bars, a quarter full packet of Fibre Flakes and a bit of Milk-Repro. 'What do you want to do, carry on or leave it for later?'

Teela weighed up the option in her mind. 'Leave it,' she said. 'I'm stuffed and I want to enjoy it, not force it down.'

Poppy nodded and pushed the small pile towards the centre of the table. She stood up and began to collect all the crumbs and odd bits of litter from where they had been sitting.

Teela walked over to the camp and lay down on the settee. She looked back towards the middle of the room. 'Who you cleaning for, Poppy?'

Poppy shook her head. 'I don't know.' She dropped the collection back onto the table and walked over to the camp, slumping on the floor underneath Teela, her body at a right angle to the settee.

* * *

'Poppy?' said Teela after a while, quiet enough as to not wake her if she was asleep.

'Yeah?'

'How long… how long will…'

'I don't know,' said Poppy, not needing all the words to know what she was saying. 'I found some relief strips in the medikit. Enough of them and it'll be like a daze.'

The room returned to silence.

'Will you sleep tonight?' asked Poppy, bringing her head up so she could see Teela's face, the underside of her chin and nose poking out.

Teela wrapped herself tightly into a blanket cocoon and flipped onto her back. 'I'm gonna try not to.' She gazed upwards towards a jungle of paper decorations and pinkish light. 'But I'm so tired.'

Poppy nodded. 'Me too.'

Chapter Fourteen

Turning in the Street

Teela woke to find Poppy sitting at the table. An anxious drum started to beat in her neck. 'How many days has it been?'

Poppy looked up from her thoughts. 'This is the third, no, the fourth... I can't remember.'

Teela placed her feet on the blanket Poppy had been resting on. With her left foot, she found the edge and slid her toes underneath. Her right foot followed. The fabric was still warm. Her body ached, her eyes feeling deep in her skull. She tried to stand up, but struggled. 'I think...' She coughed. There were polka dots of red blood across the back of her hand. 'I think today might be our last chance.'

Poppy nodded. 'I was thinking the same.'

'What's... what's the plan?' Teela paused, trying to think of a more eloquent way to phrase it. 'I mean, how are...' Her tongue tripped on the words, but Poppy knew what she meant.

'Well,' said Poppy, her voice calm and quiet, 'I think I might have a shower to clean myself up a bit, and then, I was thinking of making a final recording before...' She paused, taking her turn in searching for the right words.

Teela nodded and slowly started to stand.

'What about you?' asked Poppy.

Teela sat down at the table and thought about what needed to be done, what she had to do, but struggled to find any obvious answer. 'I'll probably just do the same.'

'Do you want to leave a recording?'

She shook her head. 'No, I don't think so. I don't really have

anything to say. At least, not to anybody outside of this room.'
Her eyes began to well.

Poppy smiled and put her hand on top of hers. 'I'm glad
I'm in this room with you.' She gestured her head towards the
door. 'You coming?'

Teela got to her feet and walked with her. Her pink curl
slowly spun in the threshold. 'Hold on,' she said.

The two of them looked back at the sporadically placed
colours that flowered themselves in uneven clusters, remaining
constant and completely undeterred.

'We did alright, didn't we?' said Teela.

Poppy nodded and went through the door, creating a small
draft that made the curl dance and drop soft pink gems of light
across her back.

* * *

Poppy limped, her head drooping slightly to one side and her
shoulders hunched forward. Teela's arm brushed against her
with each step, both of them tacitly walking closer than normal.

They reached the chamber ladder and climbed up to the
landing as best they could, Teela first, then Poppy, the ascent
agonisingly slow and painful, their bodies almost as stiff as the
rusted metal rungs that bore their weight. Teela reached the top
and pulled herself over, her lungs burning, as Poppy followed,
recalling a vague image of herself marooned in the very spot.

'Just wait a minute,' she said, as they got to their feet, catching
their breath, the two of them awkwardly staring towards the
battered remnants of her door, before quietly parting to their
respective rooms.

Poppy lifted the bruised, battered flap and clambered
underneath. The bright, clinical room was cold and bare,
lacking in all homeliness. She looked around and struggled to
find any real evidence that she had once occupied it. She sat on

the bed and thought about all the bedrooms she had belonged to. Her very first bedroom in the tiny spare room. The larger bedroom down the landing. Then, the one at the new house on the other side of town. Even the Rec. Room camp. They all held parts of her, both hanging from the walls and in the experiences that filled them, these rented spaces.

She stood up and began to undress.

The cold floor of the washroom hit the soles of her bare feet, but didn't have time to penetrate any further before she had reached the refuge of the shower. She held the rusted shower head and noticed the red tinge of a bloody occasion that seemed so long ago she couldn't really remember it at all, as if it had happened to a different person.

She switched on the shower, and the warm water cradled her skin like a soft blanket, causing her to glow with a rosy radiance. She leant back, the cool wall now refreshing, as a steamy mist fogged its way throughout the room, opening her pores and attacking the dirt. For a brief moment, she stood in total bliss, looking up towards the stream, as a pool collected around her feet in the subtle indentation left by hundreds of previous visits. She dabbed a bit of the water on her dry lips and wished she could take a gulp.

'Oh no, darling,' said her mother, as she rushed over to Catherine, who was knee-deep in a rock pool. 'We don't drink that water; it's all yucky and salty.' She took a water bottle from her backpack and handed it over. 'Wash your mouth with this and spit it out,' she said, demonstrating with an overelaborate mime. 'There you go.'

Poppy turned off the shower and crossed the floor to the sink. The sheet that had hung across, covering the nightmare, lay abandoned on the floor next to her feet. She looked in the mirror, recognising the friendly, but changed, face that stood in front of her. With the back of her fingers, she stroked down the skin of her cheeks. They were still thin, but seemed to glow in the mist of the bathroom.

She grabbed a towel and watched as the used water dawdled down the slope and into the drain, leaving silvery trails that twinkled briefly, before evaporating in the heat. She ruffled her hair into a semi-styled mess before using her hand as a comb. It felt nice as the long strands travelled smoothly between her fingers. She brought her hand back up and went for another pass, trying to tease out any knots she had missed. A curly quiff drooped onto her forehead as it always did, although this time quite a bit further, almost reaching her eyebrows.

She entered her bedroom and was brushed by the refreshing relief of cooler air that danced around her, but threatened to nip and scratch if left unbridled. She abandoned her old clothes in a crumpled heap and quickly dressed into fresh ones, trying to cover her body before the pleasant air turned to a chill.

'Poppy?'

Poppy looked towards the movement outside, visible through the gap underneath her door. 'Yeah, come in,' she said. 'I'm dressed.' She picked up her boots and sat down on the bed, wrestling to get them on over her new, thicker socks.

'I found this,' said Teela, scrambling underneath the flap.

Poppy looked up as Teela stood holding the picture of the two of them, the extra light from the landing framing her in such a way that caused flashes to play on her still wet hair. She smiled as she took the picture, sliding her finger across the top, causing the loop to play over and over. 'You look beautiful.' Poppy felt Teela lean over, looking at the photo, trying to find evidence for her remark. 'No,' she said. 'I mean now. Here.'

Teela took the photo from her. 'You too. You look good. Sort of clear.'

Poppy noticed the ruby pin fastened neatly across a curl in Teela's hair. 'I didn't know if you'd wear it or not,' she said, pointing to the stone.

Teela shrugged. 'I own it. It's not real, but it's mine.' She wafted the photo in front of Poppy's face. 'Where's yours?'

Poppy's eyes darted towards the lockers, then to the locker door that lay abandoned on the floor, before finally settling on the pile of clothes at her feet. She bent down and fumbled inside her trouser pocket, pulling out the smiling faces of her family. 'I forgot I had it.'

Teela took the picture and played the loop. She watched as Poppy's infant head repeatedly turned from her family to the camera, and then back to her family. 'You look so small and innocent,' she said, giving the photo back.

Poppy stood up and put the photo in the side pocket of her new trousers. 'I don't think I am anymore. Neither of us are.'

Teela went over and lifted the door so she could duck underneath.

Poppy emerged on the landing and waited for her to follow before placing her foot on the ladder. 'I'm not sad that I won't have to climb this again,' she said, starting her descent.

Teela smiled and followed her down, giving special attention to her chamber door that disappeared more and more with each rung. 'Feels strange, though,' she said. 'We'll never sleep in those rooms again.'

'They weren't fit for purpose,' said Poppy, setting off down the corridor. 'A sterile set of painful rooms with hospital beds and en-suite frost.'

Teela stumbled off the ladder, delighted by the honesty.

'Your camp was the greatest remedy,' said Poppy. 'It was the best thing we ever did. I don't know why we didn't do it sooner.'

Teela jovially took Poppy's hand and held it in the air with her own, before letting it droop back down as the effort to maintain the action grew too harsh.

* * *

'I'll wait here,' said Teela, leaning on the wall as Poppy had done so often.

Poppy smiled and entered the booth, sitting down at the seat for the last time.

'Speak to initiate recording.'

She listened to the automatic voice as it repeated its instructions. 'That's it,' she said, casually, and the light changed from red to green. 'It's been days since we had any food or drinkable water. The bull has nearly caught us.' She smiled. 'It was fun, though, to feel the sun on your face and the breeze through your hair. Seems like a blur sometimes, but then other times it seems so clear. The trips and falls and some of the escapes... the people, they all come flooding back.' She ran her fingers through her hair. 'I wish there didn't have to be such a chase, though. With such cruelty. Why does it have to be like that? I wish it didn't feel like you needed to look over your shoulder all the time. I wish someone could explain it to me. It's not fair on anyone. I thought I might outrun it at one point, but the truth is, it always catches up.'

She shook her head and rubbed her eyes. 'I know there isn't really anyone listening. I know that.' She looked around the room, trying to find something to say her words to. 'And, I know that if there was anybody actually listening to me, it isn't you. It isn't the detached voice coming from the corner.' She rubbed her brow and slumped forward, pushing her elbows onto her thighs, staring at the floor. 'I don't know what I'm doing here.' She lifted her head and looked towards the camera lens. 'There's no reason to be here,' she paused. 'And yet here I am, just in case... just in case. I don't know.'

Poppy leant back in her chair, dissatisfied with her mumbled words. 'When Grandad died, after all those weeks and months, finally it was the right time. He was ready. I don't know why it was that day, but it was. He knew he'd never make it to the bullring. He was too tired to run, and it hurt too much when people carried him... so, it's like he just stopped. And turned. Holding out his hand to stroke the bull's face. He accepted it.

Nobody ever really makes it to the bullring.'

Poppy positioned herself precisely in front of the camera. 'We're ready.' She brushed her fingers across her chin. 'We're going to stop running now.'

The light changed from green to red as she rose to her feet.

'Recording session terminated,' said the voice, which seemed to talk generally to the room now instead of directly to her. 'To continue recor-'

Poppy stepped outside to find Teela crouched against the wall. Her face was mottled, like her own, with tear streams and pinkish attempts to wipe them away. They laughed awkwardly, acknowledging the strange bittersweet feeling they shared.

'Well, that's that,' said Poppy, sitting down, her legs bent up and her arms dangling down between her knees.

Teela nodded and planted her head against the wall before turning towards her. 'What did you say?' Her eyes flickered in the direction of the booth.

'Nothing really, just waffled. You can go in if you want?' said Poppy.

Teela shook her head and coughed. 'No, I'm okay. I don't reckon there's much more to say.' She sat forward and looked down the corridor past Poppy's face.

Poppy followed her gaze down the hall. 'Just a short walk.' She looked into Teela's eyes. 'You ready?'

Teela smiled. 'Let's go.'

Poppy slowly clambered to her feet, Teela delaying slightly, watching the light shine on the buckle of her boot before rising herself. They stood together and looked down the corridor that seemed to be widening in front of them. Poppy felt the back of Teela's hand brush against her and, without uttering a word, delicately wrapped her palm around hers.

They began to walk back to the Rec. Room, their unified footsteps shattering against the grates, creating a drum that felt like their hearts, their grip on each other's hand increasing as the door came into view.

'This is the last door we'll ever walk through,' said Teela.

'It's a good door,' said Poppy.

A smirk grew on the corner of Teela's mouth and spread to a smile before jumping to a laugh. Poppy raised her slightly drooping head. The laugh danced across, bouncing off the walls until it landed neatly on her. They both laughed, for no real reason other than just because they could. Tears welled in their eyes and spilled onto their faces. For a few brief moments they filled the corridor with glorious, uninhibited noise, until, as quickly as it had come, the sounds softened back to a simple smirk.

'Come on,' said Poppy, leading her back inside, 'I'm tired.'

Chapter Fifteen

Stroking the Bull's Face

Teela woke, her eyes only half open. She could barely move her head, but could feel Poppy still beside her. 'How many days?'

'I don't know.'

'I think…' Teela closed her eyes. 'I think this might be…'

'Teela,' said Poppy, her voice weak and breaking, 'I'm scared.'

'I'm here,' said Teela. She looked to the ceiling. A pink curl softly spun above her. It caught the light and flared piercingly strong, reflecting briefly in the ruby stone that slept on her head, before quietly fading back to nothing.

In the quiet, they could hear their hearts. The sound seemed to fill their little worlds. They listened, focusing on each beat growing further and further and further apart.

A SHORT HISTORY OF THE FUTURE

AZ AMAZING
SCIENCE FICTION
SHORT STORIES

LIAM HOGAN

PAUL S EDWARDS

THE
TRITON
RUN

REDEMPTION CAN BE FOUND
IN THE FAR REACHES